The
Munitions
Girls

Rosie Archer is a pseudonym for June Hampson, author of the acclaimed Daisy Lane crime sagas. June was born in Gosport, Hampshire, where she still lives. She has had a variety of jobs including waitress, fruit picker, barmaid, shop assistant and market trader selling second-hand books.

Also by June Hampson

Trust Nobody
Broken Bodies
Damaged Goods
Fatal Cut
Jail Bait
Fighting Dirty
A Mother's Journey
The Crying Game

The Munitions Girls

ROSIE ARCHER

Quercus

First published in Great Britain in 2015 by

Quercus
55 Baker Street
7th Floor, South Block
London W1U 8EW

A CIP catalogue record for this book is available
from the British Library

PBO ISBN 978 1 84866 494 4
EBOOK ISBN 978 1 78429 230 0

12

Printed and bound in Great Britain by Clays Ltd, Elcograf S.p.A.

Typeset by CC Book Production

For the people of Gosport

Most of the places, street names and topography mentioned in my book are real. However, the characters are figments of my imagination.

Chapter One

March 1943

'Fancy going down the Fox tonight?' Em asked, over the noise of the wireless.

Pixie Smith finished pouring the concentrated explosive powder for the two-pound shell she was filling. Then she hooked the bomb on to the eye-level conveyor-belt. She watched, taking in the stink of the powder that misted the air, turned skin yellow and hair the colour of conkers, as the container made its way safely along the line to Em, the inspection manager. Pixie nodded vigorously. Em directed her eyes towards Pixie's mate, Rita, and gave her a look that could have frozen Hell.

'Keep your eyes on your job, Rita, else we'll be going to kingdom come instead of the pub. This work's important if we want to win the war.' Em paused, adjusted her glasses, then peered again suspiciously at Rita. Pixie looked at her friend. They'd been down to the town, drinking, the previous night. Walking to work that morning, Rita had complained to Pixie of her hangover.

'We're doing a good job in this place an' I don't want no mistakes with the TNT, you girls,' Em went on.

Pixie sighed and tucked away the stray hairs that had slipped from her white turban, standard headgear for the job. The factory fed supplies to the Armament Depot at Gosport's Priddy's Hard, overlooking Portsmouth harbour. The depot supplied ships, aircraft and troops with the explosive equipment and mines they needed.

Pixie's real name was Pamela. Her mother's then boyfriend, possibly her father, had taken one look at the hour-old silver-haired scrap and renamed her, saying she looked like a garden gnome. He'd balked at having his surname on her birth certificate, so the space remained blank. That had been nineteen years ago. Pixie had decided life was too short to worry about it, because old Adolf Hitler might blow them all to pieces at any time.

Dick Haymes, on the wireless, was singing himself to more success with 'You'll Never Know' when the buzzer sounded and the machinery slowed. Pixie stopped topping up the shell cases with the grains that reminded her of lemonade powder. The girls around the big work-bench gave a small cheer.

'Thank Christ for that,' said Rita. 'Lunchtime.' She took off her gloves and laid them on the bench. Pixie saw Rita's nails were nearly, but not quite, devoid of the bright varnish she loved. The job demanded an almost hospital-like cleanliness. If they did go to the Fox, she would painstakingly replace the scarlet colour that matched her lipstick.

'We going outside?' Pixie was dying for a breath of pure March air. She ran her fingers through her hair at the front of her turban and scratched. 'I hate this head-gear,' she said.

Rita nodded in agreement, then grimaced. 'It'll be cold in the yard. Is it worth the bother of changing our clothes and shoes?' Any article of clothing or jewellery that might cause a spark was left in the locker room. Leather shoes were banned as the tacks, or Blakey's, were hazardous.

'It's fresher outside than the smell in here.'

'Oh, all right.' Rita gave in, as Pixie had known she would. She slipped her arm through her friend's and together they walked towards the locker room and the exit. Already chatter was dying down as the remaining women left the long workshop.

3

They washed their hands and changed into warm coats. Carrying their lunchboxes, they strolled towards a low wall that overlooked the harbour and the strip of sea between Portsmouth and Gosport. Choosing a spot that seemed clean, Pixie sat down.

The sun was weak but bright, and warm enough to cause the green buds on the rowan trees to glisten. A few daffodils had braved the damp after the rain of the previous night. Primroses and late snowdrops lay beneath the gorse and over-wintering bramble bushes.

Pixie eyed the Oxo tin that served as Rita's lunch container and the glass bottle with the ball-top stopper filled with a milky brown liquid. 'Not got another flask, yet, then?'

'Nah. When I've got the money there ain't one to be had in the shops, and when there is, I ain't got the money. Bloody war! Anyway, this does the job.' Rita unclipped the top and swigged the tea straight from the bottle. Afterwards, she wiped her hand across her mouth, then grinned at Pixie. 'How's your mum?'

Pixie began to choke on her doorstep dripping sandwich. Rita thumped her across the back and the coughing fit stopped.

'Ouch!' Her glare turned to laughter as she picked

spat-out crumbs from her cardigan. 'Only come back with a bleedin' canary, ain't she?'

'What?'

'A canary in a cage and a new hat. She danced in large as life just after I got home last night, about half ten it was. Please don't laugh.'

But it was too late. Both girls were giggling fit to burst. Pixie used the hem of her blouse to wipe the tears from her eyes, then asked, 'Why couldn't I have had a proper mother, like you?'

'A mother who cares more about her new husband than her daughter, you mean?'

Pixie knew she'd been thoughtless. Rita's stepdad was younger than her mother and good-looking in a beefy way. He gave Pixie the creeps, though. There was something greasy and shifty about him and he wouldn't look you in the eye when he spoke.

She put a hand on Rita's arm. 'Sorry,' she said. She stared into her friend's brown eyes. Honest eyes fringed with long dark lashes that Pixie envied. 'You can't deny that your mum's always got time to listen, though.'

Rita sighed. 'She does her best.' The silence that followed didn't last long. 'Where's your mum been this time?' She took another swig of tea.

Pixie shook her head. 'Brighton. She was doin' all right with this bloke until his wife turned up outside the little house they'd rented.'

'I suppose he never told her he was married?'

'Course not.' Pixie looked at Rita, whose face had fallen. 'Oh, don't feel sorry for her. She's found another bloke!'

Pixie was laughing now and trying to make light of her mother's return, but inside she was crying. Every time her mum, Gladys, disappeared with her latest man, Pixie fought the loneliness that followed as she tried to act as though her life was normal. But no sooner had she got used to sorting out the bills, which usually included paying those her mother had run up while she'd been away, Gladys would return and the merry-go-round would start all over again.

'It's a good job you got that Bob living next door to you. He's a kind man. I don't know why you don't marry him.' Rita leaned across to wipe a crumb from Pixie's chin.

'Because I don't love him, that's why.' Pixie steadied the blue tin flask over its cup and poured. She thought of the dark-haired man whose presence in the next house eased her loneliness. He was a good friend, but that was all. 'When I marry, I want to be head over heels in love.'

How many times had she written those very words in her diary as she'd sat in bed at night?

Pixie liked words, liked to write them down. People didn't always listen when they were told things and conversations were soon forgotten. She wrote things down in exercise books. That way, the words became real. She twisted the stopper and set down the flask on the gravel by the wall.

A ship's siren caused her to look across the strip of grey, muddy water from which issued a salty, dank odour. Waves with white tips hurled themselves against the pontoon, making the wooden contraption rock. The small boats moored against it bobbed up and down and bumped against their buoys.

Two more ships were berthed in the Dockyard. Pixie recognized their American flags waving in the breeze. No doubt tonight the sailors would climb aboard the squat, beetle-like ferries that ran between Gosport and Portsmouth to spend money in the pubs and try their luck with the girls.

The Channel was busy with fishing craft and tankers watched over by Nelson's flagship, the *Victory*. This part of the south coast was high on Hitler's bombing list and Gosport had taken a beating. Gaps like broken teeth appeared in the streets where houses had once stood.

Buddleia, purple fireweed and nettles grew on waste-ground in the summer amid the rubble and broken bedsteads.

Pixie loved Gosport because it wasn't as brash as its neighbour, Portsmouth. It wasn't an affluent area, far from it, but the markets and pubs spilling noisily onto the pavements were gloriously colourful, and the people were rich in humour and kindness, just like her friend. Rita was trying to scratch her head through the turban's itchy material, as Pixie had done moments earlier.

'Fat lot of good it is wearing this thing when the front of me hair goes orange instead of staying black.' Rita frowned. 'Anyway, this is Gosport, not the movies. We're two girls working in a factory with about two thousand five hundred other women an' a load of men. And most of them want the same true-love miracle.'

'I know,' said Pixie. 'And one week we work days and the next we work nights. Twelve-hour shifts. But we can dream, can't we?' She didn't wait for an answer, but put out a hand and touched the soft discoloured curls at the front of Rita's turban. 'Extra bit of hair dye should cover that.'

'You reckon?'

Pixie nodded and drank the last dregs of cold tea. They watched the stream of girls returning to the workshops.

They wore different-coloured overalls and caps relating to the areas they worked in and the type of explosives they handled.

She glanced towards the railway line, with its open trucks that hauled goods around the site. The red-brick buildings were practically hidden in woodland. That was the beauty of the place, so near the town of Gosport yet not overlooked, and with excellent water access. Pixie smiled at Rita, who was picking bits of fluff off her coat. She reckoned the break was nearly over and wrapped up the uneaten food to feast on later. Em, who had ticked off Rita earlier, was walking towards them. Pixie knew Em was a good bit older than her, mid-thirties maybe. Today her face seemed more tired-looking than usual. If Pixie wasn't mistaken, she had been crying. When Em wasn't inspecting shells before they were passed into service, she had the unenviable job of putting highly toxic azide pellets into shell fuses. Her hands were boxed within thick glass panels to localize the vapour, as it presented a severe explosion risk.

'You all right, Em?' Pixie asked.

Em seemed to shrink into herself. Then she sighed. 'I'm telling you two now before it becomes common knowledge but my Doris is in the family way.'

'Jesus, Em.' Pixie sighed.

'Oh, no.' Rita put her arms around the other woman.

Pixie often wondered how Em coped. Her husband had been sent home from the war with shattered knees and spent his days in a wheelchair. Pieced together with bits of metal, he could just about stand, but he was quiet and withdrawn. He'd been rescued from a trench full of his dead mates, and Em had told them he had terrible nightmares.

Em was the breadwinner so she took any job that paid. Her eldest girl, Lizzie, didn't live at home but helped when she could. She was saving to be married. Lizzie was the same age as Pixie.

But no matter how hard Em worked, the most difficult job was keeping Doris safe. Doris wasn't like other girls her age. Cruel children taunted her. Most adults ignored her.

'Sometimes I wish I'd put her in an institution like the doctor advised.' Em twisted her hanky around her fingers and stepped back to look at them both.

'No, you don't,' said Pixie. 'That girl idolizes you.'

'I know. And I'm only letting off steam by saying that. For all her rages and the wet beds, it isn't her fault. The bloke who's had his way with her must take the blame. If I could only find out who's responsible.'

'Mum!'

Em lowered her voice as Doris bounded up to them. Her blonde curls bounced around her face, and Pixie thought again that if it wasn't for the slack mouth and faraway look in Doris's eyes, the girl could have been a beauty. Doris *was* beautiful. But she was an eight-year-old child in a young woman's body.

Rita stood up from the wall and enveloped Doris in a hug. 'Hello, love,' she said.

Pixie whispered, 'It's difficult to believe Doris isn't quite, quite . . .'

'Normal?' Em was gazing across the harbour, though Pixie could see she wasn't watching anything. She spoke quietly. 'It took me a long time to see it – until I realised she wasn't walking and talking like the other kiddies of her age. Rita chipped in: 'She can hold down a light job, can't you, Doris, my pet?'

Doris's face lit up with a smile. Rita was right, thought Pixie. For that reason Doris had been allowed to work at the munitions factory under the supervision of her mother, attending to simple duties, like sweeping up, checking in the coats, running errands. Of course, this suited everyone, especially the manager, Harry Slaughter. Em could be handed all the worst jobs and do them without complaint because she knew that if she made a fuss both she and Doris could be sacked.

'And you've no idea who the father is?' Rita persisted.

Men and women were trailing like snails to the factory's entrance.

They made their way to the open doors of the long building for the afternoon shift. From inside, the wireless was cheering the workers with the Mills Brothers' singing.

'She won't say, Rita.' Em turned to Pixie. 'She don't go out on her own and this is the only place where I can't keep me eyes on her all the time.' She stepped out of the way as Myra, a tall, well-built girl, brushed against her as she went to open her locker. Then she grabbed Myra's arm. 'Here, you've had more than tea out of your flask. Trying to disguise booze with peppermints don't always work. I can smell it.'

Myra looked at her, then at Pixie. 'Nah,' she said. 'Last night I was out for a few drinks but it'd be more than my life's worth to be caught at it in the daytime doing a job like this.'

Pixie caught her breath. One false move on the line with detonators and concentrated explosive powder and all of them could be killed. She stared at Myra but the woman's eyes were now fixed to the floor.

'You better be on the level with me,' said Em.

Myra seemed to shrink into herself. There was talk among the girls that something was going on in her private life, but as yet Myra hadn't confided in anyone. Still, the heavy bombing the Queen's Road area had taken a few weeks ago was enough to unhinge anyone.

Em relented. 'Go on. On your way.' Myra slipped off her shoes and coat. The piercing shriek of a whistle told Pixie there were only a few minutes left to change their clothes.

Em sniffed the air. 'Fags out, girls. You know you can't smoke inside.'

Myra handed over her outdoor shoes and coat for examination, then was given the all-clear by Mae, the woman who made the daily searches of bodies, clothing and footwear going in and coming out of the building.

'Such a palaver simply getting in and out of here,' said Pixie, following her. She liked the big-boned, normally jolly girl and didn't like to see her as down as she'd been lately. Myra didn't answer.

Pulling on her work boots, Pixie turned to Em. 'You must have some idea who the father is.'

'I told you. She won't say. Just goes around with that daft grin on her face.'

'I bet your old man wasn't happy about it,' Rita put in.

Em's face fell. 'No. He called me all manner of names before I got a clout. He might be in a wheelchair but he's bloody quick when he wants to be.'

'But it's not your fault,' Pixie said.

'Try telling him that.' Em sighed. 'He's so different now. Not the kind man he used to be. This bloody war has a lot to answer for.'

Pixie put her arm across Em's ample shoulders. She could smell baking on her skin. Em was a cracker of a cake-maker when she could get hold of the ingredients. 'We'll all help with the baby stuff,' she said.

Em wiped her hands on the thin towel that hung by the sink. 'I know you will.' She pursed her lips, then practically hissed, 'He's a bastard, whoever done this!'

'You wouldn't think of taking Doris to Eadie Moss in Old Road?' Rita asked.

'That bitch! I'd as soon cut me own throat!' Em's face had reddened with fury. 'Anyway, I can't afford what she charges.'

So Em had considered a visit to Eadie Moss, Pixie thought. More than likely if she'd had the money Em would think Eadie the answer to her prayers.

'How will you manage, Em?'

Em shook her head. 'I don't know, Pixie. She can't have the kiddie. Who'd look after it? I can't. Doris can't look after herself, let alone a baby.' Another buzzer sounded. Em seemed to shake herself into inspection-manager mode. She stretched herself to her full height and, in a sharp, dignified tone, called out, 'C'mon, you lot, back to work.'

Most of the girls were at their places by the time the conveyor-belt started up for the afternoon shift.

'Who would do that to a kid like Doris?' said Rita. Pixie saw her glance over to where Doris, in her own little world, was pushing a broom along the floor.

'There are hateful blokes everywhere,' Rita went on. 'But we'll find out who's taken advantage of that poor girl. I think Doris should have it taken away.' She sighed. 'Anyway, it's not our problem.'

Pixie rounded on her: 'That's where you're wrong. It is our problem! Em's our friend and a bloody good manager. But she's worried sick. Supposing she makes a mistake?'

'Em's too much of a professional to make a mistake on the line.'

'It only takes one moment of forgetfulness and we're all blown away. Why d'you think she's always so watchful of us?'

She could smell the damp in the place as she walked along the cracked lino of the passage. She shivered. The range had gone out in the kitchen, which told her that her mother had left quite a while ago. On the kitchen table was the birdcage with a tea towel over it. As soon as she whipped off the covering, the yellow bird began chirruping.

'Hello,' Pixie said. 'You're pretty, aren't you?' The poor canary was probably as fed up as she was. Amazingly, there was fresh water in a dish clipped to the side of the cage and a second dish topped up with seed. A twig with more seeds had been placed on a perch. Her mother had obviously sorted out the bird before she'd gone out.

'Don't suppose she left *you* a meal to come home to.' Rita was still admiring the canary, which was sitting quite still and peering back at her. 'Or is that bird it?' Pixie gave her mate a withering look. 'Good job you had a bowl of stew at our place,' Rita continued. 'Even if it was more vegetable than mutton.' She went to the sideboard and slid back the metal bread bin's lid. 'This would make a good bomb – not that I'm sayin' it's hard!' She let the quarter loaf fall back with a thud. 'And you was lucky me mum and stepdad weren't having one of those point-less rows they're so fond of. I wish she'd never married him. But she reckons she was lucky Malcolm took her on after me dad copped it, her being older than him.' Rita grew quiet and Pixie knew she was thinking about her real dad, who had died of a brain tumour. She had idolized the jolly man.

Pixie didn't like Rita's stepdad. There was something really creepy in the way his eyes always seemed to follow Rita, as though he was mentally undressing her. She shook her thoughts away. Malcolm had married Rita's mum because he loved her. 'My mum's enjoying the war,' she said.

Somehow it was all right for her to criticize her mother but she hated anyone else, even Rita, doing so. Pixie picked up an empty Brickwoods Pale Ale bottle, looked at it for a moment, then set it back on the table next to two dirty glasses. She'd obviously brought someone home with her.

'Isn't she just?' Rita agreed.

Pixie opened the larder door and peered inside.

'I don't suppose she left you anything to eat?' Rita said.

'You're wrong there,' said Pixie. She backed out of the cupboard with a tea plate on which sat a small mound of Spam, dried at the edges.

'It looks lonely without its tin.'

Pixie put the meat back on the shelf. 'No, she's done no shopping,' she announced. 'But there's condensed milk and tea.' She put the caddy and the opened tin of milk on the table. 'You make a cuppa while I have a wash and get changed.'

Pixie, closely followed by Rita, went out into the scullery. Rita filled the kettle at the stone sink and put it on the stove.

Pixie took her curling tongs from the shelf, lit the ring at the back of the stove and propped them over the flames. Rita went back into the other room and Pixie heard cups clattering.

Pixie had a quick strip wash at the sink in cold water, saving the boiling water for tea.

'It's ready,' she shouted. 'I'll die if I don't have a cuppa.' From a hanger on a nail on the back of the door she pulled on a green box-pleated skirt, then tucked in her white blouse with the pussy-cat bow, and added a green jacket with a peplum. 'Glad I ironed these last night,' she said.

Rita, teapot in one hand, took a rose-coloured silk camisole off the line tied across the scullery. 'When did you get this?' She put down the teapot and let the fragile silk run through her fingers. 'It's lovely. And here's the French knickers to match. Oh, my God,' she said, 'there's another set here, in peach. You're so lucky.'

'They're not mine.' Pixie grinned. 'They're me mum's.

I ain't never seen them before. She's got much better undies than I have.' She thought of her white cotton knickers growing greyer with every wash after they'd been hung outside to dry. Bomb dust settled everywhere. She'd have loved new underwear, but the clothing coupons were always needed for something more important. The frilled silk in Rita's hands had to be black-market gear. It certainly hadn't come from Woolworth's.

Pixie rubbed her toothbrush over the round block of Gibbs' dentifrice and started scrubbing her teeth. 'Must be a present from some bloke,' she mumbled, the pink toothpaste bubbling and dribbling from the side of her mouth. Pixie was always scrubbing her teeth.

'If it was a present I wonder what she gave him in return,' said Rita.

Pixie rinsed her mouth, then spat down the plughole. 'Oy! That's my mother you're casting aspersions on!' Then she laughed. 'Good thing you're my best friend! If you weren't I'd clock you one for saying that!'

Gladys liked men, lots of men. When she was younger, she had been beautiful. Pixie had photos that showed a blonde with long legs posing on the beach at Brighton. But there was no denying her mother could be very selfish.

A knock at the door shook Pixie from her thoughts.

'You go and answer it while I draw a line up the back of me legs with me eyebrow pencil. Wouldn't it be lovely to go into a shop and buy a pair of silk stockings?'

In the mirror above the sink she stared at her green eyes and blonde hair. Her face was a little too thin for beauty but she was aware she was a perfect foil to Rita's dark, sultry looks.

She searched in her make-up bag, then puffed out her cheeks with the effort of swinging a foot onto the edge of the draining-board to begin the chore. She could hear footsteps and voices in the passage. 'I bet me mum has some silk stockings. And I bet she's hidden them! One day I'm going to wear nothing but silk stockings and when I get the tiniest run in one I'm going to throw them away and simply buy loads more.'

'Is that so?'

His voice was deep, with little of the local Hampshire harshness. Bob, her neighbour, wearing horn-rimmed spectacles and still dressed in his market gear of collarless shirt, V-necked pullover and thick grey woollen trousers, stood next to Rita. A lock of dark curly hair fell onto his forehead no matter how many times he ran his fingers through it.

Pixie almost toppled over, putting her foot down.

'Don't stop on my account.' Bob grinned. 'I like the

view. I know you're going out so I won't keep you long. I came round because I heard noises and voices in here today and wanted to make sure everything was all right.'

His eyes fell on the curling tongs glowing bright red on the stove. 'Do you need them as hot as that?'

'Oh, Christ!'

He went to turn off the gas tap, grabbed a towel and moved the tongs away from the glowing ring. 'Best let them cool right down before you use them, otherwise you'll have no hair left.'

'Thanks.' Pixie smiled.

'So, was there someone in here today?'

'Oh, yes. Me mum's back.' Pixie shrugged her shoulders. 'No idea how long for, though.'

At that moment the canary gave a loud squawk.

'That's her bird,' Pixie added.

'Ah. A canary for a canary,' he said.

'Don't you start!' Rita punched him playfully on the arm.

The women who worked with explosives got yellow hair – hence the name Canary Girls. 'Though with Pixie being at work, I expect you wondered what was going on in here.'

'Mystery solved. I'd better go. Got to get some sleep. I'm at Fareham tomorrow and I need to be at the market by five.' Bob worked hard, rising early to sell whatever he could buy from wholesalers and auctions. He made to walk away, then turned back. 'There's tomorrow's dinner in here.' He pointed to the bird that was singing sweetly now. 'Won't get much off a leg, though! And mind those curling tongs.'

After the door had closed behind him, Pixie gazed longingly at the tea that Rita was pouring into enamelled mugs. She didn't say anything but went back to drawing a dark line down her leg to represent the seam of a stocking.

'He likes you.' Rita was stirring in condensed milk.

'No, he doesn't, he's just a nice person.' Pixie looked at Rita. 'I don't want to talk about Bob Roberts. Why don't you do something sensible, like go round the house and check the blackout curtains are in place while I do me hair?'

Rita stomped off. She looked like she was sucking lemons.

Pixie curled her fringe into a roll, then turned the back under, pageboy style. Then she shook a bottle of Evening in Paris perfume and touched her neck and pulse spots with it. She breathed in the sensuous smell and sighed. The small blue bottle was less than half full and luxuries were extremely hard to come by.

When Rita came down, Pixie was rummaging in a cupboard drawer.

'We're never getting out tonight at this rate,' grumbled Rita, taking a slurp of tea. 'And it's a pity Em ain't gonna be there after all. She could do with letting her hair down, but her husband won't allow it.' She drank some more tea, then asked, 'What are you looking for now?'

'Paper.'

'What for?' Rita took her lipstick from her bag and in the mirror dabbed at her lips until they glistened scarlet.

'I think I know how we can raise money for Doris's abortion, but we got to keep secret what we need the money for – it mustn't get out to a pub full of people. Some folks have very strong ideas about babies and getting rid of them.' To tell the truth, she herself had mixed feelings on the matter. But at least they'd be giving Em a choice and that had to be better than none.

Rita said, 'You seriously think I'd say anything? And you know I'd do anything to help Em . . . as long as it's honest.'

Rita, who'd changed her clothes at home, was dressed in her best black frock. It had a white motif and padded shoulders. She looked very exotic. Pixie pulled her away from the sideboard drawers and opened one.

She smiled as her eyes fell on an old exercise book.

'Aha!' she said. 'That'll do fine. Now where did I put that black eyebrow pencil?'

Then she explained her idea to Rita.

Rita pushed open the heavy oak and glass door of the Fox. Clouds of cigarette smoke, mixed with the sweet, earthy smell of beer and unwashed bodies, wafted over her and Pixie. 'Dunno why we bothered to make ourselves smell nice,' she moaned. 'This pub stinks.'

'Why, just for once, Rita, can't you look on the bright side of things?' said Pixie. She looked around the packed bar, hearing the loud voices of American sailors above Vera Lynn on the wireless singing about the white cliffs of Dover.

She spotted Sam Owen, the manager, talking to Old Fred, who was shuffling cards for cribbage and sitting with his mate. 'Let's hope he's in a good mood,' she said. Keeping her fingers crossed, she turned to Rita. 'Come on.'

They were talking about the regional football tournaments, normal football league games having been suspended for the duration of the war. Why did men always talk about football? 'Sam?' Pixie put her hand on the publican's arm. 'Can we have a quiet word?'

The bags beneath his faded blue eyes seemed to have a life of their own as he turned from Fred and asked,

'Whassamatter?' He was frowning, but as soon as he saw Pixie, a smile lit up his red face.

'I got a friend who's in trouble, and me and Rita here,' she elbowed Rita in the ribs, 'need to make a bit of money fast. We wondered if we could use the bar and the customers . . .'

She didn't get any further: Sam's face had darkened from red to purple. 'I'm not having any funny business here. I could lose me licence.'

'No, no! It's not that kind of thing!' Though what kind of 'funny business' he meant, Pixie wasn't sure.

'I get lots of married women try to pick up punters in here when they ain't got no money to feed their kids. I feels sorry for 'em but this ain't no knocking shop.' Pixie's eyes fastened on his grubby shirt collar. His wife had run off with a customer less than six months ago and he was finding life difficult.

'You have to tell him the truth, Pixie,' whispered Rita. Sam brightened.

Pixie glanced at Bert, Fred's mate, with his wooden leg, staring at them intently, and taking in every word. Fred too, was waiting for the next instalment.

'Can we go somewhere a bit more private?' Pixie asked. Bert looked put out. He took the cards from Fred and shuffled them again.

'Come through to the back.'

Pixie let out a sigh of relief. 'You'll shuffle all the spots off them cards, if you ain't careful,' she told Bert.

Sam lifted the wooden door in the counter. The three of them moved past the colourful bottles reflected in the mirrored wall of the bar. Pixie reckoned that due to the shortages the contents had long been drunk and the bottles refilled with coloured water.

'Watch the bar, Trudy,' Sam yelled to one of his barmaids. She nodded her blonde curls.

It was quieter by the stairs and Pixie poured out her story, knowing that Sam wouldn't spread the news of Doris's condition. When she'd finished, Sam said, 'You realize Em might be as cross as a tiger with a wasp up its arse if she knew what you was doing?'

Sam had been to school with Em and had walked out with her a few times before settling for his wilful missus. It was even said that Sam and Em had cosied up a few times since, taking what happiness they could salvage from unhappy marriages.

Pixie nodded. 'I'm expecting that. It's also possible she'll throw the money back in our faces, but it's a chance we have to take. Say yes. Please?'

'Poor Em, she don't have much luck, do she?' Sam bit

his lip. Pixie knew then that his soft spot for Em meant she and Rita would have their way.

For a moment there was silence. Sam's enormous belly heaved, then he smiled. 'All right, then.' He looked at them. 'I wish I had a couple of mates like you two,' he said.

Pixie was so excited she leaned up on tiptoe and kissed his salty-tasting forehead.

'Gerrorf,' Sam said. 'The regulars'll be gossiping about me next.'

Pixie opened her clutch bag and unrolled the poster she'd made. Rita had lip-sticked hearts on it as a decoration. It read,

WAR EFFORT KISSES

A SHILLING EACH

Chapter Three

After a few hours Pixie reckoned she had been kissed by the whole of Gosport's male population, and half of the American fleet! Sam's female customers had been divided into two camps: those who thought it was a laugh and those who had tried to stop their men going back for a second kiss. Any questions about the nature of the 'war effort' were fielded by Sam.

'I think I've got razor rash,' moaned Rita, tenderly feeling her chin and rosy cheeks.

'A bit of Vaseline on your face when you go to bed and you'll be as right as rain in the morning,' Pixie said, humming along to a Glenn Miller tune. 'Thank goodness it's nearly chuck-out time!'

'Too right,' said Rita. 'I feel like I've been gobbled up!' She laughed. 'What about that bloke I had to slap because he thought he could cop a feel as well!'

'Good thing Sam was here with us.' Pixie smiled at him: he was coming towards them with two gin and oranges.

'On the house, girls,' he said.

'Thanks, Sam,' Pixie said. There were still a few customers about, more than usual at this time of the night, including a table full of Americans who'd all been kissed, and two old men in the corner, playing dominoes.

An old man in a flat cap caught her eye and grinned at her. Pixie smiled back. He was quite a good kisser, she thought, but thank goodness he'd kept his mouth closed! It wasn't so long ago, she remembered, that women alone in pubs were regarded as tarts. Though the married women were often taken along by their men, once they'd been bought a drink they'd had to resign themselves to an evening sitting alone on a bench, or with the other wives, while their husbands stood at the bar with their mates. But now the men were away fighting and the women worked at men's jobs, they ventured into pubs for a good time with their friends. Sadly, some of the older men working at the armaments factory still reckoned women shouldn't be tackling men's jobs, and some unpleasant name-calling went on behind the girls' backs.

Pixie knew that since the last war, due to the yellow discolouration of skin and hair caused by the gunpowder,

'Canary Girls' was one of the least offensive names they were called.

'You did me a lot of good, you two,' said Sam, breaking into Pixie's thoughts. 'I've had a busy night. Have you raised what you wanted?' She knew he was concerned for Em.

Rita poured the money from two pint tankards onto a table and began counting. After a while she grinned. 'Plenty,' she said, and finished her drink. Then she whispered to Pixie, 'Now all we have to do is make Em take it. I reckon that's going to be the hard part.'

'We'll talk to her together,' said Pixie, staring at herself in the mirror at the back of the bar. 'Jesus, I look a state.'

Then she froze. The wailing had begun.

'Oh, no!' shouted Sam, leaving Pixie and Rita and moving quickly to the back of the bar. 'Take cover, everyone!'

The scream of the air-raid siren warning people that an attack was imminent over Gosport and Portsmouth was a dreaded sound. Pixie glanced at the windows covered with thick blackout curtains. Beneath the material the glass was criss-crossed with tape to stop it shattering if the windows blew inwards.

Some customers had already fled the building. Others hadn't moved a muscle.

'Nearest shelter is by the ferry,' yelled Sam.

Rita shook her head. 'Too far to run in the pitch dark,' she said. She tried to scoop the money back into the glass tankards without it spilling across the table.

Pixie hoped the raid wouldn't last long. She knocked back her gin for courage.

'Fancy another?' The sailor who'd asked the question seemed to have materialized from nowhere.

His American voice made Pixie think of the films. 'Yes, please.'

Rita was behind him, frantically signalling that she, too, would like another drink.

'I'll get one for your friend as well, shall I?' he said.

'Blimey! You got eyes in the back of your head?' Pixie laughed.

'We got no air-raid shelter on the premises, everyone.' Sam was apologetic. 'The public one we used, just up the road, took a hit about three weeks ago.' Pixie knew he was devastated that so many people had been killed that night. 'I don't leave the premises,' he sniffed, 'for obvious reasons,' he looked at the beer pumps, 'but you're welcome to stay here. First drink is on me.' He nodded and the bags beneath his eyes jiggled. 'If we have to be blown to smithereens, I say we go happy.'

The American listening to Sam seemed confused. Pixie

watched the tall, broad-shouldered man walk towards the bar.

'I wish this war would end,' she said to her friend. Her heart was beating fast. She should be used to the air raids by now, but part of her knew her fear would never go away.

'Did you kiss that American or did I?' Rita asked. 'He's a bit of all right, isn't he?' She'd reclaimed the money from the table and now held it in a brown carrier bag Sam had found for her. 'I wouldn't mind kissing him.'

'Behave yourself, Rita,' said Pixie.

The American came back from the bar with a drink in each hand. 'You Brits are generous,' he said. 'The girl wouldn't take my money.' He grinned at Pixie. 'My name's Cal. What's yours?'

'Pixie.'

'Like a fairy?'

'If you like.'

'It suits you,' he said, setting the drinks on a table.

Outside in the street, Pixie could hear people running for shelter, yelling for loved ones to keep up. For some reason her heart was still thumping against her ribcage, as though it was trying to escape her body. She took up one of the drinks and sipped at it, while Cal went back to the bar. She passed the other gin to Rita and was suddenly aware of another sailor, dark-haired, olive-complexioned, hovering near them.

Cal returned with two pints of beer. The barmaid, Trudy, set a candle on the table and lit it with a match. 'Sam's had to turn off the electric, gas and water,' she whispered. Her hands were rough and her red nail varnish chipped. 'We don't want to be blown to smithereens with a gas leak, do we?'

'What's smithereens?' A frown crossed Cal's face. Pixie thought he was very good-looking, a bit like Alan Ladd, though she'd heard that the movie star wasn't tall and Cal was well over six feet. 'I keep hearing this word,' Cal added.

'Little pieces,' said Pixie.

'Tiny bits,' said Trudy, before moving on to the next table.

'Ah!' said Cal. His American accent fascinated Pixie. It was a soft drawl that she found soothing. She knew the clipped nasal sound New Yorkers made, so guessed Cal came from another part of America. She stared at his smart uniform, the knife-edge creases in his trousers. Everything about him was immaculate, from his tanned skin to his short blond hair.

'This is my friend, Rita,' said Pixie. Rita was now sprawled across a chair, still clutching the precious bag.

'I kissed you.' Cal blushed.

Pixie looked at Rita and laughed. 'I believe you did.'

The blush spread to Cal's neck.

'I went back for seconds,' he said.

The other American was laughing now.

'It was all in a good cause,' said Pixie. She took her drink over to the window and pulled back the curtain a fraction. Against the near darkness in the bar and the inky blackness outside, she could see bright searchlights criss-crossing the skies. The growl of planes filled the air. 'They want to hit the dockyard and the armaments depot,' she said, taking another sip of her gin. 'They'd love to get a direct hit on the armaments, but it's on waste-ground with trees and gorse bushes hiding it, so it's difficult to see, especially as most of the roofs are painted green to blend in with the countryside.'

Cal had followed her, Rita close behind him.

'Mind you, if a bomb made a direct hit, there'd be nothing left of us.' Pixie took another sip of her gin. 'I pity the night workers.'

'We can't use the air-raid shelter at work,' said Rita. The other American had joined them. He was even taller than Cal.

'This is my buddy, Tony,' said Cal.

Pixie saw Rita's eyes linger on Tony.

'Why can't you use the shelter?' Tony had a sing-song Italian voice.

As he spoke, Rita opened her mouth to say something, but nothing came out.

Cal suddenly hissed, 'Get down.'

He grabbed Pixie's arm and pulled her beneath a nearby table. She could smell his citrus cologne and somehow it calmed her. Drinks spilled everywhere as the table rocked. Suddenly there was a huge explosion. The whole building shook and clouds of dust seemed to drift in from nowhere. Tony and Rita had dropped to the floor and were crouching together, their arms tight about each other.

'They store the gunpowder in it,' said Rita, finally. 'The air-raid shelter.'

Pixie had to re-run the previous conversation in her head so she could make sense of Rita's words. Lights bounced off the curtains and the snarling of the planes was so loud that Pixie knew they were right overhead. Half of her was too terrified to move, the other half wanted to stand outside and watch the dogfight: the air would be full of noise and colour and the sky would be lit up like it was with fireworks in November. And all about her there would be the smell of burned wood and cordite.

Inside, though, cocooned beneath the table, Pixie could see clouds of dust drifting across the candles' flickering flames. Amazingly, one candle had fallen from the table and was upright on the floor, still burning merrily. The pub's roof shook and the walls seemed to rattle, joined by the sound of china slipping and breaking.

'Oh dear,' muttered Sam. 'That sounds like me missus's best china gone at last.'

Then the whistling started. At first low, then slowly louder and louder, closer and closer it came.

Cal pulled Pixie to him and her face was smothered by material that smelt of newly washed wool. She relaxed. Cal made her feel safe, though she knew that was ridiculous, given the danger they were all in.

The droning was going on and on.

And then came the crash.

Rita screamed. The candles guttered out, leaving them in total darkness. Bottles fell and smashed.

There was a moment's silence.

Pixie felt unable to breathe. From somewhere came the noise of a window cracking and glass falling.

Then torches were flashing and voices shouting. Sam scrambled up, fumbled for the matches in his pocket and lit another candle.

'The planes have gone,' said Rita. 'But someone's copped it.'

Pixie could see a layer of grey dust clinging to her friend's dark hair. Cal crawled out from beneath the table on all fours, got to his feet, then held out his hand so that Pixie could stand upright.

'I think it's over,' came a woman's voice from across the room.

'Mind the floor!' Sam shouted. 'It's slippery and there's broken bottles everywhere.'

Pixie heard the crunch of glass beneath Sam's shoes. She saw him leave the bar. Moments later the electric light came on. Sam didn't bother with the metal drinks measure but sloshed whisky in a glass and downed the golden liquid in one. Pixie could see relief on his face. 'There's a drink here for those that want one,' he said gruffly. He helped himself to another, his whole body shaking.

Pixie walked over to him. 'You want a hand to clear up?' There were upended ashtrays, fag ends covering the floor, broken glasses and bottles.

'Thanks for the offer,' he said, 'but I know you got work to go to in the morning. Get off home.' Then he added quietly, 'When you see Em, tell her I said hello.'

'She was supposed to come tonight but her old man wouldn't let her out,' Pixie said. 'At least it gives us the opportunity to collect the money.'

'He was a decent bloke before the war got to him,' Sam said.

'You're a nice man, Sam,' Pixie said. Then she pushed herself up on tiptoe and kissed his cheek, a daughterly kiss. 'I won't forget the help you've given us tonight. Thank you.'

Rita was whispering to the Italian American. Her face was white beneath a mask of dust. Pixie mimed actions asking if Rita had the money they'd collected. Rita held up her brown bag. They'd already decided she would hang on to it. Pixie knew that if her own mother discovered it in the house, it wouldn't last five minutes.

Cal walked towards Pixie and tucked her arm through his. If a man had done that at any other time, Pixie would have thought him forward and shrugged him off. But there was something intimate about going through an air raid together and surviving.

When Cal opened the street door the sky was orange. People were crying and running along the pavement towards the ferry. Smoke filled the air. Piles of smouldering rubble lay in the road and the empty shop that had been next to the Fox lay in ruins. Pixie could hear an ambulance trundling along the high street. Then, at last, the scream of the all-clear, and Pixie breathed a sigh of relief.

She and Cal were slightly ahead of Rita and Tony, who seemed totally absorbed in each other. They walked in the road, careful of the uneven fragments of brick and glass underfoot. They talked of inconsequential things until Cal stopped and stared down at Pixie. 'So why were you selling kisses?'

'Been worrying you, has it?'

He looked embarrassed, as though he hadn't liked to ask her.

Pixie supposed it would have seemed strange, two women offering to kiss men for money. She cleared her throat. 'I'm not answerable to you or any man, but a friend's in trouble and we think the money we collected will help her.' She was quiet for a moment, then went on, 'We discussed it with Sam, the landlord, beforehand, and he was looking out for us. He knows the person in question, you see.'

Cal's shoulders dropped, as if he had been coiled like a spring, waiting for the right answer.

'None of the money is for us,' she added.

He smiled at her, showing white, even teeth. 'I'm beginning to think you're a very nice person,' he said.

The clock on the tower at St George's Barracks chimed as Pixie and Cal walked past, still arm in arm. Cal checked his watch.

'What time are you due on board?' Air raid or no air raid, sailors had to be back on ship at the designated time.

'In about half an hour.' As though on cue, a foghorn hooted in the harbour. 'But I need to see you safely home first.'

Pixie said, 'You two will never walk us home and get back to Portsmouth in time. What ship are you on?' She thought of the two destroyers she'd seen moored that morning at the dockyard – it seemed ages ago now.

'USS *Bristol*.'

'Are you and Tony on the same ship?'

'Yep.'

Although it was late, there were still plenty of people wandering about. The air raid had seen to that, displacing and disorienting many. A dust mist hung over the streets and gaps had appeared in the row of houses opposite St Vincent's Naval Barracks. People were scrabbling in the ruins, holding gas lamps that gave off an eerie glow. A tea wagon was on duty, with volunteers dishing out welcome refreshment to people sitting stunned on chairs, with blankets around them.

'This bloody, bloody war,' said Pixie.

To ease the tension she felt after the evening's events, she began to gabble on about herself and her job.

Suddenly Cal halted, turned and stopped her with a kiss, holding her head gently, pressing her body close to his. Pixie ran her fingertips along the nape of his neck, feeling the silkiness of his hair and the strength in his shoulders. She could feel, taste, smell him, and it was like fire running through her, but she knew the moment had to end even though she wanted it to continue.

Cal was the first to pull away, saying, 'I've got to go, but I *must* see you again.'

'Tomorrow night,' Pixie said. Her heart was thumping so hard she was sure he must be able to hear it. 'In the Fox.'

As Cal crossed the road to catch up with his mate, Pixie saw Rita walking towards her with a huge smile on her face.

Chapter Four

'I heard you was selling yourselves last night.'

Cedric drew the heavy trolley, piled with boxes of assorted ammunition parts, to a halt and stared at Pixie. There was frothy spittle at the corners of his mouth.

'None of your business, Cedric, and we was selling kisses, not our bodies. Get on with your work and leave me to mine!' She continued carefully pouring the TNT, then took another quick glance at the boss's son.

He was crushed, but there was no anger in his eyes. His fingers left the handle of the cart and he put his hands into his pockets. Pixie saw the movement under his clothes of his fingers edging towards his cock. She shuddered. Cedric never disguised what he was doing. Perhaps he thought the girls didn't notice him touching himself.

'Is that simpleton bothering you?' Rita shouted, and

all the girls started sniggering. Cedric was scared stiff of Rita. Maybe, thought Pixie, it was her brash personality or perhaps her quick tongue. Now, with both hands back on the trolley, pausing only to glare at Pixie, he continued on his way.

'He gives me the creeps,' said Pixie.

'His father's not much better,' returned Rita.

Harry Slaughter could always be found hanging around the women's lavatory, and it was well known that if you offered him a favour or two he'd get you a better job. 'You ever noticed his fingers?' Pixie didn't stop for Rita's reply. 'They're like fat sausages. Ugh! Imagine them all over you!'

Rita made a face. 'I'd rather not,' she said. 'It'd put me off me dinner. It was a laugh last night, wasn't it?'

Pixie nodded but her mind was still on Harry Slaughter. 'Imagine being that poor wife of his.' Eliza Slaughter was a rigid, middle-aged woman with a penchant for feathered hats. It was rumoured she was the daughter of a Stubbington farmer who bred horses and had sent her to the best schools in the hope that his plain child would rise above the local girls and marry well. Eliza had had few gentlemen friends who called more than once so when Harry Slaughter came along, with an eye to inheriting the family money, he was welcomed. Eliza's scoop from the shelf meant security for Harry. And she could hold her head high in village society. But, it was rumoured, Harry had to do as he was told and, so it was said, he was more than just a little afraid of the large-boned, domineering woman.

'Dragon she may be, but Harry Slaughter really is horrible,' Pixie said.

She remembered hiding beneath the table in the Fox to escape the falling bombs. A tingle ran down her spine when she thought of Cal and his kiss. A smile raised the corners of her lips as she pictured Sam and his willingness to help Em. Rita, too, must have been thinking about the previous evening, for she said, 'Sam was amazed he sold so much beer. He thought he was going to run out. And them two Yanks are really something, aren't they?'

She never stopped for answers, thought Pixie, but, no matter how much she chattered, she was eagle-eyed about the amounts of explosive she was using.

'When are we going to give Em the money?' Rita asked now, and nodded across the workshop to where Em was bending, closely watching as Myra filled a shell case. Myra looked as though she hadn't bothered to wash or even comb her hair.

There'd been another commotion in the locker room that morning, Em telling Myra she was on her last warning about drinking the night before work. In Em's mind, the safety of the girls was the priority. Pixie thought she was weighed down with unhappiness. Any moment now she would begin another of her walks around the room, checking that none of the girls had smuggled in anything from outside that might be a fire hazard. It was amazing how stupid some could be, hiding cigarettes, matches, so they could have a quick fag in the lavatory.

Pixie glanced towards the window. The morning's rain had eased and Portsdown Hill was a huge bulk of chalky earth sheltering Portsmouth and Gosport. The Dockyard was filled with ships that had arrived during the night, probably for repairs, bringing hundreds of troops. They would be reloaded with ammunition; the ammunition we make here at Priddy's, Pixie thought proudly. There was growing confidence among the workers and the townsfolk that Hitler was gradually being driven into retreat.

'Stop daydreaming, Pixie,' Rita said. 'We can't talk to Em here – too many sharp ears about. Shall we pop round tonight before going to the Fox?'

'Done. And don't think I never saw you kissing the face off that Tony!'

'What about yourself? I seem to remember you cuddling an American sailor too.'

Again Pixie felt the glow ignite itself as she remembered *that* kiss.

'Not just any old American. Callard Dalton the Third, actually. Like your Tony, he comes from Ohio.'

'So they're posh?'

'No, they're farm boys. I can see you were too busy kissing to find out anything about them, Rita.'

'I didn't want to waste smooching time, did I?' Rita winked.

Cedric once more stood by their bench with his trolley, having moved through the workshop handing out parts that were needed. He was looking fearfully at Rita. 'Cedric agrees with me, don't you?' She lunged forward suddenly and ruffled his greasy hair. Pixie could see the boy wasn't sure whether Rita was pulling his leg or not. He shifted from one foot to the other and blushed bright red. Both girls laughed.

Pixie turned the key in the front door and went in. Cigarette smoke greeted her. She could hear laughter, a man's voice, and the canary was chirruping fit to bust.

Wearing a loud checked suit and a pork-pie hat, a fat man had squeezed himself into the chair next to the kitchen window. For a moment Pixie wondered how he was going to extricate himself.

'Hello, girl,' he said, through a mouthful of gold teeth, as though he'd known her all his life and she was a visitor in her own house. He was chomping on a doorstep of bread and jam. Pixie wondered if that was the last of the loaf she'd queued twenty minutes for before she'd left for work that morning. 'You never told me you had a sister, Glad.' He laughed at his own joke. Pixie thought he sounded like a horse. Except that a horse wouldn't have been gawping at her breasts. The gold pinkie ring he wore seemed almost to slice his fat finger in two.

Her mother waltzed in from the scullery, holding the new cami-knickers and camisole top. A battered suitcase lay open next to the birdcage on the kitchen table. In the case, neatly folded, were some of Gladys's 'dolling-up' clothes, as she called them.

'Off somewhere, Mum?' Pixie tried not to sound as fed up as she felt.

Her mother barely glanced at her. 'Brighton. Del here's taking me to The Lanes to do some shopping. I've borrowed some money from the utility jar. You don't mind, do you, love? You'll be all right, won't you, Pixie?'

'You just came back from Brighton!' All Pixie's pent-up anger rose to the surface. She was the one who worked and brought money into the house and her mother spent it before she'd earned it. The utility jar on the shelf in the scullery held money for the gas and electricity. Pixie was fed up with paying off her mother's debts, and now here she was swanning off again with some bloke. She couldn't begrudge her a few shillings, though. She sighed.

'You're obviously going for more than a day. It might be nice for me to have the pleasure of your company sometimes. We haven't even had time for a chat since you came home this time.' Pixie took out from the case a pale blue blouse she'd never set eyes on before, then let it fall back again. 'Am I allowed to ask when you'll be coming home?'

The man got up, easing his flesh from the chair. Crumbs fell from his suit to the floor. 'Don't be cross, girly.' His voice was wheedling. 'You can come an' all, if you like.'

He moved towards her and put a hand on her shoulder. He smelt of sweat and hair oil.

'Get off me!' Pixie elbowed him in the ribs and moved back.

'Leave her alone, Del. She can be an ungrateful cow when she wants.' Gladys dropped the underwear inside the suitcase, picked up a packet of Woodbines from the table and theatrically lit a cigarette. She threw the spent match towards the grate. 'Put me other undies set in me drawer when they're dry, Pixie love.' She flapped a hand towards the scullery. Pixie noted she had on a new houndstooth check suit and black court shoes. Her red hat sported an ostrich feather, which was bouncing perkily. 'Why don't you put the kettle on, Pixie, and we can all have a nice cup of tea?' Gladys blew out a line of cigarette smoke that streamed across the small room.

'I don't want one. Unless, of course, you've actually bought some milk, Mum. And, by the way, your lipstick is smudged.'

Gladys went to the mirror over the unlit range and peered at herself. 'Damn,' she said. Del was looking at his watch. 'All right,' she said to him. 'I'm coming now.'

She flipped the lid of the suitcase shut. The cigarette hanging from the corner of her mouth, she stuck into the dregs in a teacup. 'You'll be all right, Pixie. You always are.'

The man had moved down the passage to the front door. 'Well, goodbye, girly.' His voice was small, as if he didn't want to be there any longer.

'Well, go on, then!' Pixie looked at her mother.

Gladys stared back at her, then hoisted the suitcase and looked over her shoulder to check that her stocking seams were straight. Satisfied, she walked down the passage. The front door slammed behind them. The canary on the table began to sing.

*

'That shines so bright it hurts your eyes to look at it,' Rita said to Pixie.

The brass anchor knocker on the door in Beryton Road gleamed with copious polishing – Pixie felt she oughtn't to touch it.

'This is a surprise,' said Em, answering the door. She seemed flustered.

'We're not stopping. It's just that we didn't want to talk to you at work.'

'Too many nosy parkers,' said Rita.

Em ushered them into a hallway that smelt of furniture polish, then into a room where a three-piece suite took pride of place. Antimacassars almost hid it.

'Would you like a cup of tea?'

Pixie noted the dark half-moons beneath Em's eyes. She would have been pretty if she hadn't been so careworn. Em was curvier than most but she went in and out in the right places, the way men liked.

Pixie shook her head. She hadn't wanted to come out tonight. Her mother's leaving had hurt her more than she'd ever admit to Rita. If she hadn't promised her friend to see Em and arranged to meet Cal, she would have crept into bed, pulled the quilt over her head and stayed there until morning.

'I've got a nice bit of seed cake?' Em's voice cut into Pixie's thoughts.

'No, honest, Em, but thanks. We just want a few words,' Rita said.

Em motioned for them to sit down. They took each end of the sofa, having already decided that Pixie should do the talking.

'It's like this,' began Pixie.

The half-closed door was pushed further open and Doris poked her head round. A smile lit her face. 'I'm doing a jigsaw. You can help me.' Then she rubbed her hand over her belly. 'I've got a baby in me.'

Em blushed. 'Go out to Daddy in the kitchen, darling. Rita and Pixie have come to see me. We won't be long.'

The girl's face creased. She burst into tears and disappeared.

'Excuse me.' Em got up. Pixie could see she needed all her strength to rise from the chair. 'Won't be a moment, I'll just see to her.'

Pixie and Rita looked at each other in the silence after her departure. Then Pixie shrugged and gazed round the room. Two china dogs sat at either side of the fireplace. A large mat, worn in places, covered the floor. A reproduction print of *The Blue Boy* and another of *The Laughing*

Cavalier hung on the walls in mock gold lacquered frames. It was a very clean, unused room.

Em returned. 'She's doing that jigsaw puzzle and eating a bit of cake. Sorry about that.' Pixie was reminded once more of what a loving mother Em was. Em had once confided to Pixie that Doris had been a surprise baby. She had never dreamed she was having a baby after being childless for so long after the birth of her first daughter. Pain clutched at Pixie's heart. Em thought the sun shone out of Doris's eyes. If only Gladys was a bit more considerate and loving . . . Stop it, she told herself. Say what you came to say.

'I'll get straight to the point. We got some money. Honestly got. We'd like you to have it. It's not charity. It's because we appreciate you and all you do for us at work.' Her mouth had gone as dry as an old paintbrush.

Rita said, 'If you don't want to use it for, you know, an abortion for . . .' she inclined her head towards the door that was now closed '. . . then we'd like you to keep it for a pram, bedding, whatever.' She fumbled in her bag. Out came a rolled-up brown paper carrier. She went over to Em and dropped the money onto her wraparound pinny. Em's mouth had fallen open. 'We'd be grateful if you didn't mention this to anyone,' Pixie added.

As though waking from a dream, Em peeped inside

the bag, then said incredulously, 'But I can't take this.'

Pixie nodded. 'Yes, you can.'

Rita said, 'You have to. It's not for you. It doesn't mean we're advising you to go ahead with an abortion. We all know what a terrible decision that is. But whatever you decide *is* the right decision.'

Pixie said, 'We have to go now.' She got up and smoothed down her skirt. 'We don't want it mentioned again.'

Rita picked up her handbag, grabbed hold of Pixie and moved back into the passage. She opened the front door and pulled Pixie after her, out into the night. Pixie quietly closed the door behind her, leaving the astounded Em to her problems.

Neither was in a talking mood as they walked towards North Street and the Fox.

The glazed-brick-fronted tavern was well over two hundred years old but catered to young and old alike. Its immense popularity was due to Sam, an expert host, who now waved cheerily to Pixie and Rita as they pushed open the door. Pixie made her way to a table in the corner. For a moment her eyes lingered on the darts players and two elderly men at the next table deep in the mysteries of cribbage. Rita brought two gin and oranges back from the bar and sat down next to her.

'I love Dinah Shore,' said Rita. 'Miss You' was playing on the wireless.

Pixie said, 'Let's get one thing clear. I don't want to talk about Em, money or my mother.' She took a sip of her drink.

'Well, you won't want to talk about men either, when I tell you the barmaid has just told me our Americans have been denied shore leave and can't get off the ship for four days. We've been asked to take a raincheck. A raincheck! I ask you! What kind of language is that?'

Pixie's heart sank. Cal might just have been the person to cheer her up. But he wasn't coming to the pub and it was no good wondering why, because it was wartime. She simply had to accept he was a sailor and the Americans had entered the war to help defeat Hitler and his armies, so Cal had to obey orders.

Her disappointment made her realize how much she'd been looking forward to seeing him.

Chapter Five

'Having a clear-out?'

Pixie was deep in thought and the voice startled her until she realized it was Bob's. Her neighbour was weeding in his vegetable patch. She put down the carpet beater, walked over to the wall separating the two houses and gazed into his tidy green garden. She didn't think she'd ever seen so many shoots of this and that and small plants pushing their heads up through the rich soil. Cloches had been set over fragile young leaves and he'd made the most of old window frames by building a miniature greenhouse.

'Mum's gone off again with a fancy man and I thought I'd take advantage of the weather with a couple of days off work. It's amazing how the rubbish creeps up, isn't it?' She waved an arm to encompass both gardens. 'You're definitely "Digging for Victory", aren't you?'

Her garden, surrounded by privet hedges, was a rubbish tip.

'I see you didn't burn your hair off.'

She pushed her fingers through her fringe and grinned. 'No.'

'Very smart outfit,' he said, a twinkle in his eye.

She looked down at herself. She had tied back her hair with a piece of string, put on a wraparound pinafore and wore her mother's old slippers with pom-poms on the tops. He must have read her mind for he said, 'You could dress in a sack and still look lovely.'

She smiled at him. Sometimes it was nice to be complimented, especially today. 'I've washed all me clothes, not that I've got many.' She bent down, picked up the carpet beater and a rag rug, slung the rug across the line, then started whacking it. Clouds of dust filled the air, making her cough. After a while she paused, breathing heavily. 'The house hasn't been cleaned properly for ages,' she said. 'I've been working shifts and Mum, when she's here, never has the time for all that malarkey.'

He looked fit, tanned and healthy, in a John Garfield way. But he was outdoors most days, selling on his stall at the markets.

'I'm about to make a drink,' he said, adjusting his spectacles. He brushed back the stubborn curl of hair from his forehead, leaving a smudge of dirt above one eyebrow. 'D'you fancy one?'

'Wouldn't say no.' She didn't add that she'd run out of milk and had no money until she collected her wages tomorrow to buy any more. She didn't like black tea. The milkman had stopped deliveries after he hadn't received payment for a month.

Bob propped his gardening fork against the path's brick edging. 'Do you want to come round to my kitchen or shall we have it in the garden?'

'Outside. It's a lovely day, isn't it?' Pixie looked about her as though seeing and feeling the spring sun for the very first time.

He grinned and went indoors. There were some old wooden crates piled near the wall. Pixie selected two of the cleanest and sturdiest as stools for them both.

When he came out again with a tray in his hands, she was un-pegging the washing from the two lines that criss-crossed her garden. He set the tray down on a sawn-off tree-trunk as Pixie began folding a sheet. He clambered over the low wall. 'Here,' he said. 'Give me the end and we can fold it together.'

When all the sheets were done, he helped her with the rest of the washing. She saw he was handling only the things he didn't think she'd mind him touching. Then

59

he lifted the heavy wicker basket and took it to her back door.

'I've left it on the scullery table.' He leaned back over the wall and picked up the tray. 'Better drink this before it gets cold.' He poured the tea. He'd given her a china cup and saucer. For himself he'd chosen a blue-rimmed enamelled mug. The tea was just right. They'd known each other a long time and he'd remembered that she didn't take sugar even before it was rationed.

She'd had a shock that morning and his kindness was her undoing. Suddenly tears were streaming down her cheeks.

'What's the matter?' Worry was etched across his face.

Pixie was shaking so much she was afraid of spilling her tea. He took the dainty cup from her and put it back on the tray.

She held her head in her hands for a moment, then took an envelope from her pinafore pocket and handed him the creased letter. 'It came this morning and I swear I didn't know a thing about it.'

He took it, slid out the single page and read the contents.

After a while he said, 'You've been given notice to quit unless the rent arrears are paid within seven days.'

Pixie nodded. 'It sounds like there've been other letters that I know nothing about. Mum must have hidden them, I've been searching drawers and cupboards for evidence. That's what started me on the clearing out. It helps to stop me thinking about what I might turn up.'

He nodded, then looked at the letter again. 'It's an awful lot to have to find.' He frowned. Then he turned the envelope over.

'It's addressed to Mum,' said Pixie. 'I've always given her most of my wages and she's supposed to pay the outgoings. When she's not around I put the money by.' Pixie wiped her hand across her cheek. Defiantly she said, 'We've never had a notice to quit.' Bob hadn't moved. 'Well, I have to trust her. She's my mum.'

He sighed. 'You don't have this kind of money, do you?'

'No. She's let me down again.'

'Again? You mean she's done this before?'

'Not with the rent. But she "forgot" to pay the paper bill and they stopped delivering until I settled it. Then it was the grocer – she ran up a bill that still hasn't been sorted out. I just don't have the money. That cup of tea was the first for me since yesterday when I ran out of milk.' Pixie paused. It was difficult to talk about her mother like this. She felt disloyal. 'She's really dropped me in it this time. And it's not as though I can tell her how I feel. All I know is she's gone to Brighton with a man called Del . . . You won't tell anyone, will you? Even Rita doesn't know about the notice to quit.'

Bob's face was grey and drawn as he asked, 'Is that also why you're clearing the house? So it's not in a mess when you have to move out?'

Pixie nodded. 'I don't want to leave the place dirty.' She sniffed and wiped her hand across her eyes. 'Like I said, cleaning takes my mind off things.'

He gave a sigh that seemed to reach down inside him, then picked up her tea and passed it to her. 'Finish this, it'll make you feel better. Then I'll pour another cup. It's amazing what a nice cup of tea can do. I can lend you the money and give you some milk.' His words had come out all in a rush.

'No! I'm not asking for a hand-out.'

But if she didn't take him up on his offer, what would she do? She and her mother had lived in the house for a long time. The rent wasn't high, like some of the other places she had seen advertised in the local *Evening News*, and on notice-boards in shop windows, but it did need to be paid, and regularly. Housing was at a premium, with German bombs flattening homes daily. There must be some way she could raise the money without taking up Bob's offer.

Bob took the cup from her and refilled it as though nothing had happened. But Pixie could see by the set of his shoulders and his grim expression that her rebuff had hurt him. 'I didn't mean to upset you. But I can't borrow money from *you*. That just won't solve the problem.'

He gave her the cup. 'I know you don't want to feel beholden to me. But what will you do?'

Pixie sighed, then voiced her thoughts. 'There's a scheme at work where in special circumstances they can offer a loan and take the money back from the wages a bit at a time. They won't give it to just anyone. But I've been there a while. And I'd like to think I do my job well enough to qualify.'

Bob smiled. Pixie felt the muscles of her face and the back of her neck relax. She'd been worrying about this problem but talking it through had given her new hope. And now it was out in the open she felt sure the solution was near. And, best of all, if the depot manager, Harry Slaughter, approved the loan, she could pay off the debt and no one need know of her shame. She drank her tea and gave Bob a watery smile.

He took the cup and saucer and put them on the tray. 'Good idea, Miss Independent,' he said gruffly. 'In the meantime you'll have to explain to the landlord, just in case there's a time delay.'

'I've thought of that. If I'm honest with him, it should be all right.' That was more of a question than a statement. No, she told herself, don't start letting doubts crowd in.

'Will you promise me one thing?'

'Of course, Bob.' She could promise anyone anything now her future seemed more assured.

'If you can't secure the loan that way, will you come back to me?'

Chapter Six

'I never thought your mum would go off again so soon.' Rita bit her lip. 'No, that's not true. I'd expected her to stay away longer. She's like one of those men who've been married for a long time, then go chasing a bit of skirt and desert their families. It's her leaving you in such a pickle that I don't hold with.' She put her hand across the table and patted Pixie's arm. It was cold today and they'd decided to stay inside the factory to eat their lunch.

The wireless was playing big-band music that made Pixie feel quite jolly. The women workers were all either eating or chatting, some even singing along with the melody.

Pixie was ashamed that until now she'd kept her money worries from her friend, when all Rita wanted to do was help. She had told Rita she intended asking

Harry Slaughter for a loan against her wages to pay the outstanding rent.

'Well, I mean,' Rita continued, 'most people try to escape life by having a hobby, going dancing, reading a book. Your mum, God bless her, goes gallivanting off with blokes. Give me a good book to read in bed at night. Have you started that *Saratoga Trunk* by Edna Ferber yet?' She didn't wait for Pixie to answer her. 'I'm into another really good story that you can have when I've finished with it. *Mrs Miniver* by Jan Struther – it's smashing. I think reading's like going into a different world.'

So was writing things down, Pixie thought, just like she did in the early hours of the morning when she woke up worried and couldn't get back to sleep. 'I don't remember my mum reading anything other than the racing form,' she said, putting her Spam sandwich, uneaten, back into the greaseproof paper. She just couldn't face Spam again but there was precious little in the larder.

'You can always come and live with us,' Rita looked into Pixie's eyes. 'That's if you have to get out of your house.'

'Yeah, well, thanks all the same, but let's hope it doesn't come to that,' said Pixie. 'Because I can't quite see you and me sharing a single bed.'

To share with Rita meant sharing a house with

Malcolm, Rita's creepy stepdad. Pixie shivered. Not only was Malcolm a bloke to steer clear of, but Rita's parents thrived on arguments and fights, or so it seemed to her. Mrs Brown was a jealous woman. It was nothing to see her with a black eye one day, complaining about her husband's short temper, and the next she'd be arm in arm with him, walking up Reed's Place.

Pixie wanted a quiet life and hopefully, in the future, someone to love who would love her in return. Cal slipped easily into her mind. From where she and Rita were sitting, they had an excellent view through the windows of the outside workshops, the main gate and the strip of water separating Gosport from Portsmouth. USS *Bristol* and her sister destroyer had sailed. Would she ever see him again?

Rita dug her in the ribs. 'Quick, pack away the rest of your lunch.' She gestured across the yard. 'There's Cedric and his daddy, just getting out of his mother's posh car.' Pixie looked towards the gate where the guard was tipping his hat to the boss and his wife. 'Try to talk to him before he gets to his office. You don't want the girls asking why you're in there, do you?' She took the food packet from Pixie's lap and put it into her lunch tin. 'Pity we don't still 'ave the money we earned kissing.'

'Well, we haven't.' Pixie's tone was sharp, mostly

because she was worried about facing Harry Slaughter. 'We got so much flak about it from the factory girls, not that they knew why we did it, that I could never go through that again.'

Had she and Rita done the right thing in giving Em the money so she could choose whether or not to abort Doris's baby? What would she do if she had a daughter and was in that position? A new thought entered her mind. Did Cal think she was easy because she'd sold those kisses?

Pixie watched Harry Slaughter and his son go into a building next to the narrow-gauge railway line that served the site.

'Damn!' Rita cursed. 'He's not gone to his office. Now you'll have to wait until later. But just look at that car.' She pointed to where the sleek MG TA was being driven away by Harry Slaughter's wife. 'She always looks as though she has a bad smell under her nose.'

Pixie grinned. 'Well, she does. It's called Harry.'

The two friends made their way back to the locker room to put away their things. Then, after washing their hands, they went to the workshop and their places on the lines to start the afternoon shift.

'Hello, Em,' said Pixie. The woman stood beside her writing notes on a clipboard.

Doris was sweeping up at the end of the line. Her golden curls bobbed around her sweet face unhampered by her turban and she seemed to be even more in a world of her own than usual. Her white overall was tight round her body. The bump was beginning to show.

'Hello, Doris,' called Pixie. Doris wiped her hand across her nose and looked up to see who had called her name. When she saw it was Pixie she gave her a big smile, then sneezed, scrabbling in her overall pocket for her handkerchief. In doing so, she let go of the broom, which clattered to the floor.

'She's got a cold,' said Em, as though that explained everything.

'I need to go to the office to see Mr Slaughter,' Pixie said.

Em raised an eyebrow but didn't ask any questions. 'I'll stand in for you on the line,' she said.

Pixie thought the poor woman looked more tired than ever.

'Give me the nod when you want to leave as I've got to check everyone in first.' Em moved away.

Pixie pulled a face at Rita. She really wasn't looking forward to seeing the manager.

Suddenly they could hear heated voices, and looked towards the door.

Em had Myra by the arm and Myra was trying to pull free. 'You're not coming in here in this state, Myra.'

Myra was staring about her with eyes as big as saucers. 'Nothing wrong with me.'

'You're drunk. I gave you a warning. Go home. Come back when you've sobered up.'

Myra, her turban askew, managed to extricate her arm and walk away, but she stumbled. Em caught her, saving her from falling.

'Let me go! This work's all I got. Let me go.'

Two male workers appeared, it seemed, from nowhere. Em pushed Myra into the arms of one burly man, then whispered something to his companion. Myra had shrivelled into herself and was crying. She was led, quiet and resigned, out of sight.

Em coughed. 'All right, you lot,' she said. 'This bloody war gets on everybody's nerves. Myra's road took a bashing recently so you can't blame the girl for trying to blot out the memory of bombs falling, can you?' She paused. 'I'm switching the conveyor-belt on now, so get to it.'

The chattering lulled to a more normal level as the belt started up and the machinery began to grind. So engrossed was Pixie in measuring the powder into a case that she was surprised when Em touched her shoulder.

'You can go now,' she said, sliding into Pixie's space, her capable hands steadying the half-filled case as Pixie moved aside.

In the lavatory Pixie washed her hands, then walked around the maze of corridors until she was outside the boss's office. Her heart was thumping. Her knock on the manager's door was answered immediately.

'Come.' Harry Slaughter was clearly surprised to see her. A smile crept over his face. 'What can I do for you, Pixie?' She knew he liked to believe he was forward-thinking in calling his employees by their Christian names. They had to call him Mr Slaughter. 'Sit down,' he commanded.

She sat on the chair opposite his desk, but immediately he rose, his tight waistcoat stretched across his ample belly, and came to perch on the corner of the desk, swinging one fat leg. She noticed his brown shoes had black laces.

She took a deep breath, looking around the office as though for help. The furniture was Utility, and a spider plant was perched on top of a scratched metal cabinet.

'I'm not beating about the bush,' she said. She was finding it difficult to talk because he was so close to her. But she could hardly offend him by getting up and moving away. Not when she wanted something as badly as the loan. 'My mother has gone. She's left me with a debt and I need a loan lodged against my wages.' There. She'd said it. A small sigh of relief escaped her.

His eyes were on her face. Except for his swinging leg, he was immobile.

He kept her waiting so long for a reply that she wondered if she should repeat her request. Then he stopped swinging his leg, returned to his seat, opened the top drawer and took out three pencils that he began to sharpen one by one. He bent forward a little too quickly and strands of long hair fell out of place. He brushed the greasy hair aside.

'There's a problem.'

'Oh?' Pixie said. Two of the pencils didn't need sharpening. Their points were already needle sharp.

He examined them carefully. 'I am expected to keep costs down.'

'I am aware you're expected also to keep the workforce happy.'

His head jerked up and he glared at her. 'Don't take that tone with me, Pixie. Why do you think you deserve a loan?'

'I'm never late. I've been an employee for a long time and . . .' She was near to tears '. . . I wouldn't ask if it wasn't the last resort for me.'

'You're aware we usually comply if the employee has been bombed out – we like to help the family get back on its feet. Your mother leaving the family home is hardly reason to give you government money.'

'I'll pay it back. You'll take it from my wages.'

'What do you want the money for?'

'Rent arrears.' She couldn't bring herself to say her mother had spent the money set aside for the rent.

Beads of sweat had appeared on his forehead. 'You default on your rent, then expect this war-ravaged country to help you?'

'You mean I can't have a loan.' Why, oh, why did she ever think this fat weasel would help her?

She got up to leave, near to tears, pushing her chair back so it screeched on the wooden floor. He let the pencils slide away, rose and came to stand in front of her. Then he put a hand on her shoulder, 'Wait,' he said quietly. 'I think I can see a way around this problem. How much?'

Pixie sat down again, heavily. His hand fell limply from her shoulder.

'How much what?' she asked. She was almost unable to move now, hemmed in by the chair, the table and his fat body. She was also confused. At one moment he was giving her the impression that a loan was impossible, and the next enquiring how much she needed. Why?

His meaning, however, was very clear when he said, 'I'm sure we can come to an arrangement.' He leaned in close to her, one hand again on her shoulder, the other hand, flat on the desk, fingers outstretched.

Pixie froze. The hand on her shoulder travelled down until it cupped her breast. He squeezed. Pixie's stomach heaved. Harry Slaughter's meaning was now very clear. 'If I'm nice to you, you'll be nice to me, and I'll get the loan, is that it?' She could hardly get the words out, she was so disgusted.

'Of course,' he said. His thick lips drew back in a smile as one finger circled her nipple. Pixie thought there was almost as much oil in his voice as there was on his sparse hair. She saw his piggy eyes close in ecstasy. Pixie reached around him. Her fingers touched the table and she retrieved the pencils. Carefully she positioned them in her hand as she would a knife. Then, with as much strength as she could muster, she stabbed them into the back of the hand that was still stretched out on the table, feeling the sharpened points dig into his plump flesh.

'Eeowww!'

Harry Slaughter leaped back, pushing against the desk, causing the plant to tumble to the parquet floor, showering it with dried earth. The noise was alarming. Two of the pencils had dropped to the floor but one was firmly embedded. He clasped his hand to his chest just as Pixie jumped up and faced him.

'I'll get you the sack for this,' he hissed, cradling his damaged hand.

'No, you won't,' she said, thinking quickly, 'because I've had someone listening at the door. Listening to every word you've said. You'll be the one getting the sack.'

She hoped he would believe her lie. She hated liars but that one had been necessary for self-preservation.

He was looking fearfully at the pencil in his skin. 'You still don't get the loan.' He sounded like a sulky child.

'Stick the money,' she said, turning towards the door. Already she could hear movements outside. Probably other workers investigating the noise, she thought.

But before she reached it, she stopped, turned and said, 'If I find you trying to trap any other girl, you'll find a pencil point shoved right up your arse.'

When Pixie got back to her line she went straight up to Em and confessed, 'I've just had a shouting match with old Slaughter. Can I get a drink of water and have a sit-down? I'm all shook up and I don't want to make a mistake handling the explosive.'

Em's forehead creased in a frown. 'You don't look too good.'

Pixie glanced at the wall clock and saw Em follow her gaze. Some of the girls were glancing nervously in their direction.

Em caught at her arm. 'You want to talk about it?' Pixie shook her head. Em continued, 'It'll be break time soon. You can start again on the line afterwards.'

Luckily the machinery noise almost drowned their voices and, even though Pixie was receiving peculiar looks from the other women, she winked at Rita, who was watching her worriedly.

'Check on Doris,' called Em, as Pixie strode away.

In the lavatory, which smelt of stale pee and carbolic soap, Pixie leaned her head against the cubicle's white tiles. She'd already drunk some water, cupping her hands beneath the tap at the butler's sink. Tears had risen, but she'd sniffed them away. Crying wouldn't change anything. That fat toad of a manager wasn't going to get her down. She hugged herself, still feeling his horrible hands on her body.

Now she'd have to take Bob up on his offer. There was no other way. Rita had offered to help but, bless her, she had no savings. Rita lived from week to week like most of the other workers at the factory. Pixie was wiping her face on the roller towel when Doris came in, moving awkwardly through the doorway with her broom.

'You jus' come out of Mr Slaughter's office. He's cross with you.' Doris shook her head and the blonde curls danced about her face. The made-over grey serge dress didn't do her any favours, but it hid her blossoming belly.

'Where's your white overall?' asked Pixie. She didn't want to carry on crying in front of Doris – the girl would get upset.

'The buttons keep popping open.'

Pixie smiled. Doris really was such a little girl. 'How do you know he's cross?' she asked.

Doris frowned. 'I was listening at the door when he started shouting. When I heard the big bang I hid in the broom cupboard.' She twisted the handle of the broom. 'He was cross with me too. Did he make you take your knickers off?'

Pixie looked at her in amazement. Em had said Doris wouldn't say who the father of her child was. Could it be Harry Slaughter? Was Doris confiding in Pixie because she thought Pixie had been made to do the same thing as she had?

'No, Doris. No knickers off for me.' Would Doris open up and talk to her?

'I'm not doing it again.' Doris walked over to the fly-specked mirror, the broom dragging on the tiles. 'He said I was pretty.' She smiled at her reflection in the mirror, then turned to Pixie. 'But he hurt me with his thing. I didn't tell Mum about him.'

Pixie went over and put her arms around her. 'You are pretty, Doris. And Mr Slaughter is a bad man. Why didn't you tell Mum this?'

'No! She'd be very cross again. Like when I wet the bed.' Doris swung free. 'Don't like it when she's cross.'

Pixie jumped as the bell shrieked, announcing break-time. She could hear voices. Soon the lavatory would be filled with women. She smiled at Doris. 'You did right to tell me,' she said. If Em found out about this, she wouldn't let the matter rest. She would, in all probability, be sacked. Em's wages kept her family.

Oh dear. Another dilemma. But justice had to be done. Em had to know the truth but without blowing up and losing her job.

'C'mon, Doris. Let's go and find your mum and have some tea.'

Chapter Seven

'You shouldn't feel awkward about asking anything of me.' Bob counted the last of the notes onto his kitchen table and handed the money to her.

'I'll pay you back as soon as I can.'

'I know that.'

She felt ashamed and closed her eyes to stop a tear escaping. When she opened them, Bob was watching her. It was warm and cosy in his kitchen and smelt of cooking. She let her shoulders relax.

'Put that in your purse and I'll be back in a minute,' he said. She watched him leave the kitchen, then heard him open the oven door, followed by the sound of crockery and cutlery rattling on the table in the small scullery.

She looked around the room. There was an armchair with scuffed arms next to the window, a table in the centre, with condiments in the middle, along with a sugar bowl and milk in a bottle. A flower-patterned, wipe-over oilcloth covered the table and two kitchen chairs were placed beneath it. A sideboard with one of the door-knobs missing stood against the back wall. Bob's market moneybag and keys to his van had been left on top of the sideboard, and a tall bookcase stood near the arm-chair, against the dividing wall. She went over to examine some of the titles, George Orwell's *1984*, *Mildred Pierce* by James M. Cain, and *Now Voyager* by Olive Higgins Prouty, which she herself was reading. She wasn't surprised to find that he liked books.

'Them bouncing bombs did the trick,' Bob called. 'All over the papers today. Crippled Germany's heartland, caused massive damage. Good bloke, that Guy Gibson.' She heard more rattling and a delicious meaty smell wafted into the kitchen that made her mouth water. 'I'd have loved the air force,' he continued. 'But my eyesight let me down for joining the forces.' She heard him sigh. That told her he wasn't happy about being turned down. She knew most things about him but every so often he could surprise her.

Bob's parents had died one evening at a cinema in the town just after the war had started. None of the picture-goers had stood a chance against the bomb.

On the mantelpiece stood a slate clock, some letters, and a wedding photograph of his parents. Bob was the spit of his mother. There was a snap of him with Rita and herself, a tall tower in the background. She remembered Bob asking a passer-by to take the photo one afternoon at Blackpool. He had treated the pair of them to a coach trip to see the Illuminations. It had been a good weekend. Rita had met a young Londoner and written letters to him for ages until it all fizzled out. Next to the photo was Bob's camera.

'I made two,' he said. He pushed an enamel dish towards her across the table. 'I'm afraid there's more veg than meat but I thought you could share it with Rita when she comes tonight.'

He was wrapping a couple of clean tea towels around the dish so she'd be able to carry it without burning herself. She wondered what she'd do without him.

'You got enough money to last you through the week?'

'The rent was all I needed,' she said. 'Thank you. And thank you for this.' She picked up the dish.

'Only glad I can help.' He walked Pixie to the front door. 'When Rita comes, and you've eaten, you should go out. Do you good.'

Rita arrived just after Pixie had laid the table for the two of them. She'd been listening to Valentine Dyall's *Appointment with Fear* and was glad of the company.

'I dunno why you listen to something that frightens you,' laughed Rita. She slung her bottle-green cardigan over the back of a chair. 'I'm starving. Me mum said we had fish for dinner tonight. Then she laughed and said, "Fish in the larder and see what you can find. Malcolm's down the pub."'

'Was she angry?'

'Of course she was, but what could she do? There was a tin of Spam but I couldn't face it. I'm so sick of Spam.' Rita made a face.

Pixie, too, was hungry. The enamel dish was still wrapped in Bob's tea towels.

Carefully she unrolled one of the striped cloths. Then she gasped. A pound note nestled between the next tea-cloth and the dish.

'What's that?' asked Rita, bending forward for a good look.

Pixie sighed and stepped back. 'It's Bob's way of telling me to go and enjoy myself and forget about my problems,' she said.

Chapter Eight

Bob slipped another log into the grate and sat back with the *Evening News*. Although it was May, it had been a wet, chilly day.

He sighed, reading about the latest Gosport bombings. A shell had landed on an air-raid shelter on Whitworth Road. In the ensuing panic to escape, fifty-four people were killed, including a young woman carrying her child; she'd slipped on the steps and been trodden underfoot, crushed.

Would this war never end? He brushed his fingers through his wayward hair. If you couldn't be safe in an air-raid shelter, where could you escape from Hitler's bombs?

He looked at the clock: it was just after nine. He would have been abed by now if it hadn't been for Pixie calling around. Getting up before four in the morning was one of the hazards of being a market trader. But a late night now and then he could cope with. It made his love-life a bit precarious, though. The women down the market liked him, but his romances didn't last long when he had either to take them home early or get up in the small hours, leaving them to sleep on.

He gazed around his kitchen, where he spent most of his time when he wasn't out earning money. It wasn't posh but it was home. His eyes fell on his camera, which Pixie had asked to borrow. He'd shown her how to take photographs with it. He supposed she wanted some snaps of her mates at the depot.

He hoped Pixie was out enjoying herself with her friend Rita. He'd made sure she wouldn't fail to see the pound note.

Poor kid, he thought. Bob's parents had moved into the two-up and two-down ten years ago. She'd been just a kid then, with a lot of growing up to do, and he'd been a gawky lad with glasses and his head forever in a book. He was five years older than Pixie and it had seemed a lot when he was young. Now the gap between him and her was nothing.

She wasn't a beauty but she had that elusive 'something' that made men turn for a second look. She was slim and blonde with the capacity to love and go on loving the people she cared about, no matter how disloyal they were to her. Look how she was with her wayward mother. The woman had left her daughter in Shit Street and still Pixie wouldn't have a word said against her.

He knew she'd dated a few men but they never lasted long. He wondered if her mother's infidelities caused her not to take relationships seriously. He preferred to think Pixie hadn't met the right man, the one who would love her as he did. If only he had the courage to tell her how he felt about her. But what if she dismissed him? He wouldn't be able to bear that. Perhaps it was better to be her friend, the one person she could always rely on.

He drank some Brickwoods Pale Ale from the bottle and went on reading the newspaper. Women had been advised by the government to take part-time jobs to help in the war effort.

Well, he was doing his bit, wasn't he? He was waiting for Marlene to come round so he could tell her he'd decided to take her on.

'That's good,' he said aloud, continuing with the newspaper and lifting the drink once more to his lips. Church bells could be rung again now the threat of invasion was over. 'Good old Churchill,' he murmured. 'Be nice to hear the bells again.'

A loud knock on the front door made him jump. He

folded the newspaper, got up and made his way down the passage. The banging sounded again.

'Hold your horses,' he said, to the pretty bronze-haired girl standing on his doorstep. 'I ain't got no servant to send running down the passage to let you in.'

The girl laughed and stepped over the threshold.

At that moment, Rita and Pixie walked arm in arm past his open door.

Rita giggled. 'She's eager to get into your house, Bob!'

Damn, he thought. He should have told Pixie he'd been thinking of asking Marlene to help out on the stall. He didn't want her imagining he was carrying on with the girl.

'Goodnight, Bob,' sang out Rita.

'Goodnight, girls,' he replied. Before he closed the front door, he saw Pixie look back and smile.

'Oh, it's nice in here,' said Marlene. 'Can I sit down?'

'Course you can. Do you want a cup of tea or something?'

She eyed the bottle on the table. 'Wouldn't mind one of them.'

Bob was taken aback. She didn't look old enough to drink. But that wasn't the only thing that was deceptive about the girl. Small and wiry, she was as strong as an ox.

He'd seen her unloading metal bars from vans and fixing up the stalls at the market. He went into the scullery, opened another pale ale and took a clean glass from the wooden draining-board.

When he got back to the kitchen she'd made herself comfortable in the armchair. She accepted the bottle and glass. He noticed she did a perfect job of pouring the beer, without making it froth to the top. She'd probably worked in a pub, Bob thought. He knew she wasn't afraid of hard work.

'Thanks,' she said.

'I won't beat around the bush,' Bob said. 'I want you to work on my stall, because I'm doing well and I need you to look after things while I get out and about buying up more stock.' He pulled out a kitchen chair and sat down. 'That's about it. I've been watching you. You don't seem to work for anyone in particular, but you work hard for anyone who'll pay you. Am I right?'

She nodded and her auburn hair fell forward. In the electric light it was almost golden. He'd only ever seen her in dungarees and boots. She'd taken off her Jigger coat and was wearing a close-fitting serge dress with three box pleats at the centre. The padded shoulders and white Peter Pan collar made her look fragile. Inwardly he smiled. If it wasn't for the fact that he sometimes sold women's clothing and shoes, brought straight from the sweatshops in London's Petticoat Lane, he wouldn't know a thing about ration-book fashion and Utility designs.

She took a sip of beer. 'I make pretty good money working for different stallholders . . .'

'Yes, and I know that when there isn't any work around you go home empty-handed.'

'Swings and roundabouts,' she said, taking another drink. 'One day I want to be selling second-hand jewellery and answerable to no one, but buying gold costs big money.' She crossed her ankles, her black suede shoes with the maximum two-and-a-half-inch heels, a wartime restriction, showing her slim legs to advantage.

Bob said, 'You're astute enough to get what you want. And sooner than you thought possible.'

She brightened at his words.

He glanced at the clock. If he was going to clinch the deal he'd have to work fast. It was dark outside now and raining. He couldn't let her walk home on her own, especially not when the storm that had been threatening all day was darkening the sky by the minute.

Then he had to get back and grab some shuteye before getting up early for tomorrow's work. He named an amount of money. And was quick enough to see her eyes widen with surprise.

But she was going to test him. 'Is that what you reckon I'm worth?'

'No, it's what I'll pay. I've watched you going from stallholder to stallholder begging for work. Some of the blokes treat you like something the cat dragged in. I've checked up and I know you're honest. But why do you work on the markets? Why not a regular job, like in the armaments factory?'

Marlene took a gulp of the beer and set the glass on the floor. 'I'll be honest with you.' She took a deep breath. 'I got a baby. She's six months old. Me mum takes care of Jeannie while I work, but if I had set hours I wouldn't be able to take time off when I have to. And Jeannie needs me.'

He could see she was waiting for him to dismiss her. A baby out of wedlock was a terrible disgrace. Then she looked away, but it wasn't shame he'd seen in her eyes: it was defiance.

Her revelation showed why sometimes she had to shrug off abuse. He'd heard her being told to 'piss off', and worse, when she'd asked for work, yet the following week she'd returned to the same stallholders. To him it proved her staying power. 'I'm not worried about your personal life. I need loyalty and someone I can trust.'

A smile hovered at the corners of her mouth. 'You can have that. When d'you want me to start?'

Chapter Nine

Music from the live band at the Connaught Drill Hall spilled out onto the street. Inside, the master of ceremonies wore a tight black suit so shiny it might have been polished. He had on white gloves and waved his baton, in between using his index finger to push his glasses further back on his nose. Pixie marvelled that the band still played the right tune.

The parquet flooring was slippery, the air clogged with the stink of cigarettes, beer and assorted cheap perfumes that had gelled to one overpowering smell. Pixie was in seventh heaven.

Chairs were placed against the walls all around the room, but there were only a few small tables.

'Didn't expect it to be so packed,' Rita smoothed her hair, then picked an imaginary piece of fluff from the dress she had just finished altering. She was very proud of it: blue wool with padded shoulders, it fitted smoothly to her svelte body. A belt made her waist seem even smaller than it was.

'Do I look all right?' she asked.

'You know you look gorgeous,' Pixie told her. Her own grey dress had the fashionable box pleats in the skirt front and matching box pleats across the bust. It had been a gift for her mother from a male friend. He had paid a fancy price for it at Estelle's Modes, but Gladys, once she'd got it home, had decided she didn't like the colour. With it, she was wearing a string of pearls that her mother had left on the sideboard, which accentuated the sweetheart neckline. Pixie spotted a couple of empty chairs, sat down, then jumped up again, opening her bag. 'I've got enough for two glasses of orange,' she said. 'After paying to come in I need to save enough to buy some bread and milk tomorrow morning.'

She left Rita with the coats and began walking around the edge of the floor to a table in the corner, where an elderly man and woman were in charge of selling refreshments. She glanced back at Rita and waved, as a flash of lightning lit the blackout curtains with an orange glow and a growl of thunder followed. She shuddered.

Rita was chatting to a girl sitting next to her. A lot of the men were standing with glasses in their hands around the table where the beer was. But many people were dancing and the music made Pixie feel happy. Tonight she didn't want to dwell on her problems.

She was on her way back with the drinks when she heard her name called. She turned and nearly dropped the glasses. 'Cal! What are you doing here? I didn't know your ship was in port.' Her heart leaped. He was just as tall and gorgeous as she had remembered him. This time he was in civvies instead of his naval uniform.

He took the drinks from her and together they began walking towards Rita.

'The ship developed trouble in the boiler room, and we had to return to Portsmouth,' he said. He set the drinks on the table. He smelt of tobacco and soap, like Pixie remembered. 'I didn't know where you lived, but the girl behind the bar at the Fox said you liked dancing and often came here.' Pixie nodded. 'The manager, Sam, wouldn't tell me where you lived or worked. He said, "Careless talk costs lives."'

'Quite right too,' put in Rita.

'You look very smart,' said Pixie. Cal's leather jacket had its collar turned up and he wore light-coloured trousers. He took off his hat and put it on the table. 'You can't blame Sam,' she said. She felt giddy with excitement at seeing him again, especially as he'd now slipped an arm round her waist. 'You might be a mad axe murderer! Or a spy!'

Just then Tony arrived, pushing through the crowd and holding aloft a tray with more drinks. Pixie saw Rita's eyes light up as he grinned at her and, in his musical Italian-American accent, said, 'Rita, my love, did you miss me?'

'Yeah,' she said, with a huge smile. 'Like toothache!'

Tony put the tray down and pulled her to her feet. 'If you make fun of me, you must dance with me.'

Rita laughed. 'I've heard all about you Latin lovers,' she said, as he drew her into the crush on the dance floor.

'Tommy Dorsey's "Boogie Woogie",' said Cal. He took off his jacket and let it fall on a chair, then swept Pixie into his arms.

Pixie melted into him as though it was the only natural thing for her to do.

'Never waste glorious dance music,' Cal said, 'not when anything can happen tomorrow.' She was matching him step for step. 'Hey! You move real good,' he said.

Pixie loved dancing. She let the music flood through her body, so she was flowing with the rhythm. He was sidestepping and throwing her away from him. She caught at his outstretched fingers and clung to his hands, swirling and jiving.

'You're lovely!' Cal murmured in her ear. They were

close together, dancing slowly now to Frank Sinatra's 'All Or Nothing At All'. She was still breathless, but could swear his heart was beating as fast as hers and that it had nothing to do with the music. Did he already feel as she did? She'd heard of love at first sight but never thought she might experience it.

She snuggled into his shirt-front. They seemed to fit together like the pieces of a puzzle.

When the dance finished, he led her to her chair and sat down next to her. 'I'm going to give you this,' he said, foraging in his jacket pocket and coming out with a piece of paper. 'It's my sister's address – she lives in Chichester, married an RAF fella – and my forces address because I want you to write to me.' He looked suddenly nervous. 'You will, won't you? I couldn't bear it if I lost you again. Tony and I only came here tonight because Trudy, the barmaid at the Fox, thought you might turn up. I'm so glad she was right.'

The deep blue eyes she wanted to fall into held hers. And then she didn't want to be in the crowded dance hall any more. She wanted to be alone with him. Anywhere would do, just somewhere she could hold him tightly and tell him she'd fallen in love with him, crazy as it seemed, just like in the pictures. It was the most exciting thing that had ever happened to her.

Pixie put the piece of paper into her handbag and snapped it shut. 'I'll write every day,' she promised.

He took a pull on his drink and grimaced. 'Warm beer, I don't know how you Brits can drink it.' He pushed the glass away. 'You'd better write every day. I won't get mail regularly because we'll be at sea, but I shall be first in the queue to claim your letters.' He reached for her hand and drew it to his lips. As the music changed to another fast tune, he pulled her up from the chair and they went to find a space on the packed floor.

Pixie felt herself being swept along with the music, the laughter, and the need to dance in time to the beat. The jiving was fast, the rhythm furious, and she was filled with happiness. Here, dancing, she could let herself go, forget about work and its dangers and the awful Harry Slaughter, forget about her mother, forget the debts that kept her awake at night and most of all forget about this awful war. The music, sadly, drew to a close and Pixie knew that nothing had changed and the problems were still there . . . But, yes, something had changed! She was in love!

Cal gave her a final twirl before pulling her into his arms and almost crushing the life out of her as he hugged her against his firm body.

She looked up into his eyes and knew that she wanted him as she had never wanted another man.

Confusion and panic suddenly consumed her. 'I have to go,' she said, wriggling from his grasp, picking up her clutch bag and turning to Rita, who had just returned to her seat. 'I have to go,' she repeated, and left Rita standing, open-mouthed.

It was raining as she ran out onto the pavement.

'Wait! Pixie, wait up!' Cal's voice rang in her ears, but she had to get away, escape from the feelings that overwhelmed her. She wanted him so much it hurt. All the feelings she had experienced while dancing, the freedom to live and to love, would take her over and she wouldn't be able to stop herself begging him to kiss her, to love her and make love to her. And because of this bloody war, he would leave her. He would go back on board his ship and she might never see him again. That would be far, far worse than her mother going off on one of her jaunts. No, no, no! She couldn't take the chance of being hurt by this man.

'Pixie!' Cal caught up and pulled her round to face him. 'What's the matter? What have I done?'

He didn't wait for her reply. He kissed her. And it was the most glorious kiss ever. Her nerve endings fluttered, her heart was racing and she melted into his arms as though she belonged there. The rain was falling heavily.

'Mmm,' he said, as he came up for air.

She was still being held tightly but now his lips were covering her face with tiny kisses. At last she managed to speak. 'That's just it. You've done nothing. It's me. I think I've fallen in love with you.'

His eyes held hers. Then a slow smile lifted the corners of his mouth until it showed his strong white teeth. He began to laugh. He pulled her even closer, then, like an afterthought, pushed her away, took off his leather jacket and slipped it around her shoulders. 'You goose! I love you. I'm amazed at how I feel. But I love you too.' He was laughing again. 'Fact is, I love you so much I want to shout it out loud. I think I will!' He stepped away, threw back his head and shouted into the storm, 'I love you, Pixie!'

An elderly man on the other side of the road, walking his soaked mongrel, stared, slipped a lead onto his dog's collar and moved swiftly on into the darkness.

Watching the pair, Pixie dissolved into laughter. Cal's shirt was sodden and rain ran down his face. When she moved her feet, her shoes squelched. Cal grabbed her hand and began to run in the direction of the town. She had no option but to go with him.

He kept stopping to kiss her, even though their clothes and hair were plastered to their bodies.

'We must get out of the storm,' he yelled at last, above

the noise. 'It doesn't look as though it's going to ease up.' As if in answer, the sky lit up with another bolt of lightning. Pixie screamed as Cal pulled her into the entrance of the Black Bear Hotel and pushed open the heavy door. Inside, a haven of warmth, music and cigarette smoke enveloped them.

Pixie was shivering as she plumped herself down on a padded window seat.

'Looks like it's set in for the night,' said the barman.

'Terrible weather,' said the barmaid.

Pixie heard Cal order a gin and orange and a half-pint of Brickwoods best. She heard the barman reply in a friendly manner, then turn towards her and nod. Cal took his wallet from his trouser pocket and handed over some money.

Pixie was still shivering. The air in the bar not only smelt of tobacco, but of damp clothing. There were only a few people in the room, most having decided to stay indoors because of the atrocious weather. Cal came back to her with the drinks.

'Look,' he said, 'you can shout at me if you want but I've paid for a room for the night—' Pixie opened her mouth to protest, but Cal put a finger across her lips. 'We're both wet through and I thought we could dry off. If you want to go on home after you've warmed up and had something to eat, I'll take you straight to your door.'

She shrugged herself out of his leather jacket and rivulets of water splashed to the beer-stained carpet. Now he was holding both her hands in his.

She would very much like to have a hot bath and rub her wet hair dry. She pulled a hand away and picked up her drink. A big sip began to warm her from the inside. A bigger sip, then another, and her drink had vanished. She put the glass back on the white-ringed table. She knew he was waiting for her answer.

But instead he said, 'D'you want another?' He frowned. 'I didn't think to order you a double . . .' He stammered, 'Not because you'd like a larger drink but because you need it . . .' He must have realized how stupid he sounded for he put his hand to his head. 'Look, I booked the room so we could get dry, nothing more . . . I don't want you to think . . . Gee, I seem to be making a mess . . .'

'Don't worry,' Pixie said. 'Just go and get more drinks.' She sounded more confident than she felt.

While he stood again at the counter she watched the glistening raindrops sliding down the back of his hair to his wet shirt collar. Another flash of lightning caused the electric lights to falter for a moment, but they stayed on. A young man standing beside the window cheered. The

Mills Brothers were singing 'Paper Doll'. The wireless music was suddenly drowned by a peal of thunder that made Pixie jump.

She looked over to the bar where Cal was waiting patiently to be served. Should she go upstairs with him? Regardless of what he had said, she knew if she set one foot inside that room she wouldn't leave until morning.

What was the alternative? Leaving now, with the probability of Cal returning to the ship and the ship sailing? She might never set eyes on him again. If he took her home and kissed her goodnight in an alley, she'd never be able to tear herself away from him. They'd make love while the storm raged about them. She shuddered. Making love to Cal had to be special.

Besides, it was her first time.

The small room was clean, comfortable and fairly warm. A wardrobe, dressing-table and a chair practically filled it. A faded patchwork quilt covered the iron bed. Two clean, if threadbare, towels sat on it at the foot. Cal handed her one.

'The bathroom's at the end of the corridor. A hot bath's what you need. I've ordered a plate of sandwiches and a pot of tea to be brought up.'

Pixie's heart was pounding. Would he know how

inexperienced she was? It was different for men, wasn't it? Everyone expected them to know exactly what to do in circumstances like these.

Still, a hot bath would be lovely.

In the bathroom Pixie picked up a toothbrush, choosing between the two new ones on the shelf, and a new bar of Lux soap that she sniffed. Its scent was delicate. The only soap she used at home was carbolic. To see these things, which she could use if she liked, made her feel very special indeed.

The claw-footed bath was sparkling clean, as were the washbasin and the lavatory pan. The lavatory had a long chain to flush, just like hers at the bottom of the garden. There was even a roll of Izal paper, not newspaper as she used at home.

Pixie began to relax. She turned on the taps and steaming water flowed into the bath. When it reached the regulation five inches, where there was a painted mark on the enamel, she turned off the taps. After checking the door was locked, she stripped off her sodden clothes.

Her house in Alma Street didn't have a bathroom. Not even a bath plumbed into the scullery, as so many of the terraced houses now did. She lay full length in the water looking at her toes and smiling to herself, luxuriating in the smell of the Lux soap.

Pixie was eager, yet apprehensive, to return to the room and Cal.

When she was sure her hair had been rubbed as dry as possible, she wound the towel around herself and gathered up her damp clothes. She opened the door and peeped out to make sure no one was about, then ran back to the bedroom.

A pot of tea and a plate of sandwiches covered with a clean white tea towel sat on the dressing-table.

'Cuppa?' Cal asked. Despite the warmth in the room, he shivered and his shirt was still stuck to him. She could see he was drinking her in with his eyes.

He pulled her close and kissed her. 'You smell lovely,' he said, then, disappointingly, broke away and began fiddling with the teacups. Pixie knew he'd pushed her away because he wanted her so much. She wondered if he might be as shy as she was.

'I can do that,' Pixie said. 'I can sort out the tea. You go and have your bath.' His sudden timidity made her heart swell with love.

She heard the door close behind him. She draped her clothes over the back of the chair, hoping they'd dry, then put the tea tray on the bedside cabinet, slipped off her towel and sat in bed, listening to the rain still hitting the window. She pulled the crisp sheet up to her chin.

It was peculiar to be in a strange bed without her usual flannelette nightdress.

She poured a cup of tea, drank it and ate one of the sugar lumps. It felt decadent crunching the sweetness because she hadn't seen sugar lumps since before the war. There were still eight small treats left in a flowered bowl. She didn't touch the sandwiches but saw they were a mixture of Spam and egg.

A knock on the bedroom door startled her.

'Who is it?' Pixie called.

'Me,' came Cal's reply.

'Come in.' She pulled the sheet even higher. 'Why are you knocking?'

A waft of soapy freshness preceded him as he came towards the bed with his towel tucked around his middle. He'd found a coat hanger somewhere and draped his clothes over it. He hooked the hanger over the top of the wardrobe door.

'I didn't want you to feel shy if you weren't in bed,' he said. He ran his fingers through his hair. It stuck up in all directions. 'You don't have to do this,' he said. His shyness had taken over now and he was staring down at the aged silk rug on the floor. 'I mean, er, stay in this room with me. I can still take you home.'

'But I don't want you to do that.'

He had one hand loose at his side, the other holding on to the towel fastened at his hip. She put out her hand and slid it into his palm. He gripped it and sat down on the bed. 'I have to be on board by eight in the morning,' he said. His eyes were downcast.

'And I'm working the nine till three shift tomorrow,' Pixie said. She sensed he'd been worrying about telling her about his return to the ship. 'Are you sailing from Portsmouth tomorrow?'

He looked up at her. His blue eyes showed sadness. 'The repairs should be finished. We have to catch up with our sister ship.'

'Where are you going?'

'You know I couldn't tell you, even if I knew. The guys are beginning to think this trip is jinxed.' He was very nervous now. 'We've been told to forget shore leave for ages. The boilers were acting up, so we had to return and I've never known such secrecy before on any of our voyages . . .'

'Don't talk like that,' Pixie said. 'Don't talk at all.' She suddenly mustered confidence she'd never known she had. She pushed back the covers. 'Get in here.'

He stood at the side of the bed, watching her. 'God, you're so beautiful,' he said, his voice full of emotion. He dropped the towel.

'You're not so bad yourself,' Pixie said.

His body was tanned and there were freckles across his broad shoulders. His stomach was taut and flat, his legs and thighs strong. What on earth was Pixie doing trying to put him at ease when she felt far from calm herself?

'I haven't done this before,' she admitted. 'I may make mistakes.'

He bent down and kissed her nose. His breath was sweet. 'Make all the mistakes you want,' he said, sliding beneath the covers. Pixie closed her eyes and felt the warmth and hardness of his body against hers.

His lips, soft, sensuous, rested on hers for a while, then his tongue probed, met hers and played inside her mouth until that one kiss was as hot as the fire burning inside her.

She opened her eyes. This was *not* a dream, she told herself. This was the moment every girl, including her, had dreamed of. The first coupling with the man she loved.

And this beautiful man was kissing her, now with no hesitation, no shyness. She could smell their mingled desire.

Her arms went around him, quite naturally, and she returned his kisses passionately, as though it was the most natural thing in the world for her to do.

Cal pulled away. 'You are indescribably beautiful,' he said. 'I saw you in the Fox and something happened to me. Before that I didn't need anyone, certainly not a permanent woman in my life. But there and then, I knew.'

Pixie held on to the back of his neck, pulling his head towards her. He kissed her face, her eyes, her ears. Then his hands touched her body. Inside she was screaming for more, more touching, more kissing.

He found all her secret spots, claiming her. 'I can't stop touching you, Pixie,' he whispered. 'You will always be mine. You're special, like no woman I've ever known before. There's an innocence about you, yes, that's what it is.' Pixie wasn't sure whether he meant her innocence in the art of lovemaking or that this awful war hadn't yet broken her spirit.

When he entered her, slowly, carefully, it hurt a little at first. But soon it was the most incredible sensation she had ever known. As though she'd been waiting her whole life for just this moment. Her back arched, rising to meet his thrusts until their bodies were in perfect unison.

'Marry me, Pixie,' he whispered, as her pleasure rose furiously.

She gave a sharp, muffled cry as something exploded inside her. She cried out again with joy as his soaring release became a final miracle of delight.

After a time of intense quiet, Pixie moved. Cal's face was buried in her damp hair. He slid away, curving himself around her.

She ran her fingers over his arms. There was no chill in his body or hers, not now. The sweet smell of their lovemaking came up from the ruffled sheets. He raised himself on one elbow, looking down at her. At last he touched her upraised mouth with his lips, tasting salty, of sex and perspiration.

Pixie was lost in him.

He stroked her hair and murmured into her ear, 'I meant what I asked earlier, I want you to marry me.'

Pixie stretched fully, like a cat. There was so much to find in each other. Her fingers touched his beautiful mouth, then his broad forehead and tangled through his golden hair, curling it and winding it around her fingers.

'Yes,' she breathed.

Chapter Ten

When Pixie woke up she was alone.

Cal had left as she slept. She discovered, when she pulled back the blackout curtains, that the ferocity of the storm was over, leaving a wet, dull start to the day.

She thought of the night of madness, helped along by a war in which nothing could be planned or taken for granted. Later, when she wrote in her notebook, she would relive every blessed moment of their lovemaking. She regretted nothing, except that Cal was on board his ship and she was alone. It was time to go home and get ready for another gruelling day at the factory.

A sharp knock on the door and a female voice interrupted her thoughts. 'Do you want breakfast? It's extra.'

It was the barmaid from the previous evening.

'No, thanks,' Pixie called back. She listened as footsteps receded along the corridor, then peered at the clock on the bamboo bedside table. It was gone seven. The teapot and uneaten food looked forlorn. Straightening the tangled bedclothes she noticed a note on Cal's pillow.

Pixie, I didn't want to leave you but saw no reason to wake you so early. Last night was terrific. I'll write. Remember your promise to marry me. I love you, my darling.

Cal

Tears swam in her eyes. She remembered his kisses, his fingers sliding through her hair, his hands roving over her body. She had no regrets. They'd dozed and talked, then made love again, repeating that bliss all through the night. No regrets because he loved her and she loved him.

'Where the hell have you been? I've been knocking at your door for ages.'

Pixie could see Rita was staring hard at her. Her coat was slung over Rita's arm and dangling from her fingers was a carrier bag. It was pretty obvious she, Pixie, hadn't been home all night, for she was still wearing her box-pleated grey dress. Putting it to dry on the chair hadn't done it any favours: it was a misshapen mess.

She pulled the key through the letterbox and opened

the front door. She could smell Rita's strong violet perfume.

Rita frowned. 'You've been out all night!'

Pixie couldn't meet her friend's eyes. 'So you got home all right despite the storm.'

'No thanks to you,' said Rita. 'Are you going to tell me why you left me there at the dance?' Rita threw the coat across a chair and then tipped out a loaf from the carrier bag. 'Got that on the way over here,' she said.

Pixie gave her a grateful smile. Get the kettle on, Rita, will you? I'll tell you all about it while I change for work . . . Oh! What's this?' Pixie bent down and picked up an envelope lying on the doormat. 'I'll look at it in a moment after I've had a wash and changed.'

She could see her mother hadn't returned. Everything in the place was just as she'd left it. The bird in its cage chattered away as Pixie took off its tea-towel night cover. 'Hello, Bird,' Pixie said. A bag on the sideboard contained a piece of cuttle-fish and Pixie wedged it through the bars, then set about refilling the canary's water and seed dishes. Rita started the business of tea making. Her silence told Pixie she wasn't happy.

After a good sluice beneath the cold tap in the scullery and a frantic scrub of her teeth, Pixie ran a comb through her blonde hair then went upstairs to find clean clothes.

She decided on a grey skirt and a darker grey jumper. She'd bought the jumper at a jumble sale at Sloane-Stanley Hall, near the Criterion picture house, from the WVS stall. It had little puffed pads at the shoulders and was hand-knitted. Pixie thought she could unpick it and use the wool for something else when she got fed up with it. Anyway, it had been a bargain at sixpence.

Rita had switched on the wireless, and the news was telling them of how the average family of four spent thirty pounds a year on clothing, which was just seven pounds and ten shillings per person during the two years since clothes rationing had been introduced.

'I'm fed up with making do and mending,' Pixie said. She looked lovingly at Rita busy filling her flask with tea and making her a dripping sandwich for lunch at the factory. The smell of toast browning beneath the gas stove's grill was delicious. She went over to her and slid an arm around Rita's waist. 'I'm sorry about last night,' she said. 'All of a sudden I felt my head was going to explode. My brain was telling me *not* to do something and my heart was urging me to *get on* with it. I just had to go.'

'Cal ran out after you.'

'I know. And he caught me.'

She thought of the battle she'd fought against her

conscience, in allowing herself to fall for a man who'd sailed away today.

Then she continued telling Rita about Cal, that she loved him and he'd asked her to marry him. Even thinking about him and the previous night seemed to put wings on her heart.

But as she stood at the kitchen table, sipping her mug of strong tea, she saw that Rita's face was pale and drawn. Her mouth was a thin line. Beneath her eyes, which today had no sparkle, there were grey shadows. When her friend began spreading margarine on the toast, Pixie noticed her hands weren't steady. She wondered if Rita had drunk too much the previous evening. Rita, dispensing with plates, shoved a slice of toast towards Pixie. Her voice was sharp. 'Eat that. You can't make love to a bloke all night, then go to work on an empty stomach.'

'Aren't you happy for me?' The words slipped out.

Rita slammed the knife onto the table, making the remains of the loaf jump into the air. Then she put a hand to her head. 'Ouch! That didn't do my headache much good.' Pixie knew then that Rita *was* hung over. Her friend had tried to disguise the smell of stale alcohol with lots of perfume. The anger in Rita's voice further confirmed it. 'Have you forgotten you ran out of the Connaught Drill Hall without telling me what was happening, then left me to wonder where the hell you were when you never came back? For all I knew a mad axe murderer could have sliced off your head and hidden you in Walpole Park's boating lake!' There were tears in Rita's eyes.

'I've said I'm sorry,' Pixie said, putting down her mug and gathering Rita close. Rita's body was stiff and unyielding. She wriggled away from Pixie, then used her hand to wipe away a tear.

'Later, when I realized I'd run out into the storm and was wet through, I was too caught up with Cal to think of anything.'

Pixie stared at her friend. Rita wasn't usually mean-spirited. Something else must have happened, as well as her getting drunk. 'What is it?'

Rita gave a big sigh that made her whole body shake. 'Tony and me decided it wouldn't work.' Her arms hung at her sides. Suddenly she looked years older.

Pixie's heart went out to her. 'Oh, Rita, I thought he really liked you.' She wondered what she could do or say to make things better for her friend.

'So did I, but apparently there's a girl back home he likes more.'

This time when Pixie put her arms around Rita, her friend let her hold her tight.

'And all this time I've been going on about me and Cal. I'm so thoughtless . . .'

'You didn't know. Did Cal say anything about Tony's girlfriend? Or that he was going to ditch me?'

'We didn't talk about anything like that. Not about my mum, or money problems, we just enjoyed each other.' Pixie knew she was blushing.

Rita sniffed, then smiled at her. It was almost as if her old friend was back to normal again. 'Finish your tea – drink it quickly. We don't want to be late for work. You can tell me all about it as we walk to Weevil Lane. I shouldn't have snapped at you. It's not your fault.'

Pixie picked up her mug again. 'I didn't really like Tony anyway,' she confessed. 'His eyes are too close together and his eyebrows are too long and black. Me mum says, "Beware the man whose eyebrows meet, for in his heart there lies deceit." She got that right, didn't she?'

At her words Rita smiled but the smile didn't quite reach her eyes.

Pixie's tea was finished and she took a bite of the toast. Then she saw the letter on the table.

'I forgot about that.' She swallowed another mouthful and slit open the envelope, read for a few moments, then frowned.

Rita had gathered up the crockery and taken it through

to the scullery. Pixie heard a clatter as she left it in the sink. When she came back Rita said briskly, 'Come on. We mustn't be late.'

Pixie handed her the letter. 'Read that. We're not going to work. Em needs us.'

Rita read the note aloud:

I want you both to help me with Doris this morning as I've contacted Eadie Moss. Doris is too strong for me to handle alone if she decides to play up. Already she knows something is going on and won't do anything I ask her. I've told Harry Slaughter that the four of us are needed at the Dockyard in Portsmouth. We are supposed to be going to a talk on how to get more work output from factory girls. In any case the police will be at the depot this morning asking questions and Harry Slaughter will have to stop our line while information's gathered. You won't lose any pay or be out of pocket. Please don't let me down – there is no one else I can turn to. Come to the house at half past nine. Please. Em.'

Pixie looked at the clock on the mantelpiece. There was plenty of time to walk to Em's house. 'She must be in a right state about things to ask for our help,' she said.

'You all right about this?' Rita asked her.

'Can't say no, can we?'

Rita shook her head. 'What's this about the police coming to the depot?'

'No idea,' said Pixie, slipping into her shoes.

'That Harry Slaughter's a bastard.' Rita handed Pixie her coat.

'Don't you worry about him.' Pixie ran her fingers through her hair. 'I've got an idea that'll put him in his wife's bad books.'

'What d'you mean?'

'If it comes out that Harry Slaughter raped Doris, he'll deny it. Men get away with all sorts of stuff unless they're caught in the act.'

'So?' Rita was frowning at Pixie, who put a finger to her lips.

'Wait and see,' she said, with a smile. 'Harry Slaughter needs to be taught a lesson. The women in the factory are all scared of him. He must be stopped from thinking we're there to have his grubby paws all over us whenever he wants.'

Just then the letterbox rattled.

'What's that? It's too early for the postman.' She went to the passage and saw another envelope on the doormat. 'Today's the day for hand-delivered notes,' she said, picking up the letter with 'Mrs Smith' and the address written in pen.

Slitting it open, her heart started beating fast. 'A bill from the corner shop,' she announced to Rita. Then she saw the amount outstanding, with the words, 'An early settlement would be appreciated.' She handed it to Rita. 'Mum's ticked this up, gone off and, of course, it's not been paid.' Pixie gave a long-drawn-out sigh. If only she could use her wages to live properly instead of paying her mother's debts.

'It's a big bill. What are you going to do?'

'Pay it. I have to pass the shop every day. Imagine how I'd feel knowing I owed them so much.'

'But look at all these fags.' Rita shook the bill. 'You don't even smoke!'

'No, but I ate the food that isn't paid for. And what if I need to put something on the slate myself? They certainly wouldn't give me credit, owing so much already.'

Rita looked thoughtful. 'I've got some money, not a lot. I've been saving for a new coat, but you can have—'

Pixie broke in: 'I don't want *your* money. Thanks for offering, though.' She smiled at Rita. 'Anyway, I can pay it out of the money Bob lent me. I can leave the rent and make up the shortfall when we next get paid.'

'Perhaps you should have asked Bob for more.'

'Certainly not!' said Pixie. 'I'll manage somehow.' She slipped back to the kitchen and looked at the clock on the mantelpiece. 'We'd better go,' she said. 'Em must be out of her mind with worry.'

As she opened the door and they trooped out into the drizzle, it seemed to Pixie that the glory of last night, with Cal, had happened years ago. It was almost as though she wasn't allowed to be happy.

As she closed the front door, she heard the canary singing its heart out.

Chapter Eleven

Bob eyed Marlene as she struggled with the canvas top sheet, pulling and straightening it so she could peg it onto the stall's metal bars. She stepped down from the wooden stool and stared at him, her hands on her hips.

'That high one's a bugger! But it'll never defeat me!' She grinned at him, and he dropped the heavy box of books he'd been carrying onto the flat surface of the display shelf. He smiled back at her. She was a hard worker – honest, too – and he hadn't once thought he'd made a mistake in hiring her. He returned to the van and began unloading boxes of ex-army blankets he'd bought at auction at Minstead in the New Forest.

It was half past four in the morning. A few lights run from generators brightened Gosport high street as traders erected their stalls for the day's trading. The weather forecast had promised a fine day. A sudden peal of laughter caused Bob to turn in the direction of a nearby stall. Alec 'the Fish' was always ready with a joke. The small balding man wrapped in a white and blue apron waved at Bob, who waved back. It didn't seem to matter how early it was, there was always a bit of fun going on somewhere among the traders. It was what Bob liked about being his own boss and running a stall. Especially as he never knew what he'd be selling, one week to the next.

The sky was lightening now and the birds had woken up, and were chattering away like nobody's business. The first customers coming into the market would be the workers catching the ferryboats to Portsmouth and walking through the town. Then came the early birds, women who rose and shopped at daybreak. The ordinary punters came after them, buying groceries and bargains. Often they were pushing prams or had their elderly mothers with them. That was where the money was, with the ordinary housewives, and they liked a natter and a joke.

Second-hand books took pride of place on Bob's stall. He couldn't always get hold of as many as he could sell. The war and the shortage of paper had hit books badly.

At auctions he bought up anything he reckoned he could make a profit on. And house clearances provided all manner of items people needed, especially if the buyers had been bombed out and needed to start again.

His stall was made up of metal poles that slotted together to make a shed-like frame that he covered with canvas to keep the goods dry when it rained. He was a regular stallholder, rather than a casual. Regulars paid less, kept a certain place, but if they didn't turn up they still had to pay their pitch fees. Casuals were taken on only if there was space in the market. Their stall could be erected anywhere, but was usually in the least visited parts of the high street.

Marlene was covering the selling surface with a sheet. Since he'd taken her on she'd put quite a few of her womanly touches to the stall to make it more 'customer enticing', as she called it. He had noticed, though, that some of the customers preferred him to serve them. It didn't particularly worry him: he guessed it was their way of shunning Marlene because she was an unwed mother. He simply thanked God he didn't depend on such small-minded folk for his living.

'What's in the boxes?' She waved towards the stuff he'd bought the previous evening.

'Blankets,' he said. 'If you want a couple for yourself take them before the public buys the lot.'

'I'll pay,' she said. 'Can't go giving away profits.'

She was strong-minded, and it was hard to give her any of the few perks of the job.

He'd like to take home a couple of blankets for Pixie. Warm bedding always came in handy.

The smell of frying bacon attacked his senses. The tea van had opened. He'd go and buy a cuppa for him and Marlene in a minute and something hot in a couple of doorsteps of bread. The bacon smelt good but it was usually very salty and of poor quality. God knew where it had come from, definitely black market. Nevertheless, his stomach rumbled in anticipation. He pulled out another box of blankets from the van and set it on the street. He thought of Gladys.

Now there was a funny bugger. She was sassy, easygoing and a looker for her age, but you couldn't believe a word she said – and even though you knew she was lying, you wanted to believe her because she had a way of making you feel you mattered. He wondered how old she was; perhaps early forties? She couldn't go on thinking she could twist any man around her little finger, could she? Perhaps one day she'd regret trying to recapture her youth by swanning off with any bloke who asked her.

'I hope you got more besides these. They'll soon go,' Marlene said. She'd pulled the grey woollen blankets from the boxes and now began folding them neatly into piles.

He told her the price he wanted. 'Knock a bit off if the punters buy a couple,' he said. 'I got some pots and pans in the van. Will you help me unload? The sooner I get rid of the vehicle, the better.'

After unloading, the stallholders parked their vans on a bombsite near the swimming baths.

'Cor, these'll fly off the stall,' Marlene said, taking a saucepan from a sturdy cardboard box. 'What's wrong with them?'

'Ain't nothing wrong with the goods I sell. I buy in good faith. Don't touch no dodgy stuff. The auctioneer said they was "fire-damaged" stock. There's some whistling kettles in that box there.'

Marlene nodded and a swathe of bronze hair fell across her face. She was an attractive girl, thought Bob. The bloke who had let her down and left her with a kiddie must have been a right bastard.

'You going off today?' Marlene asked. 'How much for the kettles?'

Bob told her the price, then said, 'I'll be back by lunch-time. I'm off to Littlehampton – a clothes shop got caught in the bombing night before last. The owner's got stock in a shed and wants to offload now there's no shop to display it. It's all big sizes so should go fast, if I can get it at a reasonable price.' He lifted the last of the boxes onto the road and stretched. 'You going to be all right?'

Marlene was making a display of the some kettles. 'Course I'll be all right. Always am, aren't I?'

He didn't answer straight away. The market was coming to life now with goods set out to tempt customers. The place was getting noisier and punters were already milling around looking for bargains.

Marlene had worked briefly for Alec the Fish and for Dennis on the tea stall. If anything untoward happened while he was away he knew his mates would help her. They all looked after each other on the market, didn't they? Even Kitty on the flower stall was a good friend – Bob had let her down gently after she had wormed her way into his bed. The affair had lasted only a few months but the friendship carried on. Kitty liked young Marlene.

'Yes,' he said. 'I know you can handle things. But just to keep on your best side I'll treat you to a bacon sandwich and a cuppa before I go.'

'I'm sorry you've got to see her playing up like this. I wish I'd never told her what was happening to her.' Em threw her wrap-around pinny on the chair and ran to the door of the living room to chase after Doris, who hadn't stopped her high-pitched screaming since Pixie and Rita arrived. Em had been crying: her face was strained and her eyes puffy. 'I thought she'd be pleased that her life wouldn't be changed by having a child she wouldn't be able to look after. But she's set her heart on it. Even got a name for it, Lily. She's convinced it'll be a little girl.'

Pixie watched Em disappear and the screams continued, only louder. 'Not going to be easy to get her to Eadie Moss in Old Road, is it?' she said to Rita, who was standing on tiptoe and studying herself in the mirror over the mantelpiece.

'I bet her old man put this mirror up,' said Rita, 'before he got injured and had to stay in the wheelchair. It's too high up for any normal-sized woman.'

Pixie didn't answer her. Instead she asked, 'I wonder what made Em change her mind and decide on Doris having the abortion?'

'All kinds of things,' said Rita, shrugging. 'Em don't have an easy life.' She gave herself a last look, then came towards Pixie and whispered in her ear, 'I heard that since he come back from the war, he's a different bloke and makes Em's life a misery.'

'You don't know that's true.'

Rita sniffed. 'And you don't know it ain't.' She went back to the mirror and began fiddling with her hair, curling the ends around her fingers. She was taller than Pixie and very pretty in a Dorothy Lamour way. When they entered a dance hall it was always Rita who got the first looks from the men. Today she had on a spotted cotton dress that she'd had for ages but was too short. She'd unpicked the hem and sewn some ribbon around the faded bit. She'd made a wide blue belt that was almost the same colour as the spotted material. It had a point that ended just below her bust and the belt gave her old dress a brand new look. She wore her blue and white shoes with the two-inch heels.

Pixie didn't know how much walking they were going to do, so she'd worn her lace-ups with wide-legged grey slacks and a grey blouse that her mother had given her because she didn't like it.

Doris was still screeching.

'I'm going out to the scullery – I think that's where they are. See if I can help.' Pixie walked down the passage that gleamed with polish and in the living room saw Em's husband in his wheelchair, reading the paper. He seemed quite unmoved by all the noise. 'Hello,' Pixie said cheerfully. The man, dressed in grey flannel trousers and an open-necked collarless shirt, ignored her. Pixie went through into the scullery where Doris lay on the floor, her eyes tight shut, kicking and screaming.

'Sorry you've got to see this,' Em said. She was bright red in the face. Though she spoke calmly, Pixie could see she was at the end of her tether.

Pixie shook her head. 'Don't worry. I have an idea.' She knelt down on the faded scrubbed lino. Keeping one wary eye on Doris's flailing arms and legs, she said, 'You know my red dress?'

Doris immediately stopped yelling, opened her eyes and said, with a sniff, 'The one with the frilly bottom?'

'The tiered one,' Pixie added.

Em sat back on her heels, relieved. Pixie was glad of the silence: the screeching had begun to hurt her ears. 'Would you like it?'

Doris's eyes opened wider than ever. She was like a large floppy doll. Jesus, but she was a pretty girl, thought Pixie. Life could be so cruel sometimes. Here was a beautiful child, but flawed. And Harry Slaughter had damaged her even more.

Doris threw her arms around Pixie's neck. 'You mean it? You'd give it me?'

Pixie nodded. She'd tried it on last week and decided she was fed up with it. Anyway, she'd lost weight and it was too big for her. Then she frowned, looked at Em, picked up Doris's hand and held it. It was hot and sweaty. 'Oh dear!'

'What's the matter?' Doris's face was creased with anxiety.

'I'm sorry but you can't have it, after all. It won't fit you.'

Doris threw back her head. 'It does fit me. I tried it on. It does.'

Pixie had let her try it on one day back in the spring when they were getting changed at the factory to come home. Pixie remembered how she'd been thrilled by the poppy red brightness of the material, just when the war was trying to leach the colour from clothes. It had a sweetheart neckline and a tie belt. One of the girls had told Doris she looked just like a film star.

'It did then, but you've got a baby growing inside you and you can see you're getting bigger and fatter.' Pixie expanded her hands to exaggerate a huge belly. Doris nodded sadly. 'Today we can take the baby away and you'll be able to fit inside my lovely dress.' Pixie felt the tears rise at the back of her eyes. She sniffed, groped for Em's hand and squeezed it hard. This is a baby I'm talking about, she thought. Here I am, trying to persuade a child-like woman to get rid of a baby she wants to keep. The tears began spilling over. She let go of Em's hand

and brushed her fingers across her face. Em wanted only what was best for Doris.

'I want the dress!' Doris, on her feet now, stamped hard on the lino.

Pixie's voice felt as though it was being strangled. 'Do what Mum says and I'll bring it for you tomorrow.'

Pixie didn't know why Em had changed her mind about the abortion. All her reasons for not going to Eadie Moss had been valid. But Em was a sensible woman. If she'd changed her mind it was good enough for Pixie.

'Promise?' Doris was staring hard at her.

'I promise, darling.' Pixie leaned forward and squeezed Doris in a bear hug,

She heard Em say quietly, 'Thank you.'

Pixie went back into the living room where Rita, almost oblivious to the drama that had gone on in the scullery, looked up from the scuffed magazine she was leafing through. 'Thank God she's shut her gob!'

'Sometimes, Rita, you can be bloody callous,' Pixie snapped. Then she realized that Em's husband, Doris's father, had shown not the slightest bit of interest in the kerfuffle that had been going on in the room next door. What a strange man!

She stood on tiptoe in front of the mirror and

smoothed her hair. 'You're right, this mirror's no good for short-arses like us,' she said.

'Is Doris all right?'

'She is now,' said Pixie. As if in answer, a red-eyed Doris came clumping down the passage, followed by Em, with her black handbag hooked over her arm.

'He's just switched the news on.' She nodded back in the direction of the kitchen. 'Leslie Howard's dead.'

Rita gasped. Pixie knew she had a crush on the actor after sitting through *Gone With the Wind* at the Forum Cinema.

'Thirteen passengers were lost when his plane was shot down over the Bay of Biscay on the first of June,' said Em. 'He was such a handsome film star.'

'He'll always be remembered as Ashley Wilkes,' said Pixie. 'This bloody war. Will it never end?'

Outside, the sun was still shining and Doris held tightly to Pixie's hand.

Rita said, 'Em, you said something about the coppers being at Priddy's Hard. What's it all about?'

Em gave her a hard look. 'Didn't you see it in the *Evening News*? It was in the late edition.'

No wonder she'd missed it. She and Rita had been dancing, then she'd spent the night with Cal.

'What?' Pixie looked at Em.

'I found a lady,' chimed in Doris. 'She was tied to a bit of rope in the stairway at work. Her face was all black and her tongue was hanging out.'

'Oh, my God!' Pixie stopped walking and stood very still on the pavement, her hand raised to her mouth in horror.

'You must try to put it out of your mind, love. Forget it.' Em pushed Doris forward to get her walking again. She sighed. 'It was Myra,' she said.

'Jesus!' Rita's face was chalk white.

'Poor girl said the job was all she had. When I wouldn't let her on the line because she reeked of booze and might be a danger to others, she went to pieces. Doris here,' she nodded at her daughter, 'found her.'

'Her poor parents,' said Rita. 'What an awful thing to happen.'

'That's not the half of it,' Em said. 'The coppers went round to her parents' house in Queen's Road to break the news and get one of them in to identify her – that's what they do, even though we all knew it was Myra. Well, when they got to the house she was supposed to be living in, it wasn't there. There was a bloody great crater and only the garden shed was left standing. Remember when we had that bad bombing a few weeks back?' Em paused, obviously waiting for someone to say something.

Pixie nodded. 'Queen's Road took a bashing, half a dozen houses gone, just like that!'

'Yeah,' said Em. 'Well, Myra's parents copped it. The poor girl's been out of her mind, livin' in the shed. She never told nobody, just drank herself senseless. I feel real bad sending her away. Like it was all my fault. The coppers told me not to be so bally stupid, that I had a job to do and keeping her on the line squiffy would have been stupid.' There were tears in Em's eyes. She put her head on Pixie's shoulder and the tears came thick and fast. 'If only I'd known the poor cow was out of her mind with grief . . .'

Pixie rubbed her back. 'You wasn't to know. Myra'd got strange. She wouldn't talk to nobody.'

Rita said, 'I told Pixie she'd been drinking and was a danger. You did the right thing, Em.'

Em sniffed. 'I been worried sick about this.'

'Em, Rita's right,' Pixie said, 'and you got your own family to worry over. Let's hope Doris don't have no nightmares about finding her.'

Em gave a little smile. 'You're right. C'mon, let's get this over with.'

Em knocked loudly on the door of number seventy-one Old Road.

Pixie saw a long line of unwashed milk bottles that looked as though they had been there forever. Bits of screwed-up paper and other rubbish were spread over the diamond-shaped clay tiles by the front door. It was impossible to see through the window because the curtains were drawn, even though the sun was now high in the sky.

Em knocked again. There was a horse's head door-knocker but it was broken. 'She knows we're coming.'

Pixie was holding Doris's hand and Doris was straining to pick the heads off a few weeds brave enough to grow between the tiles.

A voice rang out, 'Come round the back!'

Rita tutted.

Pixie saw the corner of the dingy net curtain flicker.

Em said, 'How do we get round the back?'

'I think there's an alley,' Pixie said, pulling Doris away from the weeds and back up the street to a gap between the houses. She walked down the alley, careful to avoid the dog mess and the muddy puddles left by the recent deluge. Em and Rita followed.

At the end a brick wall enclosed the backs of some of the gardens. Pixie counted the houses, then paused outside a broken fence surrounding an unkempt garden. Guinness bottles were grouped outside the back door and a tin bath was nailed to the wall.

'Got to be this one,' Pixie said, as they went up the path. She banged on the door.

Almost immediately it was opened and the stench of stale cabbage flowed out.

'Don't like that smell,' said Doris, wrinkling her nose.

'Sssh!' whispered Pixie, as a large woman filled the doorway.

Pixie pushed herself forward. 'Are you Eadie Moss?'

The woman spoke, revealing rotten teeth: 'Yes. Where's the girl's mother?' Her eyes sought out Em. She nodded.

'I am. We're here for—'

She didn't get any further because the woman pulled her inside, saying, 'Don't tell all the bloody street my business. Why d'you think I keeps the front door locked? You was lucky I talked to you in the week. Only coppers and debt collectors come to the front.'

Pixie and Rita followed Em and Doris into the scullery. The sink was full of unwashed crockery.

'You two might as well wait in the living room,' Eadie Moss said. She waved a fleshy arm towards an open doorway. Pixie squeezed herself as small as she could to get by the woman, who was as round as she was tall.

Her hair was like wire wool, and her eyebrows had been shaved off and pencilled on again but they weren't even, so her face seemed lopsided. The scullery was a tip and the living room, with a three-piece suite so filthy that Pixie knew Rita would refuse to sit on it, was worse. No smell of polish in this house, thought Pixie. She caught Em's eye.

Em was clearly horrified, yet resigned. 'Stay, Pixie,' she commanded.

Rita said, 'Look, I'm only going to be in the way. Why don't I go for a walk? I'll go back to your house, Em, sit on the wall in the sun and wait for you.'

Pixie knew she wouldn't go into Em's house while Em's husband was on his own there. Em nodded.

Rita kissed Doris and said, 'You'll be all right.'

Pixie said, 'I've got a better idea. I've left the key on the string in case Mum comes home. Why don't you go and get my red dress so Doris can have it later today?'

'Good idea,' Rita said.

Pixie saw Doris's eyes light up. And worry slide away from Em's face.

After Rita had gone, Pixie noticed there was another bath in the scullery, a cast-iron claw-footed one, plumbed in, with an old door covering it so that it served as a table.

'Have you brought the money?' Eadie Moss asked.

Em foraged in her bag and came up with the brown envelope. She laid it on a low wooden shelf next to an open packet of Woodbines and an overflowing ashtray.

The woman said, 'I'll trust it's all there.' She stared at Doris, who was doing her best to hide behind her mother. 'Look, I'll be honest with you. I've done another girl who wasn't all there.' She touched the side of her head.

Pixie saw Em bristle and grabbed for her hand. 'Let her speak, Em,' she said. Em gave a long-drawn-out sigh.

'The girl was a bloody nuisance. Wouldn't keep still. I need quiet to do the job right. So I want you to give her a good drink first, to relax her.' She didn't look at Em but held Pixie's eyes. It was as though she sensed Pixie was more open to suggestion because she wasn't personally involved.

'I don't like it here.' Doris had turned towards the back door and was trying to lift the stiff latch.

Pixie took Doris's hand away and said, 'I wonder if Rita's found my red dress yet?' She doubted Rita had got very far but her words seemed to do the trick, for Doris suddenly smiled.

After a silence, Em said, 'All right.' No doubt she was remembering the screeching that Doris had treated her to not an hour earlier.

The woman opened a cupboard and took down a bottle of gin. She rinsed a grubby cup beneath the tap and filled it. She handed it to Em, who gaped at her. 'She had drink before?'

'No, Mrs Moss. I ain't in the habit of giving me kids strong drink.'

'Not even a drop to get 'em to sleep at nights?'

Em shook her head. 'Got anything to put in it to make it taste better? Drop of orange juice?'

'This ain't a bleedin' café and, no, I got no lah-di-dah juice.'

Em put her hand on Doris's shoulder. 'Drink this down, love, as quick as you can.'

Doris opened her mouth and swallowed about three big mouthfuls before she realized it tasted horrible. She pushed the cup away, sending the small amount of gin left in it flying towards the grease-encrusted gas stove. She gave a scream that sent Eadie Moss to her knees with her hands over her ears. Pixie pulled the girl round to her and pressed Doris's face into her breast.

'Quick – got a glass of water?'

'Here you are.' She was handed another grubby cup containing water.

'Try this, love.' Doris refused to open her mouth.

'It'll make the nasty taste go away.'

Doris shook her head. She'd clamped her mouth shut.

'At least she's stopped screaming.' Eadie Moss was now laying out on the draining-board stuff from a brown carrier bag that she'd taken from the kitchen cabinet. She hadn't wiped it, simply placed her instruments where she could find a space. There was a rubber tube with a pump at the end, a stained glass jug, in which she sprinkled a fair whack of Fairy soap powder, and a long thin spatula. The fresh scent of the washing powder helped to dispel the stench of the scullery.

'I don't feel well,' said Doris. 'The room's moving. I want to go to bed.'

'Good. She's feeling tired,' said Eadie Moss. 'Get her up on the bath top. Take off her knickers first.'

'What do I need to do when I get her home?' Em asked. Her voice was very small.

'Put her to bed with some old towels beneath her. It ain't gonna be an easy ride the first couple of days because she's gone more months than I usually like to do 'em. She'll be as right as rain later. C'mon, I ain't got all day.'

Em didn't move. Pixie could see the pain and worry in her eyes.

Suddenly Em grabbed Doris and pulled her close.

'No! You ain't gonna touch her!' Em wrapped her arms around her daughter. 'You ain't even washed your filthy hands.'

Doris looked confused as her mother now wagged a finger in Eadie Moss's face.

'You got all the time in the bleeding world, Mrs Moss, to give young girls all sorts of infections in this filthy hole. My girl ain't gonna be one of them.'

Pixie was stunned. But Em seemed to know exactly what she was doing as she grabbed hold of Doris with one hand, pushed up the door catch with the other and frogmarched her daughter outside, where she immediately took a breath of fresh air. She tramped down the garden path, Doris wailing that she wanted to be sick.

Eadie Moss had stumbled to the back door and was shouting, 'Don't try coming back 'ere cos you won't be welcome. Bloody time-waster!'

Pixie stared at them. Then she grabbed the money from the shelf and pushed past the irate Eadie Moss, who was still shouting obscenities into the back garden.

Pixie didn't stop until she saw Em at the corner of Mayfield Road, holding Doris's hair and rubbing her back while Doris violently spewed down the wall and over the pavement. Pixie pushed her handkerchief into Em's hands.

'If you didn't want to put Doris through it why did you let that woman give her drink?'

Em looked at Pixie. 'I wanted her to have the abortion. I really did. I can't carry on no more getting up so early to wash me husband, change his bed and get him dressed for the day before getting meself and her ready.' She nodded towards Doris, who was still throwing up. 'She ain't easy.' Doris was holding her head, dry-heaving now. 'Then I got a full day or night's work to do and then I'm juggling me wages left, right and centre.' Em paused for breath. 'As yet I've seen not hide nor hair of any government pay-out for my old man's war injuries. And right up until that moment when she swallowed that gin, trusting me, her own mother what's supposed to look out for her, I wanted rid of this kid she's carrying. Then I saw her little face, mouth tight shut, and knew I'd failed *her.*'

Em gathered Doris to her. Trails of spit marked their clothes. 'We're going home and you're going to have that lovely little baby, Doris, and I don't care how hard I have to work. I'm sorry, so sorry, my love.'

Pixie felt tears prick the backs of her eyes. She put her arms round Em and Doris and said, 'You're a good woman, Em, the best.'

Doris, unsure of what all the fuss was about, said, 'I don't like gin. I didn't like gin before when Mr Slaughter gave it to me with orange juice in.'

Em began using Pixie's handkerchief to wipe Doris's face. She stared first at Pixie, then at Doris. 'When did Mr Slaughter give you gin?'

'When he made me take my knickers off. I liked the orange. It was like that stuff they gives to babies.'

'So now she's finally told me,' said Em. 'You're a good girl, love.' She sighed. 'But what good is knowing who the father of her baby is? That bastard will deny it and he'll get away with it.'

Pixie said, 'Look, Em, I'm glad she's told you. It's not news to me. He's a slimy, wicked man. And before you think Doris confided in me instead of you, it came out when Doris found me in the lavatory after he tried it on with me the other day.' The thoughts that had been formulating in Pixie's mind were becoming clearer. 'Will you help me with an idea that'll make Harry Slaughter's life a misery?'

'I can't afford to get the sack.'

'You won't. I might. But nothing will incriminate you . . . or Doris,' Pixie added.

'In that case, yes.'

'Right. I'll explain as soon as I've worked it all out. But in the meantime it's a secret, right?'

'Right.' Em finished spitting and wiping Doris's face with the hankie, just as Pixie handed her the brown envelope containing the money.

'What's this?' Em turned the envelope over in her hand. 'This is . . .'

'Yes. This is yours and you're going to need it now for a cot, pram and stuff.'

Em shook her head. 'You and Rita gave it to me for an abortion, which hasn't come about. And I've heard through the grapevine that you've got a few bills of your own to pay.'

'Grapevine?' Pixie laughed. 'That's Rita, mouth like Wookey Hole.' She loved Rita but her friend couldn't keep a secret to save her own life. 'You're going to need it, Em, more than me, so shut up.' Pixie curled Em's fingers tight around the money. She grabbed Doris's hand and began to walk her quickly down the alley.

Em followed.

'I got an 'eadache,' Doris whined.

'You're not the only one with a headache, pet,' said Pixie. She would be glad to get home. She was beginning to appreciate the canary and its singing! She'd start writing a letter to Cal, yes, that's what she'd do. So much had happened since they'd been together. She hoped he was thinking about her, wherever he was. She would also find out when Myra's funeral was. Poor Myra, she thought. What a sad end to her life

A tug on her hand made her look at Doris. 'It's a very bad headache, Pixie.' The girl's blue eyes were screwed up with pain.

Pixie squeezed Doris's fingers. 'Perhaps a new red dress might make it go away.'

'Oh, yes,' said Doris, with a big smile.

Chapter Twelve

Gladys sat in the passenger seat of the Wolseley and listened to Del telling her about the flat racing at Goodwood. She smoothed the skirt of her dark blue dress with the puffed sleeves and caught the reflection of herself in the car window. She marvelled that Del always had plenty of coupons for petrol. She flicked back a loose lock of dyed blonde hair and touched her wrist against her new broad-brimmed hat.

The bruise on her arm was turning a delicate shade of purple. She must remember not to antagonize Del when he was drunk.

'This horse, Sugar Palm, won it last year. It's a race for three-year-olds and upwards, and the gelding's tipped to win it again this year.' Del's hand, as he spoke, crept over her knees and squeezed. His hands were always sweaty.

'Mind me nylons,' she said.

'If we win, girl, I'll buy you a whole box of nylons, off a mate of mine down the docks.' Del laughed.

He was in an exceptionally good mood today, thought Gladys. But after he'd had his way with her, like he had last night, and hurt her, he was always most apologetic. On the back seat was a shopping bag and in it another blue dress and a smart black twin-set. No coupons. Del didn't worry about coupons. He seemed to have contacts all over the south coast that could get him anything he wanted. It was all a case of supply and demand, Gladys thought. Like her and Del. He demanded, she supplied. The only thing he couldn't get was a place in the forces to fight the Germans. It had shattered his confidence that he wasn't fit or young enough.

'It's the Stewards' Cup race of six furlongs. When I win I'll take you out to a slap-up meal.'

Gladys squeezed his hand. 'That'd be nice,' she said. She hoped he wouldn't lose his bet. He'd be hell to live with if that happened.

Most of the country had long ago given up eating slap-up meals. With food in short supply and everything on ration, a decent meal was something to be remembered for everyday folk. But Del wasn't an everyday person: he knew places where food was plentiful, at a price.

'Do the horses get hurt? Fall?'

'Sometimes,' he said. 'But this is a flat handicap race. No fences at Goodwood.' He rubbed her hand and pain shot through her wrist.

'Ouch!'

He must have realized he'd touched her tender bruise because he took his hand away and sat back in the driving seat with a stony look on his face. Then he said quietly, 'Perhaps that will teach you not to contradict me when we're in the presence of my friends.'

She was about to say she was only correcting his mistake when he had said she'd come from Portsmouth. She'd wanted to put his friend right about where she lived. Most people didn't know Gosport existed. But everyone had heard of its bigger brother across the water, Portsmouth. She hadn't meant to show Del up. Thank God this time he hadn't marked her face. 'Sorry, Del. It won't happen again.'

The summer was in full flow. She watched as they drove by villages with stone cottages and pretty gardens filled with colourful flowers amongst the vegetables. The war seemed far away here in the countryside. She glanced back at her new clothes. At least Del wasn't mean with his money. But he *was* heavy-handed. Well, she'd just have to make sure she didn't upset him again. He also had a nasty habit of eyeing up other women. When she was talking to him he'd be only half listening, looking past her to see what else was on offer.

After they'd driven through the main gate of the racecourse and Del had parked the car, they walked to one of the buildings overlooking the track. Once they'd gained admission to a stand, Gladys stood looking through the wide windows over a balcony, where she could see other race-goers below. There were pretty girls galore but the lack of young men in civilian clothing was obvious. With the men away at war it was left to the servicemen and the retired and war wounded men to bet on the horses. Del pointed out the winning post and the gathering crowds, then asked an assistant to bring him drinks and some food.

'It'll be pot luck what we get to eat and drink,' he said, 'not like before the war when we had champagne with strawberries and cream.'

Gladys would rather have been out in the open air surrounded by the other people, but she didn't voice her feelings. She thought Del was trying to impress her with his money, especially when he said, 'I used to work from this track, and others, of course, taking bets and giving odds. Now I got blokes to do it for me and I can take a busman's holiday to enjoy the races.' He spoke loudly, hoping other people might hear his bragging.

The man returned with a bottle in an ice bucket, glasses and two covered plates, which he proceeded to set out on a small table along with napkins and shining cutlery. Then he popped the cork on the bottle. 'Do you need anything else, sir?' As he spoke he handed Del race cards. Gladys saw silver change hands in a tip and the man left to return to his post behind the bar, saying, 'Call me if you require bets placing, sir.'

Gladys, now sitting at the table, said, 'So we put on our bets through him? Not that I have money . . .'

'You have now.' Del took from his wallet some pound notes and pressed them into her hands. 'But we can bet from anywhere,' he said.

She was flustered. 'What if I lose the money?'

Del shrugged. 'It's what gambling's all about,' he said. 'We'll have a drink. Then, as we've plenty of time, we'll go down to the parade ring and see some of the horses as they're shown off to the public.'

Gladys's feet hurt in her new shoes. She had a bunion and it was giving her gyp. She would have been quite happy to sit watching the other punters through the windows.

On the way down to the parade ring Del did his best to explain the difference between betting each way or to win. Then he helped her write out a betting slip for the horse she fancied. She'd picked it because it was called Summer Garden and reminded her of the pretty cottages she'd spotted as they'd driven through the Sussex countryside.

Del placed a hand on her bottom as she stood among the crowd. She turned and smiled at him. There was perspiration on his forehead and top lip. His hair beneath his trilby hat was stringy and greasy. She wondered how old he was. At first glance he looked middle-aged, his weight and fleshiness ironing out facial wrinkles. But when he wasn't smiling she thought he might be more like sixty.

He was a very uncouth man. She wasn't refined, but the clothes he wore were loud and his hands always seemed to be searching into her feminine places. He was kind, in his way, but she wouldn't trust him as far as she could throw him, not with other women. She wondered why on earth she had taken up with him. For a second she wished she was at home, with her feet up in her comfortable slippers, waiting for Pixie to come home from work so she could have a gossip and giggle with her daughter.

Eventually, with her bets placed and her money gone, Del took her back up the steps of the stand to their table.

'When the racing starts can we stand on the balcony?' She wanted to be among the crowd, shouting for

Summer Garden and the other horses she'd backed to win. Del produced binoculars and handed them to her and as soon as the first race began they joined the other excited punters on the balcony in the sunshine.

She'd never been horse racing before, though when Pixie was young, they had played a horse-racing game with miniature lead horses. Suddenly she had a vision of Pixie, her head thrown back, her hair in disarray, laughing fit to bust. A sharp pain went through her heart. Pixie was a good girl and she didn't deserve the rotten mother Gladys had turned out to be. Trouble was, it was always money that was at the bottom of it – or, rather, lack of it. All Gladys wanted was for someone to love her and, as proof of that love, buy her pretty things.

Gladys reassured herself that Pixie was all right. Pixie was strong and she had her life ahead of her. Just as Gladys had once thought she had. She'd been sixteen when she'd had Pixie. With a baby to look after at such a young age, she had felt as though her own childhood had been taken from her. And now? She was still young enough for men to find her attractive, wasn't she? And it only needed one man to be that special person, didn't it?

She was brought back to reality by Del pointing out each of the horses as they went up to the starting line.

When the Stewards' Cup race began, she could feel

and smell the excitement it engendered. Del had backed Sugar Palm.

She began shouting along with the crowd and jumping up and down to the commentator's voice.

As the race ended Del threw his arms around her, lifting Gladys off her feet. Groans and shouts of joy came from the other punters.

Then it was all over.

Torn-up betting slips littered the ground, like fallen snow. Del had collected a wad of notes as his winnings and was in high spirits as they left the racecourse.

'I've lost all your money, Del,' Gladys said, as they crawled in the traffic waiting to join the main road.

Almost without taking his eyes from the steering-wheel, Del foraged in his inside pocket for his wallet. Then he opened it and tossed her some notes.

'And now you have some more,' he said. 'We're off to Littlehampton and a lovely little hotel that don't ask questions when its patrons make a bit of bedroom noise.'

Her heart sank.

'And I know just the way for you to pay me back,' he said.

Chapter Thirteen

'So you haven't heard from Cal yet?'

Pixie shook her head. 'It's July already and I've written him letters that I can only think are held up somewhere.' She replaced an uneaten spam sandwich in her lunchbox; she might toast it for her supper. It would be a shame to waste it, she thought.

Other girls were sitting outside in the grounds of Priddy's Hard, talking and eating before going back in to work on the lines. She stared at Rita: her cheekbones were prominent and she was wearing way too much make-up. 'You don't look well.'

'I'm fine. Nothing that a drop of gin wouldn't sort out.'

Pixie looked across the harbour towards Portsmouth. For once there were no ships in the Dockyard. However, the tiny strip of water that separated Portsmouth from

Gosport was filled with all sorts of workboats. There were the ferries, like squat beetles, transporting passengers back and forth, their funnels belching thick smoke. When it was cold it was lovely to get a special place to stand near the hot funnels, out of the wind. Not that it was at all cold today. The warm summer days were going on and on.

Pixie took a deep breath. The air smelt faintly of smoke and, of course, the tang of salt from the sea that washed against the low wall, lapping and rolling over the shingle. From somewhere music was playing and Pixie listened hard. It was 'A String Of Pearls'. The dreamy music made her think once more of Cal. Surely by now she should have heard from him. Mind you, she hadn't heard from her mother either, but Gladys wasn't one for letter-writing.

'I reckon you still got a hangover from last night. You was in the Fox pouring drink down your gullet like it was going out of fashion.' Pixie eyed her friend.

'No, I wasn't!' Rita shouted, so loudly that a group of women lying on the grass, sunbathing, turned to stare. Rita put a finger beneath her turban and scratched her head. 'Bloody thing drives me nuts.'

'Don't change the subject.'

Rita sighed. 'I may have had one over the eight last night, but I'm fine now.'

'Just don't let Em catch you with trembling hands. She can smell drink coming through women's pores, Em can. You got something on your mind?'

Rita shook her head. 'It's this bloody war. Won't it ever end?'

That was the question on everyone's lips. 'It was on the news that Hamburg in Germany has been almost wiped off the map by our boys. Six thousand dead and twenty-five thousand injured. Our lads got the docks, U-boats, factories, shipyards and a major tunnel. And just think, Rita, you and me,' Pixie spread her arms wide, encompassing the armaments yard, 'we're helping to win this war!'

Her friend gave a watery smile that ended too soon. There had to be something else Rita was worrying about.

'Everything's set for later this afternoon,' said Rita. 'John on the gate has promised to let us know as soon as old Slaughter's wife gets here.'

'What we're going to do to him isn't going to make up to Doris for what the dirty bloke has done to her, but if it stops him having a go at another girl, it'll be worth it.' The two friends looked at each other conspiratorially.

'We'd better get back to the building – lunch break's almost over.'

Pixie closed the lid of her lunchbox. Suddenly the blare of the air-raid siren and the drone of planes filled the air.

'Jesus,' said Rita, 'what's happening?'

Planes passed overhead, their shadows huge and distorted by the sun. 'Let's run for the shelter,' Pixie yelled.

Rita swept up her belongings. 'That's a bloody laugh, ain't it?' she said. 'Have you forgotten? We can't go in the air-raid shelter here at Priddy's Hard because that's where they store the bleeding gunpowder to keep it safe! Never mind about us!'

Girls were weaving to and fro looking for cover. Some, Pixie could see, were plainly terrified, others resigned to just another dogfight over Portsmouth and Gosport.

'Come on,' Pixie said. 'Let's hide over there.' She pointed to the Camber, a stone dock serving the depot. 'We'll be sheltered by the wall and the wooden posts of the jetty. Anyway, it don't look like them Luftwaffe aircraft is bothered about us and this place. They're more worried about being shot down by them Spitfires.' The sight of the familiar little planes was like balm to Pixie's soul.

Hand in hand the two girls ran for cover.

There was a wooden crate filled with empty paint tins near the wall and Pixie pulled it in front of the posts, making a sort of hidey-hole for them.

'Do you see what's happening, Pixie? It looks like them Germans was coming this way over the Isle of Wight, and our boys are intercepting them. Cheeky buggers, them Germans! In broad daylight too.'

The noise was terrific, the smoke and smell of cordite filling Pixie's nostrils and ears. She had a sudden fear that she would die without ever seeing her mother again. She remembered Myra's funeral at Ann's Hill Cemetery and everyone crying. Rita's voice made her jump.

'Can you count the Spitfires? I make it thirteen.'

'Well, that ain't going to be very lucky for someone, is it?' Pixie yelled, the noise filling her head. 'I s'pose they're after the radar stations along the south coast.' She could see the planes chasing each other at high speed, flames coming in bursts from the aircrafts' guns. Ground-level anti-aircraft began returning the fire.

She felt Rita's hand creep into hers.

'I don't want to get killed,' Rita said.

And Pixie, until that moment, hadn't realized how much she too wanted to live. There were so many things she wanted to do with her life and, possibly, so little time to do them.

The blue, blue sky was cut about with silvery trails and black smoke, almost as though some sky-bound snail had woven paths across it.

Some of the factory girls, braver or more foolhardy than Pixie, were standing in the grounds of the armaments yard, cheering on the RAF and yelling insults at the Germans. Most had more sense and had taken cover, hiding from the shrapnel falling from the skies. Then red flashes rent the air – a German plane had been hit.

It turned, smoke and flames belching from its body, and flew across to the island, towards its home country. Before the crowds had finished cheering, a second German plane was smoking. Soon it was covered with flames. More cheering filled the air and Pixie felt sadness overwhelm her at the inevitable deaths of the enemy airmen in their disabled planes.

And then, almost as suddenly as it had started, the remaining German fighters turned away, as though losing interest. Soon the sky was clear, empty of noise and colour, and only the stink of burning metal and spent shells remained.

'Whew, that's that, then,' said Rita, 'I couldn't half do with a gin now.'

'Me and all,' confessed Pixie. 'Them German planes won't get home, will they?'

Rita shook her head. She was pushing the wooden pallet away so they could now escape from their shelter. 'They'll go down in the Channel.'

'We helped kill them boys,' Pixie said.

Rita pulled Pixie to her feet. Pixie had never seen her look so cross.

'And if we didn't do our part, them Germans would have killed our boys!'

Callard Dalton lay on his bunk, the pen slipping from his fingers. He'd written six letters to Pixie and one to his sister, Ruth, during his time back on board, and had just started a seventh letter to the girl he loved. Yesterday the mailman had handed him a letter from Ruth. Although he loved his sister dearly, and her cheerful chatter about the guesthouse in Chichester made him smile, it was Pixie's letters he was eagerly awaiting.

Tony, below him on the bottom bunk, had been reading the James M. Cain novel *Double Indemnity*, but its excellent storyline hadn't kept him awake. The pen hitting him on the forehead resurrected him.

'Jeez! Betty Grable was telling me she wanted my body and you wake me up!' He glared, found the pen and held it out so Cal could take it. His dark, curly hair was still damp from the shower he'd taken after his turn on duty.

'Sorry, pal!' Cal sighed, as he looked at the small square photograph of Pixie taken at a Lee-on-the-Solent dance at the Tower Ballroom. It showed a slight, green-eyed blonde and didn't do her justice, but was all she'd carried in her handbag the last time he'd seen her. Pixie stood with her arm linked through her friend Rita's. It sat next to a family group photograph taken back on the Ohio farm. His mother stared out at him – she was a skinny little thing, too. He knew she was going to fall in love with Pixie just as he had.

He looked at his watch. Another ten minutes and it would be chow time. The radio was playing a medley of Glenn Miller music. It made Cal feel sad that it would be a while before his ship, the American Navy's most up-to-date destroyer, USS *Bristol* sailed back to Portsmouth in England. He heard Tony still grumbling below him about being woken up.

'You can go back to sleep again, you know.'

'Yeah, and this time my dream'll be Bela Lugosi wanting to suck my cock.'

Cal laughed. 'Whatever turns you on, pal.'

'You told your sister about Pixie?'

'Of course! Tony, she knows I want to marry my girl and I intend to start the ball rolling as soon as possible.'

It's a shame you couldn't get it on with Rita. She was full of fun.'

'That's the trouble, she *was* full of fun. I'd have been worried all the time I was away that she was having fun with some other guy.'

'I don't think Rita's like that.'

'How d'you know? You only got eyes for Pixie.'

Cal nodded. Pixie filled his dreams. 'Hey, you think we'll get back to Portsmouth?'

'No, Cal. I reckon we'll get torpedoed and sunk. What kind of stupid question is that? This is the sister ship to *Ellyson*, and was committed to the water in 1941 in good old New Jersey, the US of A. I don't have to tell you what a lucky ship this is, do I? Already she's got a credit list as long as your dick! Oh, I forgot, pal, you only got a little—'

Tony didn't get any further with his insults, for Cal had slid down from his bunk, whipped Tony's book from his hands and put a pillow over his buddy's face to smother him.

Chapter Fourteen

In the workshop the girls were quietly chatting while they went about their duties. There was an air of excitement in the room and the wireless was playing a programme of big-band music that suited the atmosphere. Pixie loved Jimmy Dorsey and was trying to hum along with 'Tangerine'.

She was pretending to herself that everything was going to work out fine.

The workshop reeked of new paint and new rubber conveyor-belts. Newly built workbenches and seating had replaced the old tables, which were worn and splintery.

Mr Churchill wanted production speeded up. Pixie had heard on the news that morning that a strategy conference between the prime minister, President Roosevelt and Prime Minister Mackenzie King of Canada had resulted in preparations for imminent new operations.

As usual the news was late in reaching England's work force, as Hitler mustn't know of Britain's plans.

Pixie had decided on a ruse to lure Harry Slaughter's wife to his office. She thought the forceful woman should know how badly he treated the women who worked with him. The new workshop was the perfect excuse to get her to visit the armaments depot.

The women involved in Pixie's scheme had been sworn to secrecy. Since everyone admired Em and loved Doris, it hadn't been difficult to persuade them to play their parts.

'What time is Harry Slaughter's wife supposed to be here?' Rita knew the answer but was just making sure. Again she stuck a finger beneath the itchy material of her turban and had a proper good scratch.

'Three o'clock,' Pixie said. 'I hope after all the excitement this morning she doesn't let us down. All that fighting with shrapnel and bullets flying about is enough to make people scared to go out. I went round to the Slaughters' house this morning and said we'd been let down by one of the stars performing at the Empire theatre in Portsmouth, so could she do the honours instead? She was thrilled to bits to open the new workshop. Of course I didn't go round until I knew Harry had left for work!'

Pixie remembered the woman's face and her excitement. She'd swallowed every word and Pixie had felt bad about deceiving her. But Harry Slaughter deserved to be taught a lesson. Eliza wasn't stupid and Pixie was banking on her knowing what a rat her husband could be.

'Suppose she phones to talk to Harry?'

'Taken care of. All calls have to go via the switchboard. Elaine will be monitoring personal calls. She'll make sure Harry Slaughter doesn't find out.'

'Oh, well done,' said Rita.

Pixie thought she looked more tired than usual. 'You all right?' A thought struck her. 'You haven't been drinking, have you?'

'No, I bloody haven't! Why do you always think the worst of me?'

Pixie put an arm around her. 'Sorry Rita, but I do worry about you.' She gave her friend a little smile. 'Forgive me?'

Rita pushed her away. 'Get off me, you daft lump!' They both laughed. 'Who's meeting her when she arrives at Priddy's?'

'Cedric.'

Rita gasped.

'I've told him his mother's visiting and he needs to take

her straight to his father's office when she arrives. He might as well see what we're up to, Rita. Just to stop him getting ideas. There's a new pair of rubber overshoes for Eliza to put on. She knows the drill about being careful in this place.' Pixie had had a job persuading Em to stop the conveyor-belt for an hour or so.

'I'll be there at the gate to welcome her too,' said Rita. 'Is that her bouquet?' She stared at the bunch of mixed summer blooms, tied with a red ribbon, on the bench. Their scent filled the air.

Pixie nodded. 'Ann got them off her allotment. That nice bit of ribbon was supplied by one of the other girls. It looks quite professional, doesn't it?' She marvelled at how all the women were eager to help put Harry Slaughter in his place.

'Got your clothes?' Rita asked.

Pixie nodded, then looked at the clock on the wall. She shivered. In truth she was a bag of nerves. She hoped she'd covered the women's tracks well, so that blame could be attached to no one but herself. It wouldn't do for anyone to lose their job over this. 'I'm not sure I can go through with it,' she confessed.

'Yes, you can,' Rita said. She, too, looked at the clock. 'The old bat'll be here soon. I'm going down to wait for her. I'll join Cedric and bring her to the office, so make sure Em's ready. Does she know how to work Bob's camera?'

'I've shown her enough times,' Pixie said. When she'd told Bob why she wanted to borrow his camera, he'd laughed loudly. But he'd explained all about the flash and wished her luck. He'd also told her he'd get the film developed for her.

'Good luck, Pixie,' said one of the girls, and everyone else joined in.

Pixie went into the lavatory and undressed, ripping off her work clothes and turban. Em followed. Using a hand mirror, Pixie caked her eyelashes in mascara and firmly outlined her lips in a bright red lipstick. She was glad her mother and she were practically the same size. The silk cami-knickers and embroidered top fitted her beautifully. They felt seductive and glamorous against her skin as she fluffed her hair loose and stared at herself in the mirror. In the high heels she'd also smuggled in, she looked like a film star, or at least like Jane, the lovely blonde cartoon girl in the *Daily Mirror*.

There was a knock on the cubicle door and Vi, one of the workers, shouted, 'Mrs Slaughter's coming this way. Rita's already given her the welcome flowers.'

'Bugger!' said Em, from outside the cubicle. 'She's

earlier than expected. We'd better get into his lordship's office, Pixie.'

Vi asked, 'You're sure Mr Slaughter don't know his wife's out there?'

'I hope not!' said Pixie, coming out of the cubicle.

The catcalls started.

'Wow! Don't let me old man see that!' And 'You look bloody gorgeous!'

'I'd better get in his office quickly,' Pixie said, moving into the hallway, and glancing about to make sure there were no unwelcome visitors.

She'd picked this time of day to play the trick on Harry Slaughter, knowing he'd be in his office until six when he left the factory to go home. Later in the evening he popped back to check on the night shift.

Pixie knocked on the door. Her heart was beating fast. Around her women were trying hard not to giggle.

'Come.'

Cocky sod, thought Pixie. He couldn't even be bothered to finish his sentences and call, 'Come in.' She went in and closed the door behind her.

His gasp could have been heard in the corridor.

Pixie's mouth was painfully dry. She felt nauseated by the cheap perfume she'd thrown over herself. She thought of the times that this odious man had tried to touch her and had to force herself to say, 'Mr Slaughter, I've thought of all the times in the past you've tried to get close to me.' She paused while she moved closer to him, her heart beating like a drum.

He stood up from behind his desk. She could see by the way his eyes were almost popping out of his head that he was too startled to say anything. His slack mouth hung open, almost drooling at the sight of her in the skimpy, silky underwear. He closed his mouth and seemed to gather his senses. 'What are you saying?'

Pixie, now so close that his breath was on her, started unbuttoning his navy blue dungarees, first one shoulder clip dropping down over his shirt, then the other falling to his round belly. Then she was pulling down the dungarees over his fat hips until they fell to the floor in a puddle at his feet.

He gasped again. His off-white underpants were stained and she could see he was aroused.

The smell of sweat coming off his pasty skin was making her feel sick.

He must have gathered some wits, for he stepped out of his overalls and moved closer.

His *thing* was pushing against the grey cotton of his underpants, making a tent in the baggy material. Sweat was beaded on his forehead. He was so taken aback that he hadn't uttered a word to her since she'd entered his office.

Her silk suspender belt held up a pair of sheer silk stockings donated by one of the girls, Patsy, courtesy of her Canadian boyfriend.

Pixie took one of his sausage-fingered hands and rested it on her silken thigh. He gave a sharp intake of breath. She lifted one leg and put her foot on the chair he had vacated.

Pixie tried not to breathe. All she was praying for was that the entourage outside would quickly bring his wife to the office so this farce could end. She gave him as dazzling a smile as she could summon.

She heard voices in the corridor outside and the door opened at the exact moment she threw her arms around his neck and leaned into him.

His arms went around her just as the door swung open and Eliza Slaughter stepped inside, closely followed by Em, with the borrowed Kodak Brownie Hawkeye camera at the ready. A flash lit up the office and a cry from his wife rent the air at the very moment Pixie called out, 'Oh, Harry!'

'Harry Slaughter! You bastard!' shouted Eliza Slaughter. The workforce had crowded into the room, craning their necks to see what was going on. Em had taken another couple of photographs, one with a new flashbulb, and another just for luck!

Pixie sprang away from Harry and rushed from the room, barging through the women, who were laughing and jeering as Harry Slaughter struggled to put on his dungarees.

Surprisingly, after her initial outburst, Eliza Slaughter seemed quite composed at finding her husband in a compromising position with a factory girl. She turned on her heel and walked out, pushing through the crowd much as Pixie had done. Pixie saw her open a door to a small storeroom and enter, closing it behind her. Then she heard Rita yell, 'Now keep your slimy hands to yourself, Harry Slaughter. Try anything else on poor unsuspecting girls and these photographs will go straight to your bosses. You'll never get a job where there are women employees again!'

Pixie realized the enormity of the trick she'd encouraged them all to play on their manager. She hadn't thought it through properly. She hadn't meant to hurt his wife. *Of course it would hurt her.*

Back in the lavatory cubicle Pixie quickly dressed in her factory clothes and pushed the pretty underwear into a bag. Respectable once more, she ran back in the direction of the storeroom that Eliza Slaughter had entered.

It was empty. On the floor were the crushed blooms of her bouquet.

Further down the corridor the factory women were still jeering at Harry Slaughter. Pixie knew it would take him a while to regain control. She ran out of the building past the railway line, its train trucks stacked with bombs, and down to the main gate. She was relieved to see the Slaughters' car.

'Please stop!'

Eliza Slaughter was just about to step into her vehicle after exchanging the rubber boots left at the main gate for her own shoes. Pixie ran past the gatekeeper, and stood panting beside the open door of the car. The smell of expensive leather engulfed her.

'I'm sorry,' she said.

Eliza paused. Pixie could see she'd been crying. Eliza's fox fur, which had been casually slung across one shoulder, had slipped down and she tried to shrug it back into place. The mean glass eyes in the stuffed fox's head glittered in the sun.

'That was a cruel thing to do to me.' Eliza looked Pixie straight in the eye. 'I don't even know you.'

Eliza turned away to enter the car. Pixie knew she couldn't let her return to her home without knowing how much her husband was disliked. And also that Pixie had not meant to hurt her. 'I've been exceptionally unkind to you. I'm very sorry,' she blurted.

Eliza stood quite still, staring at her. Then she said quietly, 'Get in the back of the car. And what's your name, girl?'

'Pixie.' It came out as a strangled sound. Pixie turned the handle and climbed into the immaculate interior.

Eliza got in at the other side and dropped her snakeskin handbag on to the floor. 'You think, Pixie, I don't know what kind of a man my husband is?' Her face was heavily powdered, her brows pencilled Joan Crawford arches. She exuded an air of sadness, but also of intelligence.

'I – I never thought,' mumbled Pixie.

'No, you never thought. But I did. And yet I married him anyway. Look at me.' She peered into Pixie's face and Pixie could see the thick mask of make-up that didn't disguise the sagging skin. 'I'm not like you. I don't have a slim, firm body, a pretty face, a head of enticing blonde hair to upsweep in the latest Victory Roll hairstyle. Compared to you and most of the women working here, I'm an ugly old woman. Even when I was young, I was plain.'

Pixie opened her mouth to protest, but what was there to protest about? What she said was true. But for all that

Pixie had no right to rub her nose in it. 'I'm sorry,' she said again.

Eliza took a lace-trimmed handkerchief from her sleeve and began to dab at her eyes. Her shoulders heaved, and Pixie tentatively put a hand on her back. She began to pat. Eliza leaned in towards her.

Pixie's eyes welled with tears. What had she done to this poor woman?

Eliza was making strange, strangled sounds.

It was then she realized. Eliza wasn't crying. She was laughing! Pixie pushed her away and stared at her. 'I don't understand . . .'

Eliza took a deep breath. 'No, I don't suppose you do,' she said, dabbing at her eyes. Then she bent down and picked up her handbag, opening the snap fastener. She took out a small silver hip flask and loosened the top. She handed it to Pixie. 'Take a sip,' she commanded. 'It'll make us both feel better.'

'I can't,' Pixie said. 'My shift's not over yet and Em, our manager, can smell drink a mile off.'

'Very noble of you, Pixie. Though I doubt much work will get done for the rest of this shift.' She held the flask to her lips and took a long draught, almost as though she was inhaling a cigarette. Then she sighed. 'How many of you were in on this farce?'

Pixie thought quickly. She wasn't about to tell on her friends. 'It was my idea,' she said. 'And I think I deserve to know why you think it's so funny.'

Eliza wiped her mouth with the back of her hand, transferring a smudge of lipstick to her skin, but not answering the question. 'Am I right in guessing that the photographs will be shown, when developed, of course, to Harry's superiors, if he ever attempts to lay a finger on another girl?'

Pixie nodded, confused at Eliza's quick grasp of the reason for their jape.

'Then, Pixie, you've done me a great service. A creep of a man Harry Slaughter may be, but he's *my* creep. And no longer will I have to worry about him when he's at work here. He'll keep his hands to himself from now on.'

Pixie couldn't believe her ears.

'This will be our secret, Pixie. He must never know we've had this little chat. I must admit I was angry back there when I was shown into that office. I honestly believed I was wanted to do a service for the armaments depot in opening the refurbished workroom. But I'm not a woman to bear grudges, and Harry will be begging forgiveness from me until kingdom come.' She took another swig from the flask and handed it to Pixie, who again shook her head. 'There is, of course, the matter of the child.'

Pixie couldn't believe her ears. She sat up quite straight on the bench seat. 'What d'you mean?'

'C'mon, girl. I'm not stupid. I hear gossip like any other woman. The backward girl who's with child? Is my husband responsible? I don't think it would be my son – he hardly knows what it's for!'

'It's not my place . . .'

Pixie bit her lip. She didn't want to tell tales, but now the whole depot was awash with suspicion. 'We believe so. I mean, her mother and I believe that to be so.'

Another sigh escaped Eliza. She flipped the flask closed, then returned it to her handbag. As she settled herself in the seat, she said, 'I'm going to make an allowance of a few pounds a week to the girl's mother. But I don't want to see or talk to them. I'm aware you and she are close, so I'd prefer secrecy. Would you be prepared to talk to her for me?'

'I doubt she'll take charity . . .'

'This isn't charity. It's her right.'

There was a silence while Pixie considered this. 'Put like that, I'm sure she won't refuse. Of course I'll talk to Em, and she'll want it kept quiet, too . . .'

For a while, Eliza sat looking at Pixie. Eventually she leaned forward and, almost as if she thought she might be rebuffed, put her arms around Pixie in an awkward embrace. Then she pulled the handle down to open the car door.

Pixie got out of the car, followed by Eliza, who climbed into the driving seat. She started the engine. Pixie watched as she circled the car to return the way she'd come. Before she drove away, she put a finger to her lips. Pixie watched and waited until the car was out of sight.

Chapter Fifteen

'That was a gorgeous meal and any other time I'd have munched my way through all of it,' Pixie said, pushing away the remains of her sausage and mash. 'But I feel a bit queasy and I haven't been sleeping so well lately.'

Bob picked up the plate, stacked it on top of his empty one and stood up from the table. 'I can't say I was all that keen on the sausages. More breadcrumbs than sausage, I reckon. I bet you'd like a cuppa, though.' He took the plates out into his scullery.

'I certainly would,' she called. 'Never say no to a cuppa.' She heard the water going into the kettle, then the pop of the gas as it was lit.

'Have you heard from Cal?'

Her tears rose and Pixie quickly wiped them away with her hand. 'Not a word.'

Bob stood in the doorway. 'That's not good.' He

looked genuinely sad for her. The wireless was on and from it came dance music that made her think of Cal and the way she'd fitted so perfectly in his arms, like they were pieces of a jigsaw.

Pixie shook her head. 'I write nearly every day. I don't know what else I can do. He has a sister living in Chichester, but I can hardly go and tell her that her brother hasn't written to me like he promised, can I?'

'There's probably hundreds of reasons . . .'

'You sound like Rita.'

'Do I?' He went back into the scullery. Pixie heard the clatter of the old brown pot-bellied teapot, and cups rattling on saucers. He was a good man, Bob was, she thought. She and he had fallen into the habit of a cup of tea and a chat. It certainly made her feel less lonely at home. He worked hard and deserved to make a success of his market business. She knew he'd taken on a girl who was also hard-working and one day wanted her own market stall. He often spoke of Marlene and how he trusted her, not just with the money but because she was loyal too. Pixie had met her and was surprised that such a little thing had so much strength in her.

She looked around the room. It really was a very comfortable kitchen. Her eyes fell on the Morrison shelter, the wire monstrosity that sat in almost every house to protect the occupants from the perpetual onslaught of bombing.

Bob came back with a tray. 'I saw Rita yesterday,' he said. 'There's something wrong with that girl. She's lost her fire and bounce.'

'She won't confide in me,' said Pixie. 'Anyway, how's your helper getting on?'

Bob seemed confused for a moment. Then his face cleared. 'Oh, Marlene?' Pixie nodded. How many helpers on his stall did he have? 'I'm glad I took a chance on her. You'd be surprised how many people look down on her because of the kiddie she has. She's brought the little one with her a couple of times as a last resort when there's been no one to mind Jeannie. Marlene's a good mother. But when she makes enough money to get hold of some decent gold jewellery she'll leave me and start up on her own.' He looked thoughtful. 'How about your mum? Heard from her?' He gave the pot another stir to settle the tea leaves.

'No. But you know what she's like. Blows hot and cold like the wind. I miss her, though.'

'Course you do,' said Bob, pouring tea into the cups. 'She's your mum.'

Pixie stared at the hot brown liquid swirling in the cup. Then she rose, put a hand to her mouth and bolted through the scullery for the back door. It took barely a second to raise the sneck and be out in the garden. She reached the privy just in time.

'You all right?' Bob had followed her.

'No,' she managed, before she heaved again. She grabbed some torn-up squares of paper from the string hanging on the wall and wiped her face. She breathed deeply, then tugged at the chain. 'I feel better now,' she admitted.

The smell of the late honeysuckle climbing the lavatory wall was soothing as she pushed open the wooden door and practically fell into Bob's arms.

'Never thought my cooking would affect you like that,' he said.

'It's nothing to do with the sausage and mash. I was poorly yesterday,' she said as they walked up the garden path and back to the house. As soon as she'd spoken the words out loud, she knew.

Pixie stood in the long, narrow back yard. It had been her first time with Cal. But one time was all it needed. She could indeed be pregnant.

A baby! A tiny piece of Cal, the man she loved, growing within her!

And then a black cloud settled above her.

Bob was looking at her strangely.

'How can I have a baby, Bob? I can hardly afford to keep myself with all the debts eating my money up, let alone take time off work to bring up a child. Oh, how stupid I've been.'

He continued to look at her. 'You haven't been stupid. You fell in love. Think yourself lucky. Many women never experience true love.'

Pixie smiled. Every word he spoke was the truth. There was a trace of wistfulness in his voice. She knew Bob cared for her, but he'd got past that and was genuinely glad for her. It didn't stop him taking his chance with the pretty customers who threw themselves at him – after all, he was a good looking man, with needs. Sometimes she'd heard girlish laughter coming through the wall from Bob's bedroom as she'd been trying to sleep.

But if only Cal had written . . .

'Do you have his parents' address? If something's happened to Cal, they'd like to know about the baby.'

Pixie shook her head. 'He was going to write to them about me.'

They'd reached the back door now and suddenly Pixie felt very tired. 'If you don't mind, Bob, I think I'll go home and get to bed.'

He lifted her over the low wall so she wouldn't have to walk around to her own house. When she was facing him with the wall between them, he kissed her chastely on the forehead. He hadn't said much about the baby, she thought. Still, it was probably just as much of a shock to him as it was to her.

He stared at her hard and another smile lit his face. 'When you get in, best look at yourself in the mirror. The newspaper you wiped your face with has left its print all over you.' He laughed. 'Goodnight, Pixie.'

Pixie turned away, then felt tears rise so she looked back, gave him a watery smile and went in through the scullery door.

She fed and watered the canary and put a tea towel over him, telling him it was time for bed. Loneliness had made her become quite attached to the bird. She wondered if her mother had known that might happen.

It didn't take her long to get ready for bed, but the moment her head touched the pillow she was wide-awake, her mind whirling about the debts. Those her mother had left were almost paid up. Pixie ate very little and had taken to going to bed early to write her diary or read, thus saving on the utility bills. Visits to the Fox with the girls were a memory. She couldn't pretend she didn't feel left out when they joked about the sailors and airmen they'd met in the bar, and even Rita had stopped begging her to come out in the evenings. Her aim in life for the moment was to get her debts paid off as quickly as possible.

She'd practically cleared the rent – well, half of the arrears – but she was still getting letters from the landlord: she'd used some of the borrowed money to pay off the more pressing accounts, like the grocer's. Then other debts had quickly eaten into the borrowed money. Her mother seemed to owe shopkeepers from way back. Pixie was amazed that she'd managed to keep her debts a secret.

But however could she afford a baby? She'd need things like a pram, a cot, bedding – the list was endless. And how could she work and look after a child?

Harry Slaughter had taken some time off after his come-down, leaving Em in charge. This had produced a bumper work output and the atmosphere had been calm and happy. He'd returned with a hangdog expression and the remains of a black eye. He'd never so much as looked at a woman since that day.

Pixie had noticed that she, Em and Rita were never on the overtime rota that Harry Slaughter prepared. Just when they could do with the extra money, there wasn't any to be earned. Still, it was a small price to pay for peace in the workplace.

Pixie turned down the corner of her library book's

page to save her place. She was enjoying James M. Cain's novels very much: they were all about people with problems caused by their love tangles, and were set in America, which made her think of Cal and his family. But the characters' problems were universal. Regretfully she blew out the candle, aware that downstairs just one remained in the cupboard. Candles, like other household items, were in short supply. Pixie slid down under her patchwork quilt, which was worn but comfy.

She was just dozing off when the air-raid siren started screaming, announcing an imminent attack. She pulled the quilt over her head.

The nearest shelter was close to the Criterion picture house. She knew she should get out of bed and put on some warm clothes, make a flask of tea, slip her gas mask over her shoulder and run to it. 'Damn Germans,' she mumbled. She didn't want to leave her comfortable bed. She felt tired and queasy. She'd overheard women at work talking about being pregnant and how some had been sick almost to the time they'd given birth. How would she cope with that?

She thought about Eadie Moss in Old Road. Perhaps it might be better to get rid of it. No, she told herself. Apart from not having the money to pay the woman, she would never think of having an abortion. Remembering the filth in the woman's scullery made her heave and she managed to pull out the chamber pot from beneath the bed just in time.

She pushed her hair behind her ears and wiped her mouth and eyes. A knock at her front door made her jump. She went to the bedroom where her mother slept when she was at home, and peeped through the curtains. She breathed a sigh of relief when she saw Bob in his dressing-gown. She went downstairs and opened the door.

'I knew you wouldn't go to the shelter,' he said, adjusting his glasses above his nose. Pixie thought he looked like a schoolteacher wearing them. He had to move out of the way as the family from number thirty-two trundled their pram and four children along the pavement on their way to the shelter. The street was alive with people running and families hurrying, hopefully, to safety. 'Get what you need and come into my Morrison.' He stepped into her passage and closed the door behind him. 'You can put the light on,' he added. 'I've shut the door.' Then he said, 'Don't worry about bringing big stuff. I've got all the essentials, like bedding and food.'

He took her work coat off the hook by the front door and put it over his arm. Pixie smiled at his thoughtfulness that she might need extra clothing for warmth. She went into the scullery and grabbed her toothbrush and tin of Gibbs' dentifrice along with her make-up. Back in the kitchen she fumbled in the cupboard and took out a shoebox that contained her birth certificate, ration book and personal papers, plus a few photos of the man she thought was her father, with her mother and herself, when she was a baby. She dumped everything into a brown carrier bag with string handles.

She grabbed the birdcage, sprinkles of seed cascading over the table.

'I'm ready,' she said.

Already the bombs had started falling. Far away, thumps sounded irregularly. They were still a long way off but the drone of aircraft was growing closer.

'Turn off the light,' he hissed, as she opened the front door. 'Then wait for me. I need to turn off your utilities.' He ran through the house and she heard the slam of the door to the cupboard where the meters were. He'd turned off the gas, water and electricity supply. Swiftly he returned and, grabbing her hand, ran into the street. The bird was squawking. There were still people about, racing for cover, shouting to each other. Bob pushed open his front door and almost threw her inside, then closed it behind them. For a second he leaned back against the wall. His eyes were shut and he was breathing deeply.

Then, as if he had woken up again, he pushed her down the darkened passage into the kitchen. By candlelight, she left the birdcage on the kitchen table and crawled into the metal contraption that was the Morrison shelter. There was a mattress as a base, pillows and several blankets. 'If you don't want that stuff in the carrier bag in with you, I'll leave it on this chair beside the shelter,' he said. After making sure the water and seed were still intact in the canary's cage he re-covered it with a tea towel. 'Goodnight, little birdy,' he said. 'Perhaps he'll sing us to sleep.'

Pixie nodded. 'I could do with a cuppa,' she said. Then she screamed as a particularly loud bang shook the house so heavily that dust flew about in the room.

'There's a flask in the corner of the shelter,' he said. 'Don't spill it; else you'll be sleeping in the wet patch. I need to go and turn off the gas, electric and water.' He went off into the darkness.

Pixie decided she was too nervous to be steady with the flask, so she got inside the makeshift bed. She thumped the pillows into place. Somewhere nearby another terrific bang assaulted her eardrums. She could hear bricks and rubbish raining down on the roof and saw red and orange light flare skywards even through the heavy blackout curtains. A sharp crack told of a pane of glass splitting in one of the windows. She prayed it would be the worst of their worries. Through the dull light of the fire burning in the range, she could see the green-fringed ceiling lamp swinging crazily in the middle of the room.

Even indoors the smell of cordite had seeped into the air. She reckoned Bob must have left a window open somewhere. More quick bangs were added to the drone of planes and the ack-ack of returned ground fire.

Just as her fear was mounting, Bob returned. 'Move over,' he said. 'There's got to be room for a little 'un.'

Pixie laughed and immediately felt better. 'You don't usually invite me to join you in your shelter,' she said. She pulled up the blankets again. He'd got in at the other end and was sitting facing her. 'Why is it that old Hitler won't let us alone here in the south?'

'We wouldn't get the bombing so bad if it wasn't for the Dockyard and all the ships, not to mention the submarine base at HMS *Dolphin*,' he said. Then, 'I'm usually asleep because of my early work starts and you're not always at home when the Luftwaffe's prancing about. Your mum sometimes knocks me up so she can come in the shelter, though – she gets scared on her own.'

'That's news to me,' snorted Pixie. 'It's not often she's by herself.'

'You'd be surprised,' he said. Pixie caught the hint of

a reprimand in his voice, as though he was telling her something she ought to know but had somehow overlooked. 'We'll just have to hope she's all right. Now she's about to be a grandma!' He looked uncomfortable. 'Oh dear. I don't even know if you're really pleased about the baby. I'm just assuming you are . . .'

'Actually, I am,' Pixie said.

Another huge crash made the house shudder to its foundations. Pixie screamed again and threw herself forward into Bob's arms. She pulled back. It was almost intimate, like being in bed together. But that's what this war was doing, she thought, making strange bedfellows of people.

Silence seemed the only option between them as Pixie listened to the thwump-thwump of bombs falling and watched the searchlights brighten the sky, filling the kitchen with an eerie glow.

Pixie saw Bob had put a pack of cards next to the big torch that was near his pillow. Sometimes the bombing went on for ages. Most people found concentrating on a game of cards helped take their minds off the danger. He seemed to have thought of everything. He was a good man to have about in a crisis. She wasn't silly, she knew Bob liked her. She liked him, too. But it was Cal who had stolen her heart. She was still deep in thought when Bob surprised her by asking, 'I know I mentioned it earlier but have you found out what's the matter with Rita?'

Pixie shook her head.

'Sticks out like a sore thumb that something's troubling her,' Bob persisted.

'She'll tell me when the time's right,' Pixie said. She wasn't convincing herself. 'I shouldn't say this but she's been down the Fox, drinking with the girls, almost every night. Em told me she gave her a warning for being shaky when pouring powder into the shell cases. I'm worried about her.'

'You can't make someone talk if they don't want to.'

He was right. She would have to share her secret about being pregnant with Rita, then maybe Rita would confide in her.

Outside, suddenly, there was silence. The planes had gone.

'It's quietening down out there.'

At his words, new but familiar sounds rent the air. Ambulances, engines, voices.

'It'll be awful walking about and seeing the fresh damage,' Pixie said, just as the ear-splitting wail of the siren announced that the raid was over. Until the next time, Pixie thought.

'Go to sleep here, Pixie, if you want. There's nothing we can do tonight, not in the dark. I'll pop out and check your house and mine as best I can. And I'll switch on the utilities. Just thank the Lord that, apart from being shook up, we've lived through another raid.'

She closed her eyes. She wouldn't go back to her own cold bed and house, she'd stay here in the warm where the heat from the range's dying fire comforted her. Bob was now rattling cups in the scullery. Pixie smiled to herself. She felt safe. And, as if in agreement, the canary began to sing.

Chapter Sixteen

Cal sat at the table, writing.

'Not another declaration of your feelings towards that pretty little girl.'

Errol, the chief gunner's mate put his hand on Cal's shoulder. 'At this rate it'll take a sack to carry your letters to the mailman.'

'Just because we're escorting a convoy to Algeria in the back of beyond, it doesn't mean that *eventually* we won't be able to post and receive our mail.'

Cal looked at Errol, fresh from the shower. Droplets of water clung to his dark hair. 'Now we finally know our destination is Oran, we can look forward to a bit of shore leave when we dock.'

Big-band music from the wireless was making Errol tap his bare feet. Cal knew he thought he could dance the feet off most of the other sailors on board. Sometimes they teased him, calling him Fred Astaire.

Errol made a face then threw his damp towel at Cal. 'Yeah, I know, you're gonna marry that girl so picking up the local whores ain't your thing.'

'Maybe it's time you settled down,' Cal said, throwing the towel back at him.

Errol caught it, and tossed it over the back of a chair. He pulled on a white undershirt, patting it into place over his hairy chest. Cal thought he was like a good-natured mountain bear. 'All the while there are women out there, I'll see to their every need. Wonder what they're like in Oran.'

'Full of pox and ready to take your money.' Cal laughed. A sudden spasm of fear made his shoulder-blades clench. 'What's that noise?' The crunching sound alien to the usual ship's noises reminded him of a twig being sharply snapped in two. He clutched the writing pad to his chest. 'I think we've been hit!'

The sudden rush of water swept Errol off his feet. It had pushed in the door as though it was made of balsa wood.

Cal yelled, 'We've got to get out of here.'

Sounds of men running and shouting competed with the ship's echoing warning bells. Then the lights went out. The bells were suddenly silent. All Cal could hear in that split second, besides the water slurping and slapping, was a sailor calling for his mother.

Errol was holding tightly to the fixed iron strut of the table leg in an effort to stop himself being swept away. Cal grabbed at the other. His knuckles were white with the effort of trying not to let go as the rushing water knocked him about. He was swept upwards and flattened against the table top. His brow smacked against the wood. Still he managed to hold on. He looked at the split in the floor, which was growing ever wider. 'It's been broken in two,' he yelled, as if Errol couldn't make that out for himself. The constant roar of the water filled his ears, his brain. Errol's eyes were ringed with terror.

The smell of the invading sea was dank yet salty-sharp and stung his skin. 'Got to get out of here,' Cal repeated. The gap in the floor was sucking him downwards. He was terrified to let go of the table leg, knowing it could be his only chance of survival. To hang on, to stay in the room, stay alive. No, better to swim out and make it towards the ship's life-rafts.

He took a deep breath and let go, then half slid, half swam against the tidal wave of water towards the corridor. Where he could, he hung on to stable fittings.

Errol was close behind him.

The body of a floating dead sailor bumped into Cal. The man was unrecognizable. He'd lost half his face. Black oil covered his body.

In the corridor the smell of burning was intense.

'Fuckin' explosion,' shouted Errol. 'Never heard a goddam thing!'

Cal glanced back at Errol. The blood from his head wound hindered his eyesight. He kept shaking the blood away and droplets of red discoloured the grey-green water that now was rising rapidly. There seemed to be so little space between the roof of the corridor and the water level.

But now the water was flowing swiftly in the direction they were heading, towards the safety of the outside and the life-rafts. Unhindered and floating down the passageway, Cal looked back again to make sure Errol was behind him.

'I don't think I can make it,' Errol shouted, 'I feel so . . . I don't—'

He got no further for there was a crack, and then a ripping sound.

'It's breaking up,' shouted Cal. He put out his arm to divert a wooden plank from tumbling towards Errol. The ceiling was falling. Whole sheets of metal began crumpling like paper.

Cal looked up just as the roof came down to meet him. Metal fell on his face, his head. He heard his nose crack. Then came the pain, like a hundred knives twisting in open wounds.

Errol was holding him. 'Don't close your eyes, Cal. Stay with me.'

He wanted to tell Errol he couldn't see, but his mouth wouldn't work. He was beginning to feel as light as air. It certainly felt good in Errol's arms. Or were they Pixie's arms? They might be, he thought.

He leaned his head to one side so that he could breathe above the water. And still the rushing, swirling coldness wouldn't leave him be. It was colder than that night in the thunderstorm with Pixie. He closed his eyes.

'Don't leave me!' Errol shouted.

Cal opened his eyes. He could just make out a letter floating past him. He hoped it was one of his to Pixie and that it would float all the way to England, taking him with it.

Cal saw Pixie then, her face smiling and loving because he *was* in her arms, in her warm arms. He tried to catch at the letter and hold on to it, as her welcoming presence settled about him. Her lips touched his mouth and her body melted into his.

Chapter Seventeen

Gladys nodded at the dark-haired man who had asked her to dance. Del had gone to the bar ages ago – she could see him standing there, one shoe on the brass foot-rail and sweat discolouring the armpits of his blue shirt. He was leering at the blonde barmaid, no doubt chatting her up.

'Are you on your own?' He put out a hand to help her up from the chair.

She could smell the orange tang of his cologne, a pleasant change from the cigarette smoke and stale beer that pervaded the ballroom. 'No,' she said, 'but I might just as well be.'

He was taller than her, slim with long fingers. She wondered what he did for a living – it certainly wasn't a manual job, not with hands as well kept as those. His eyes were dark, deep pools and his slightly olive skin made him seem glamorous yet dangerous. If he had a moustache, she decided, he would look like a spiv.

'You look very nice,' he said. He had a well-modulated voice, not posh, but certainly none of the Portsmouth roughness. It had just the right uneven sound to make him seem foreign. His words caused her to look down at her blue two-piece suit with the parachute silk blouse beneath. The skirt was just below her knees and slightly fishtailed, its belt cinching in her small waist. The matching jacket was bolero style with shoulder pads. It was new. Del had been out all night while she had waited for him in the scruffy room over the St Mary's Street fish-and-chip shop in Southampton. He'd come in stinking of drink the next morning, throwing a bag containing the suit and a pink wool dress onto the bed as though they more than made up for his absence. Then he had given her some money, waved her away and got into bed. When she had returned after shopping in the Kingsland Market he was still asleep, the smell of his sweat filling the room and mixing with the frying fish from the shop below.

'I like your hair, as well.'

Gladys had fastened it in a Victory Roll. 'You're full of compliments,' she said. She was well aware of the admiring glances he was getting from the wallflowers sitting around, waiting to be asked to dance. She was also aware of the pain in her back from Del's ardent lovemaking that morning, before he'd collapsed flat out on the bed. He had shown her the large wad of money, winnings, he'd secreted in his pocket. Winnings she knew he'd never be able to hold onto. His money came in and flowed out like the tide.

'We'll be able to get out of this flea-pit,' Del had said. 'The weather's changing and this place has got more draughts than a bloody tent.'

He'd gone through a run of bad luck. But he'd kept on gambling until his luck turned, even though he'd lost her jewellery, such as it was, his watch and gold chain and his car.

He'd told her he was unmarried and a bookie. Lies simply dripped from his lips. He was married and had been a bookie. The profits from the betting shop he'd opened in his wife's name had gone on operating pitches at greyhound racing circuits. The losses from these had overtaken the profits. He was extremely lucky his wife, Rose, had her head screwed on and was able to run the betting shop, look after their three teenage children and go on paying the mortgage on their house in Littlehampton.

Gladys had felt every admiration for her when Del had confessed all, after he'd slapped her about.

Del and Gladys were celebrating his card-game win at the Mayflower Hotel in Southampton. He'd slept off the drink, and reckoned his gift of pretty clothes would soften Gladys up. The icing on the cake would be a dance in the grand ballroom. So here they were, except he hadn't danced a step with her because he was too busy chatting up the barmaid and making deals with the American servicemen who'd swamped the hotel.

The first GIs had arrived in boats at the docks last year and now they were everywhere. The US Army Transportation Corps had made the city its supply centre. Illegal deals were rife because the Americans had access to food and goods England had been without for some time. They were looking for fun, pretty women to spend their money on, and ladies of the night, who'd give special favours in return for cash.

'I've been plucking up the courage to ask you to dance,' the man persisted. His teeth were very even, small and white.

'Did you think I might bite you? My name's Gladys,' she said. 'What's yours?'

'Terrence.'

'Do you come here often, Terrence?'

He laughed. They'd reached the ballroom floor. Gladys had been sitting at a table on the balcony upstairs.

The resident band, Henry Cavell and His Swingers, were playing. The happy tunes floated through Gladys's mind and made her think suddenly of how she and Pixie had danced together in their small kitchen to music on the wireless.

The thought was quickly replaced by the pleasure she took in her surroundings. Gladys had fallen in love with the blue velvet seats and gold chandeliers at the Mayflower. The dark wooden walls of the ballroom, painted with gold scrolls, and the smoky atmosphere were, to her, very glamorous. The parquet flooring was perfect for dancing and the room was packed with entwined couples and the smell of cheap perfume.

She was easily one of the best-dressed women there. Make do and mend was part of the war effort, but Gladys wasn't one for sewing, and clothing coupons didn't allow for regular clothes-buying. Yet she admired the ingenuity of the women's ideas for altering their dresses so that they had different outfits to wear at the dances.

The music changed: a tango started up.

'Can you do this dance?' he whispered.

'You bet,' she replied. When she was younger she'd had dancing lessons and the tango was her favourite. It made her think of Rudolph Valentino.

Quite a few of the dancers had left the floor, to buy

drinks or to sit out the dance, as the tango was extremely difficult to get right.

Terrence put his arm around her, his hand on her back. As the music played, their steps were so suited to each other that Gladys felt she was dancing on air.

'This is a lovely song, but I've never heard it before,' she said.

'It's from my country, written by Homero Manzi.'

'Oh,' said Gladys. 'Where do you come from?'

'Buenos Aires.'

Gladys had no idea where that was and didn't care. She was swept along with the dance and was determined that his steps wouldn't allow her to lose her timing with the beguiling music. She looked over his shoulder and saw they were the only two dancers on the floor and that all the other couples were watching them.

'This music tells the story of a gold-framed picture removed from a wall and replaced by a painting of an autumn scene. Reflected in the music are the love, loss, and regret that this brings. Similar to the loss of true love.'

Gladys could feel the sadness in the music and knew she was drawn to Terrence. Usually when a man danced with her, the object for him was to cop a feel, but this was different.

He pulled her close, his arm encircling her body, then said, 'The last *colgada*.' Gladys didn't know what he meant but was flattered he'd said it to her.

Then he threw her away from him in a spinning movement, causing her to lean back, copying his movement. Terrence finished the dance with a back step.

The crowd clapped and roared. Even the musicians in the band stood and bowed towards the pair.

'Oh, my!' said Gladys. Her head was still spinning.

'Well done,' said Terrence. He slid to his knees and bowed his head in deference to her. The people clapped even louder as Gladys stood, unsure of what to do.

'Thank you,' she said. 'I need the lavatory.'

Dancers were again crowding the floor as she swept through them. But not before she'd seen Del standing alone, a pint in his hand, watching her.

She remembered the Ladies was downstairs. Ignoring Terrence calling, 'Wait!' she ran out into the foyer and down the marble steps.

Smoothing her hair back into its roll at the nape of her neck, she stared at herself in the mirror. Her face was flushed with excitement. The accolade she'd just received had made her feel twenty years younger. She gave a silent thank-you to her aunt, who had been determined that Gladys should learn to dance at the Miracle Maids Dancing School.

Aunt Peg had taken over the role of parent when Gladys's mother had died: Gladys had been three. Her father had been killed in the Great War. Aunt Peg had been Gladys's idol. A chorus-line dancer, she'd given up her career to look after the little girl. When Gladys broke her heart by falling in love with Pixie's father at the age of fifteen, something had snapped inside Aunt Peg.

Until then she'd never denied her niece anything, but she'd shown her the door when Gladys announced she was pregnant. Her boyfriend had refused to have his name on Pixie's birth certificate. Gladys was seventeen when he had walked away.

'You aren't exciting any more,' he had told her. At the time Gladys was working four cleaning jobs, supporting the baby and him.

She gave up the cleaning jobs and became 'more exciting', as she persuaded men who picked her up to give her money in return for favours. She deserved a good time, she told herself.

She loved the adulation she'd just received for her dancing. She felt as glamorous as Ginger Rogers when she opened the door and stepped out to the sound of raised voices from the Gents next door.

'She might be mutton dressed as lamb but she's mine! Take your filthy ideas and try somewhere else!' Del's voice. 'So who are you pretending to be this week? A greasy spic? Don't suppose you've told her you were born down Dock Road?'

'What's she to you? Just a pick-up, Del. I can make it worth your while.'

Terrence's voice. Only this time it was pure Southampton. He was still speaking: 'The punters like an older woman. She knows what's what better than the young bits of stuff and she'll be grateful for any bloke to pay her for a session.'

Gladys's heart was beating fast. It was obvious the two men knew each other.

Again Terrence spoke, 'Some men like a woman they can dominate and knock about before a bit of how's-your-father. Gladys is one of them, isn't she?'

Gladys grabbed at the door handle to stop herself sliding down the wall. She thought of the applause she'd received in the ballroom. People weren't clapping because she was dancing the tango, but because she was a middle-aged woman trying to prove she still had the special something that drew the men to her. Oh, how stupid she was! A silly old woman pulling any man sooner than being left on her own.

Two women were walking down the corridor towards the lavatories. A whiff of Evening in Paris mixed with gin reached Gladys. She moved aside as the giggling girls pushed past her and into the Ladies, apologizing – 'Excuse me, sorry, excuse me.'

Gladys let them pass her as though she was half asleep. Her brain was whirling as she tried to put together the pieces of conversation to make sense of it all. A cistern flushed. Gladys was still listening at the door to the Gents.

'Keep away from Gladys. She's all right with me. You want some old tarts for your knocking shop in Derby Road, find your own, Billy Manning! Oh, sorry, it's Terrence this week, isn't it?'

The two girls opened the door. The blonde frowned at Gladys who, flustered, immediately walked away, ahead of the pair of them and back towards the ballroom. She practically ran up the wide staircase. The band was playing 'Smoke Gets In Your Eyes'.

Gladys sat down heavily at the table, glad to see her drink hadn't been cleared away. She took a gulp and felt the soothing gin warm her throat.

So, Terrence was looking for girls. Girls he could persuade one way or another to become prostitutes at his place in the red-light district of Southampton's notorious

Derby Road. He was a pimp. He was odious. She prayed with all her heart that Pixie, her little girl, didn't come into contact with such awful men. Men who kept girls locked up in houses in the city so they could sell their bodies. Men who got women to care about them so much that they would sleep with other men to give their pimps the money they earned. How Del knew him didn't matter. What did was that Del had warned him off her.

Looking down over the balcony, she saw the two men walking up the steps into the ballroom. It's so easy to understand when it's all made clear to you, isn't it? she thought. Terrence, or Billy Manning, as Del had called him, was a con man, not a nice bloke at all. But Del had told him to leave her alone.

She was useful to Del. He kept her sweet with gifts. It was give and take.

She watched a perspiring Del climb the stairs. His forehead was covered with sweat. His big belly strained at his shirt. His eyes searched for her.

'Be a good girl and get some fresh drinks,' he said when he reached her, waving a pound note.

Gladys got up to do as she was told.

Chapter Eighteen

Marlene tucked the candlewick cot cover around her child's sturdy body.

The autumn winds rattled the window pane. These old houses were a bugger to keep warm, she thought. Jeannie lay on her back, arms stretched above her head, her chubby knees making a tent of the bedclothes. The few freckles across her nose were so adorable that Marlene bent down to kiss her. 'You are so gorgeous I could eat you,' she said softly, and was rewarded with a hiccup of a snore that made her smile.

The clock said five past seven; the alarm was set for half past three in the morning.

On the bedside cabinet lay a terrycloth napkin, a muslin square and a clean cotton nightdress. During the day, Jeannie knew what a potty was for but at nights she often wet the bed. When she woke at two, as she usually did, a quick change soon sent her off to sleep again and Marlene cherished the hour and a half of extra sleep before she had to get ready for work.

Stallholders had to arrive early at the markets. By seven in the morning, all the stalls were set up and vehicles removed from the marketplace to the parking area. The summer months had been lovely, the early mornings a delight, but it was fast growing colder and already she was wearing more clothing to keep warm. The winter, she knew, was horrendous. Ice from your breath formed on scarves and made your face sore, and your feet got so cold you couldn't feel them.

A noise behind Marlene caused her to turn. Her mother had stepped into the bedroom, her arms full of newly ironed washing. Marlene could smell its freshness.

'Thanks, Mum.' Marlene yawned – she was tired. 'I could have done that.' Where she would be without her mother's help, she didn't know. She took the pile of clothes and laid it on top of the chest of drawers to put away later.

'You've been on your feet all day. It weren't no bother.' Her mother's voice was low, so she wouldn't wake the child.

Marlene and her mother were as alike as two peas in a pod, even down to the glorious wavy orange hair. Beth had been born in Cork, Ireland, and had told Marlene it was a family trait, the hair. Every day Marlene searched the fine hairs on Beth's head, at her insistence, to see if it was changing colour or going grey. Both women were small and wiry, but Beth's eyes were ringed with dark circles and lined at the corners.

Marlene knew that tomorrow Beth would take Jeannie with her when she cleaned for Mr Wilson. He lived in a bungalow, so there was no chance that Jeannie would toddle off to fall down the stairs. On Tuesdays she cleaned the offices of Hutfield's Garage in Forton Road, and on Fridays she cleaned another bungalow down Parham Road for Mrs Jefferies. Mrs Jefferies wouldn't throw anything away, so it seemed to Beth. She said to Marlene that when she'd finished cleaning it never looked any different.

'Still, we're in town tomorrow at the market, so if you get a minute you should bring Jeannie to the stall,' said Marlene. 'Bob likes to see her.'

'You like working the markets.' It was a statement, not a question, and Marlene smiled. Her mother waited while Marlene closed the cupboard door after taking out her clean clothes for the morning. They left the sleeping child and went downstairs for a cup of tea. Marlene was aware her mother was insinuating that Marlene liked Bob. She did.

Bob flirted with his customers; some he'd bedded. Women were always giving him the eye. He worked hard, expanding his business. He was a kind man and a good boss, but not at all interested in *her* as a woman. She often wondered what appealed to Bob about Pixie. She sighed. If Pixie wasn't around, maybe it would be different.

'I'll make the tea, Mum,' Marlene said. 'Bob's a mate and a stepping-stone to my future. One day I'm going to have my own stall, selling second-hand jewellery, mostly gold. The punters like a bit of glitter.'

Her mother smiled at her. 'I know you will, love,' she said. Marlene felt Beth's arm snake across her shoulders. She knew she was lucky to have had her mother stick by her when she'd become pregnant. If only some of the customers were as forgiving.

A few of the older women were downright hostile to her. She had a baby and she wasn't married. It was a stigma. Sometimes she'd seen women walk away from the stall sooner than be served by her. Bob had told her not to worry about the old biddies. But she did worry. She didn't like to think of him losing money because he'd been kind enough to take her on.

Out in the scullery, Marlene lit the gas and set the kettle to boil. The blue and red of the flames were the only hint of colour in the room, with its blackout curtains tightly shut. She got down two willow-pattern cups and saucers and the matching teapot, then walked over to the doorway. Her mother had settled herself in the chair nearest the range and dozed off.

In the centre of the kitchen there was a table, with two chairs either side of it. A blue and white cabinet housed their food, and a cupboard built into the wall near the range held crockery, pots and pans. Beth was a house-proud woman who hated dirt. She cleaned for other people and liked the sparkling freshness to continue through to her own home.

Marlene listened carefully: there was no sound from upstairs. Jeannie was fast asleep. She would go to bed after she'd had her tea. Early rising meant early nights. Both women worked hard and Marlene knew she'd have to wake her mother soon or she'd quite possibly stay asleep in that chair until the early hours, then wake up with a stiff neck.

Marlene wouldn't have coped if her mother hadn't done everything in her power to help her keep her child.

Her mother had been overjoyed when she'd passed the hard exams needed to gain a place at the local grammar school. No one in their family had ever been to one before. Times had changed now. The government were talking about introducing a special exam, all over the country, called the eleven-plus. Children who passed it would go on to grammar school, while those who didn't would attend other local schools. Marlene remembered how proud she'd been of her grey gabardine raincoat, her green gymslip and white blouse, the uniform that showed she was a grammar-school girl.

She'd loved school, loved learning, and was determined to make something of her life, especially since her father had been killed in Africa. His death had hit her hard. But she'd been unable to confide in her mother. Instead she'd moped at school. Peter Ford, in her year, was a top football player and had invited her along to watch a few matches. She had gone with him because she felt she could talk to him. His elder brother, his hero, had died at sea. They took to meeting outside school, walking along the beach at Gilkicker, until the barbed wire was set up and the area filled with mines as a deterrent to any Germans trying to land on the beaches.

Almost as though Beth had tuned into her thoughts, she opened her eyes and said, 'Peter's mother came around this morning. Brought a toy for Jeannie.'

'Did she say how Peter's doing?'

Her mother took the cup of tea from her, set it on the arm of the chair and stirred it. 'He's doing so well at university, now he's got over not being allowed to join the air force because of his hearing.'

Suddenly Marlene felt like crying. If she'd gone on to higher education and university, like she'd hoped, she'd be doing well, too. Then she thought of Jeannie asleep in her cot upstairs and knew that keeping her little girl had been the best decision she'd ever made.

Somehow the two families had managed to stay friends. And every so often Peter wrote asking about Jeannie. He was studying law, so he couldn't contribute to Jeannie's upbringing at the moment. His parents, however, sent a postal order to Marlene every month. It wasn't a great deal of money, because they weren't a rich family, but it certainly helped.

'You should have gone back to school after . . .'

'We've been through this before. I couldn't concentrate on books and exams while worrying about how you were going to look after my baby and feed us every week, could I?'

'We'd have managed.' Beth sipped her tea.

Marlene sighed, remembering the past. She and Peter had gone for a walk to Stanley Park. Peter was upset because his history marks were down. His thin face was drawn as he told her that Mr Green had accused him of spending too much time listening to the wireless and reading instead of studying. She'd sat on the grass with Peter, holding him while he'd let his anger out. He didn't like to be at any other place in the class but top.

He'd kissed her. It had been her first proper kiss. She'd liked it and kissed him back. And in that secluded glade, one thing had led to another.

Marlene was ashamed that she'd let herself get carried away. But she knew she'd trodden one step further on the road to womanhood.

She missed a period, then another. She was appalled. One single act, her first, of sexual contact was about to change her entire life. Finally she plucked up courage to tell her mother. Beth was calm, loving and supportive, but broken-hearted.

His parents had accused her of leading their son on. There was no question of them getting married: they were both fifteen and Peter's studies were too important. Marlene was told she could have the child adopted. But immediately she laid eyes on her daughter, after a long, difficult labour, she knew she would give up her life sooner than be parted from her baby.

'It's just such a shame that a clever girl like you is missing out on all the learning you could have caught up with.'

Marlene sighed. Beth liked to remind her every so

often of how well Peter was doing and how hard she and Marlene had to work. 'I can use my brain in other ways. I'm going to earn big money. We won't always be scraping by. You, me and Jeannie are going to want for nothing. Just you wait and see.'

'I got a backache, Mum.'

Em looked at Doris. 'I gave you an aspirin before we came out. Has it not worked, love?'

Doris shook her head. She stood up straight and her huge belly stuck out like the windblown sail of a galleon.

Pixie called, 'Doris, quick, sweep this powder up I just spilled on the bench. Don't want no accidents, do we, love?' Doris waddled over to Pixie and collected every grain with her dustpan and brush, then took it to the water barrel where it dissolved and couldn't do any harm.

'Can't take risks, can we?' said Em, when Doris returned. 'The slightest spark in that lot and we'd all go up in smoke.' Em put her hand to Doris's forehead. 'You're a bit hot.'

'Not me head.' She shook away her mother's hand. 'Me back hurts.'

'Go and sit down for a while.' Em watched her walk heavily away, dragging the broom in one hand, the dustpan and brush in the other. The hem of her dress was uneven where her belly dragged up the material at the front. 'Poor little bugger,' Em murmured.

She'd tried to explain to Doris about giving birth. Doris wouldn't or couldn't understand the basics. She'd be scared stiff when the baby decided to make its appearance. Every day Em cursed Harry Slaughter for what he was putting the whole family through.

Doris's father wouldn't look at her now. He'd told Em he was disgusted by what had happened. His imbecile of a daughter was born of Em's side of the family and Doris would only produce another imbecile. 'I want nothing to do with any of it,' he'd said, turning his wheelchair so that his back faced them.

Em couldn't understand how he could be so cold towards his own daughter.

Now she turned back to Mo, busily filling a shell, who said, 'I reckon we ought not to be worried about a shell exploding in here cos we could all die in our beds from Hitler's bombs, anyway.'

'It's being so cheerful that keeps you going, isn't it?' Em observed.

Laughter erupted from the girls at the nearby bench.

Sometimes it was very hard to keep a happy face, Em thought. Her husband, Jack, couldn't walk. He could stagger about using the arms and backs of chairs, but was more at ease in his wheelchair. He'd gone to do his duty a cheerful husband and father and returned broken in mind and body. Sometimes his cruelty scared Em. She tried to tell herself he didn't mean to frighten her with the vicious things he said and did. That was the only way she could go on feeling positive about everything. But sometimes it was so damned hard that she sat in the lavatory at the bottom of the garden and cried her eyes out.

'Coming down the Fox tonight, Em?' Mo asked, bringing Em's thoughts back to the workshop.

She picked up the pencil attached to her clipboard and marked the card. 'Dunno. I'd like to.' It was the only outlet she had, that and listening to the wireless. She liked the comedy shows best because they made her laugh, especially *ITMA* with Tommy Handley.

Unfortunately, now that Jack was home he didn't like her going out. There were almighty rows when she came in and he would accuse her of going to the pub to pick up men. It wouldn't have been so bad but the only man she ever spoke to at the Fox was Sam. Whatever had been between them had ended the moment her husband had returned from war.

'Want me to come round and call for you?' Mo asked.

'Best not,' said Em. 'My Doris is a bit poorly.'

She'd hardly got the words out of her mouth when her daughter screamed.

Doris was standing in the corner of the workshop, still holding the broom. 'Mum! I wet meself!'

Em let the clipboard fall to the floor and ran to Doris, who was bent double with pain. Her waters had broken.

'It's the baby, Mum. My tummy's all tight and funny – and I hurt!' Doris's eyes were full of tears.

'It's all right, my love. Mo, go and find the duty nurse, or try phoning for an ambulance,' Em yelled.

Somehow the machinery was switched off and Doris was made as comfortable as possible on the floor in a nest of overalls and jumpers donated by the women. She flatly refused to move from the corner.

'At least let me get you into a room out of the way of all these people,' Em implored.

'Not going nowhere. I hurt.' Doris screamed as another contraction overtook her.

'The baby seems in a hurry to get here,' said Pixie. 'I reckon Doris has been in labour quite a while and didn't know it. If that ambulance don't get here soon, she'll have the little one on the workshop floor.'

'Anyone told old Slaughter?' came a voice.

'Cedric ran off at the first mention of the baby,' said

Rita. 'I reckon he'll have told his old man. Anyway, this ain't no place for blokes.'

'Nah, they're more nuisance than help at a time like this,' Em said. 'How about the nurse? Has someone been to get her?'

'There's a notice on her door. She's not in today,' Pixie said. 'For a resident nurse she's never here when she's needed,' she grumbled, putting down a cushion made of rolled clothing for Doris to lean her back on. The girl's face was wet with sweat and she was breathing heavily.

'Wouldn't you just believe it?' cried Em. 'And here's me thinking Doris had another month to go at least.'

'Ooooh,' yelled Doris.

Em looked at all the women crowding around. 'For God's sake, give her some air.' A thought crossed her mind. 'Take a break everyone. You can't work while this is going on.' To Pixie, she added, 'If Harry Slaughter wants to have a go at me, he can. I'll take full responsibility.'

Most of the women filed out, chattering, glancing at Doris, who was curled up in pain, but one portly lady planted herself in front of Em. 'I was a midwife before I decided the pay's better here. Do you want me to stay?'

'God bless you,' Em said, just as Doris yelled again, this time thrashing her legs and feet on the cold floor.

'I'll just wash my hands,' the woman said calmly. 'My

name's Freda.' She hurried off in the direction of the lavatory but within moments was back with the roller towel, which she spread beneath Doris. 'Put the lights on,' she said. 'I need to see what I'm doing.' The electric light was switched on. 'On your back, dear,' she said to Doris. Obediently Doris slid down. Her breathing was now shallow, and Em could see her tensing for another contraction. 'Get her underclothes off,' said Freda.

'Nooooooo!' wailed Doris. But Em won in the tugging contest and Freda breathed a sigh of relief as the knickers came off and the thick stockings and garters were rolled away.

Pixie came back with a cup of water and a wet cloth. She got Doris to take a drink, then pressed the cloth over her forehead.

'No time to get her to hospital.' Freda peered at Doris, then pulled her dress down to cover her. 'Even supposing there's room, with the wards full of war wounded. Best get someone to telephone the doctor.'

Rita ran from the room. Pixie put her hands on her own expanding girth and thought about the baby she would have in a few months' time. Now that she had stopped being sick, she felt very well. She knew that Doris had been collecting bits and pieces for the baby, even trying her hand at knitting. She, however, had done nothing in the way of preparation for her child. Pixie knew it was time now to put thoughts of Cal into a box in her memory and throw away the key. Whatever had happened to make him deny her existence had to be accepted. Now she must look to the future without him.

Freda allowed Doris to do what came naturally and push hard while screaming. Every so often she pulled up the voluminous dress to see what was happening. Em knelt at Doris's shoulder and held her hand.

'Stop pushing, dear,' commanded Freda. 'I said, stop!'

Freda made Doris lie flat, then said to Em, 'Hold her away from me. There's something . . .'

Em grabbed her daughter, keeping her as flat as possible while watching Freda examine her. The woman looked concerned. When she removed her hand it was bloody.

Em's heart started to race. 'She's all right, isn't she?'

'She is now,' she said. 'Cord was round the little mite's neck. Go on, love, you can push now,' she said to Doris.

The girl gave a yell, and out of her slid a little boy, covered in a bloody, greasy substance, plump and already crying.

'Give me your cardigan,' Freda said to Em, who struggled out of it and handed it to her. She wrapped the child in it, then placed him on Doris's breast where he continued to scream lustily. The cord was like a long grey rope joining mother and child.

Doris, quiet now, was looking at the baby with big round eyes that brimmed with love.

'So many tears of happiness,' said Freda, looking around her. Not one of the women was dry-eyed.

Em couldn't speak. She could feel nothing but amazing love for the scene about her and the tiny scrap shrieking and waving his little hands in the air.

Freda pressed Doris's stomach and said to Rita, who had returned from phoning for the doctor, 'Give us that paper over there.'

Rita replied, 'It's yesterday's.'

'I don't want to read it. It's to wrap the placenta in.'

For a second there was silence, then laughter took over.

'I don't know how I'm ever going to thank you,' said Em, when they had quietened.

'No matter how many babies are born, it's always a miracle,' Freda said. Then, to Rita, 'Go and find some tea, love. I'll die if I don't have a nice cuppa soon.'

'I do know the secretarial section has a kettle and a Bunsen burner,' Rita said. Then, 'Look at Doris.'

The girl was fast asleep, as was the baby, tired out after his journey into the world.

'Few more weeks and she'll be wearing Pixie's red dress,' said Rita, walking away.

Em picked up the baby and cuddled him. Immediately the little boy opened his eyes and gazed up at her. Em stared back. Her heart was filled with a feeling that warmed her whole body. It eclipsed all the horrible heartache at home, the money worries, the dreadful war. Em knew that this child had brought with him true happiness. 'Hello, my love,' she said.

Chapter Nineteen

The letter sat accusingly on the doormat. Pixie picked it up and opened the envelope. Four weeks' notice, then Pixie must leave her home. The landlord had given her all the time she deserved to pay the arrears and she hadn't complied. She stuck the letter behind the mantelpiece clock, noting it was ten minutes slow and she ought to put it right.

She sighed and scratched at her wrists. The rash from the TNT had spread up her arms to her neck and chest. Even Rita had asked her if she was lousy. She'd tried hard to keep the itching at bay by stroking petroleum jelly on herself at bedtime before she put her nightdress on. She wondered if the baby was making her skin more sensitive, as the front of her hair was bright yellow now and so were her eyebrows. Her brows she darkened with mascara, spitting on the little brush and stroking it across the hairs, but the bright yellow fringe caused the rest of her blonde hair to look cheap and nasty. She looked down at her swollen ankles, wondering if untying her lace-ups would cause her feet to loosen and fall like jelly all over the floor. She ate as well as she could and drank milk, as the girls who worked in munitions factories were advised to do, but the itchy rash, the hair discoloration and the swellings were, in truth, work-related hazards.

With no overtime and the money she'd borrowed from Bob gone on paying bills, she could do nothing but move out when the time came. But where could she go?

She couldn't rent a room. An unmarried pregnant woman wouldn't be welcome anywhere. Anyway, she'd need a deposit, which she didn't have. If she sold the furniture she wouldn't get much for it. Not enough to raise the money she needed. Pixie went out into the scullery to make herself a pot of tea. Hopefully a strong brew would cheer her up. The wireless was playing a Frank Sinatra song, 'Looking For Yesterday', which reminded her of Cal and further depressed her, so she turned it off.

She could hear her name being called and went to the back door to investigate.

Bob shouted again.

'I'm making tea,' she said, walking into the garden. 'Want a cup?'

He hopped over the fence and together they walked back into her house. She made him sit in the kitchen while she finished making the tea. When she carried in the tray, he was standing in front of the range with the landlord's letter in his hand.

'Before you get your dander up, I didn't nose around. I picked up the clock to set it right and this,' he waved the envelope, 'fell on the hearth.' He handed it to her. 'It had slipped out the envelope and I couldn't help but look at it.'

Pixie put the tray on the table. She could smell coal tar soap. He must have had a bath – his hair was still damp. 'The money you gave me went on more pressing bills. I thought I could sort it all out.' She took a deep breath, then started to cry. Not little tears but great big sobs that made her chest heave. 'I thought I could manage. Now that there's no overtime for me, Em or Rita, I can't.'

'Stop it,' he said, taking her hand. 'Why didn't you come to me for more money?'

'I've borrowed enough,' she said. 'I've no way . . . no way of ever paying you back.'

'That doesn't matter.'

'It does to me. I'll be getting further into debt. I don't know what to do.'

'If you won't take my money – I understand why you won't – why don't you move in with me? Just until your mum comes home. I'm sure she'll have some good ideas about making money.' He smiled down at her. 'I mean live with me, not sleep with me.' He paused, laughed. 'Though if you insist . . .'

She smiled damply at him, then sniffed. 'I do want to be here for my mum,' she said, 'if and when she decides to come back.'

'Of course. You'll also have someone around if the baby decides to make an appearance in the middle of the night.'

She thought of Doris and her baby. It would be horrible to be on her own or in a strange place when she went into labour. It was all quite terrifying. Especially as she didn't feel happy about the changes to her body and skin that the gunpowder was causing. Even the nurse at work had been giving her funny looks just lately, so she'd taken to avoiding check-ups in case she was told she was unfit to work.

'Yes,' she said. 'I'd like that.' Then she asked, 'Would I be able to store some of our furniture in your big shed at the bottom of your garden?'

'Course.' He took her hand again and began stroking

it. 'Have you heard from Gladys?' She shook her head. 'No.' Her voice was small and sad.

'It goes without saying,' he said, 'that if Cal comes looking for you, he'll find you.'

'Can the canary come too?'

'Only on one condition.'

'What's that?' There was suspicion in her tone.

'That you take a break, have a bit of time off, a rest. That's the only way you'll get rid of that nasty rash. You don't want to harm your unborn baby, do you?'

'No! Of course I don't . . . but how will I live?'

'I'm doing fine at the moment. It'll help me if you could do a bit of cooking and cleaning, nothing heavy, mind. But getting away from the dangers at work is important for you. I'm pretty sure that's a bad thing, them swollen ankles. If you're at home you could rest when you wanted, go out when you wanted, enjoy a bit of fresh air in the garden. I know the winter's coming, but a walk over to the recreation ground and kicking through the fallen leaves must be better than standing up for twelve hours surrounded by poisons.' He took the lid off the teapot and gave the contents a stir with a teaspoon. 'What d'you say? After you've had the little one, if you want to go back to work, you'll be fitter than ever. There's plenty of women willing to look after kiddies while the mother works.'

Pixie thought about it. 'What can I say?'

'Is that a yes?'

'Thank you, Bob,' she said. 'I don't want to be beholden to you, so how about I cut down on shifts?'

He smiled in agreement.

She'd known he cared about her, but it wasn't until today that she'd realized how much. She thought how nice it would be if she could get some eggs and dried fruit – there must be some food somewhere that wasn't rationed or on coupons. She could make a cake for Bob. She liked cooking.

The thought of having a lie-in and becoming a proper housewife appealed to her. But when she gave up work she'd be a kept woman. The neighbours would have something to snigger about behind their curtains if she lived in Bob's house. But surely it was their business, hers and Bob's, not anyone else's. Pixie thought of how the narrow-minded people talked about Marlene because she was an unmarried mother. Well, soon they'd be talking about her as well.

She thought of what her mother might say. 'If they're talking about you, they'll be leaving someone else alone.' Pixie suddenly missed Gladys very much.

*

Bob left Marlene in charge of the stall while he and Pixie spent the day clearing out her house and moving the furniture into his dry shed.

'You sure you wouldn't rather I lent you money to pay off the rent arrears?'

'No. The landlord said that as I'm moving out he'll cancel the arrears. I thought that was pretty good of him. All the other debts are sorted. Soon I won't be able to work,' she said, 'so now I'm buying bits for the baby while I can.' She scratched her neck. The rash had broken and some of the sores were weeping. She looked down at her legs, which seemed like miniature tree trunks, stuffed into a pair of her mother's old pom-pom slippers.

'If I had my way you'd not be working at Priddy's *now*,' he said fiercely. He upended a chair so it fitted on top of the one below it and stacked it neatly in the corner. 'Trouble is, you're so stubborn!'

Pixie sat down on the wall. She didn't feel too good.

'Go into my house, make a pot of tea, then lie down in the front bedroom. The sheets are clean and it's aired. I can finish here.'

Pixie got up and, feeling like an old woman, made her way to the back of Bob's house. At the door she turned. 'Don't forget the canary,' she said.

*

'You shouldn't be working in your condition,' said Rita. She was helping Pixie fit herself into her work overalls.

'You sound like Bob,' Pixie said. 'And I don't think you should be here either.'

'Why?'

'Why? Because you haven't got last night's drink out of your system.' Pixie tied her turban round her hair, then began tucking the stray locks inside. She looked at Rita.

'I'm all right.' Rita tried to smile.

'You'd better be.'

'This Yank was buying me port and lemon last night down the Fox. I honestly thought I was on to a good thing and that he really liked me. Then he started talking about his wife and kids, even took out his wallet and showed me pictures of them.'

'So you got drunk?'

Rita hung her head. 'You got Bob falling over himself for you and, I don't care what anyone says, Cal loved the bones of you.'

Pixie swung round in an ungainly fashion. 'What are people saying?'

Rita went very red. 'That he was a married man and stringing you along. After all, it happens all the time.'

'I hope you put 'em right, whoever these people are?'

'As far as I could.' Rita sighed. 'Oh, Pixie, I miss you. You're no fun any more now you're fat and pregnant. I don't like going down the Fox without you.'

'I'm still the same,' Pixie said. But she was aware that she'd changed. If only she knew why she'd never had a letter from Cal. He'd seemed so in love with her. She wiped her eyes with the back of her hand. 'When I've had the baby I'm going to see his sister, Ruth, in Chichester. I can't make the journey now but I will when the baby's born. She'll be my child's auntie, won't she?'

Together they walked into the workshop where the gossip was all about income tax.

'Soon the Inland Revenue will be deducting PAYE. It means, pay as you earn,' said Em, reading from an official letter. 'The tax office will take income tax from your wages. This way there'll be fewer defaulters on tax bills.'

'That means we can't get away from the taxman.' Pixie giggled.

'Stop laughing, you idiot!' Rita snapped. 'It also means instead of paying what we owe at the end of the year, like now, money will be taken from our weekly wages. That means there'll be less in our wage packets.' Rita stopped her tirade and angrily slammed down an empty shell case, ready to be filled.

'Oi! Stop that! Gently does it, girl!' Em shouted.

Pixie had never seen Em so angry, but she composed herself quickly. 'Anyway, don't shoot the messenger. In your wage packets this week there'll be details of the forthcoming changeover.'

But there was still something else on Rita's mind, Pixie knew. She determined to get Rita on her own and force her to tell her what was going on.

Now Em was walking towards her. 'Pixie, will you come with me to old Slaughter's office during break?' Her voice was little more than a whisper with the machinery drowning the sounds. Pixie frowned, then nodded, and Em walked away to her desk.

'What's that about?'

'Dunno, Rita. I'll tell you when I get back. Can't be anything to do with Doris and the baby – Em loves the little one to bits.'

Rita looked away, scowling.

They worked without speaking until break-time. Filling the shell cases and using the tamper to get the right amount in demanded full concentration.

When the buzzer sounded, Rita slammed away from the bench, leaving Pixie to wonder what she'd done wrong. Em came over to her. 'Don't worry about Miss Fancy Pants. She's got a bee in her bonnet about something and it'll come out in the end.'

'It's all right for you, but she's my best friend and I hate to see her like that.'

'Well, Pixie, I can't be worrying about all of you when I've got enough on my plate at home.' She strode off, expecting Pixie to follow her. When they arrived at Harry Slaughter's office, Pixie heard raised voices. Em knocked on the door anyway. Sudden silence, then a woman's voice shouted, 'Come in.'

Eliza Slaughter was sitting behind the desk as though she was the one in charge. Her husband stood with his hands behind his back, looking out of the window into the yard beyond. In the distance the small train could be heard chugging along, taking goods further up the line. The sun had come through the clouds after the night's rain.

'Sit down,' Eliza commanded. Em and Pixie sat on high-backed wooden chairs. Harry Slaughter hadn't acknowledged their presence but continued staring out of the window.

'I've invited you,' she said to Pixie, 'to witness what I'm about to do for the child belonging to my husband.' She turned to Em. 'You have a name for him?'

'James. But I don't understand.'

'I'll be as brief as possible. I know it's your break and the other women will be waiting to start work again soon.' Em nodded. 'Who is looking after the child at present?'

'Doris. She's coping quite well. Of course she can't be left unsupervised, so I pay a neighbour to keep an eye on her.'

'Quite so.' Eliza was dressed in a high-necked black taffeta blouse and a long grey skirt. A string of black pearls and a black hat, with what looked to Pixie like a raven's wing stylishly tilted to one side, completed the outfit. 'I have made a few cash payments to you, but I'd like to . . .' she looked towards her husband, who still hadn't moved from his stance at the window '. . . *we'd* like to help you in a more permanent manner.'

Em stood up. 'I can manage,' she said. Pixie heard defiance in her voice.

'You'll manage better with regular money coming in, not just the few pounds I've been giving you. You can choose to look after the child yourself, or go on paying for someone to keep an eye on the mother. The girl might even like to return to work, later.' Eliza added haltingly, 'I trust the doctor has pronounced the child fit?'

'You mean, is the baby an idiot?'

That word made Harry Slaughter swivel round, but he didn't speak. He turned to resume his watch on the yard.

'Well, James is as bright as a button. Thank you for asking but I can manage.' Em looked at Pixie.

Pixie knew she was waiting for her to say something. 'I know you're proud, Em, but it makes sense. And why should he,' she pointed to Harry, 'get away scot-free?'

Eliza smiled. 'Quite so,' she said.

'And why would you want to do this for us?' Em asked.

Eliza gave a cough. 'I have no children of my own. I'd like to be involved in James's welfare. I certainly don't intend to poke my nose in. You wouldn't be doing the job you're doing today if you couldn't cope admirably with a family and your work.'

Pixie could see that Eliza was winning Em over. But there was something she wasn't sure about. She couldn't help herself: 'What about Cedric?'

Eliza began laughing. 'You don't think that clown of a boy is *mine*?'

Em was staring at Harry Slaughter now. 'You mean . . . ?'

'I married my husband, then out of the woodwork came the boy's mother with the child. She was a common street girl. The child had been left with a slovenly child-minder while she plied her trade. Their situation was quite different from yours, my dear.' Eliza adjusted the arms of her spectacles and then replaced them, gazing at Em. 'Perhaps if I'd had the chance to look after Cedric earlier, he wouldn't be such a liability. Oh, my dear, your

237

daughter isn't the first.' She stared at Harry Slaughter's back. 'But she will be the *last*.'

Harry Slaughter turned again. His face was red. 'Nothing that has been spoken about in this office will go out of it,' he growled.

Pixie coughed. 'Excuse me,' she said. 'We can promise that only if we get our names put back on the overtime list.'

Eliza was clearly confused.

'Since we played that trick on your husband, our names have been wiped off the overtime rota. The extra money we can earn means a great deal to our living standards—'

Pixie didn't get any further for Eliza broke in: 'My God, Harry, you made these women suffer . . .'

His face was almost purple. 'Oh, for God's sake, yes,' he said.

'I think I like you,' Em said to Eliza, who gave a weary sigh. 'Now I've got to get the girls back to work.'

'Is all this agreed, then? You're a witness to her answer, Pixie?'

Pixie nodded, just as the buzzer sounded.

'It's a deal,' said Em. 'You come round to our house any time you want to see James. Maybe you'd like to take him out some time.'

'Thank you,' said Eliza, with more than a hint of a

smile. 'And, if I may, I'll bring a bottle of brandy to toast him.'

'Excellent idea,' said Em. She had the biggest smile on her face that Pixie had seen in a long time.

Chapter Twenty

Pixie sniggered at Gert and Daisy's chat on the wireless. The irrepressible duo, Elsie and Doris Waters, were a great favourite with the workers.

'They ought to broadcast this more than three times a week,' she said to Rita. She got no reply, for Rita was living, it seemed, in a world of her own. Pixie could also smell stale gin on her friend but didn't want to comment and get a snappy reply. 'It certainly makes the day go quicker,' she added.

'I like Charlie Chester,' said Em, coming up behind them.

'Yeah, but he's a bit naughty at times,' returned Pixie.

'What about Gert and Daisy singing, "She's A Lily But Only By Name"? That's a bit near the knuckle.'

Pixie laughed and Em joined in. Rita just smiled.

'Thanks for being with me in the office, Pixie,' Em

said, changing the subject as she nervously shifted from one foot to the other. 'Eliza Slaughter's a real toff. She'll give James a proper background. A solicitor is sorting things out so the boy will never want for anything. You've been a tower of strength with my Doris. If it hadn't been for you, things would have turned out quite different.'

'Oh, go on,' said Pixie, colouring up. 'You'd have done the same for me.'

Rita coughed. Em looked at her feet. 'And you, Rita. You've both been good friends to me.' She looked hard at Pixie. 'Which makes it all the more difficult for me . . .'

'What?' Rita spilled a couple of grains of the yellow powder. She blew them quickly away from the bench. 'So now we've got our overtime back, you're going to tell us some bad news?'

Em sighed. 'Not you, Rita. I'll be honest with you.' She looked Pixie up and down, her gaze lingering on her belly. Then she took a deep breath. 'Pixie, you're in no fit state to be working. How long is it before the baby's due?'

Pixie frowned, trying to add up the months. She'd met Cal in the spring, in early March, wasn't it? It was now September so the baby could be born in November. 'Couple of months at the most,' she said. Her heart was banging away like a drum. She knew what Em was going to say. There was a nasty sore on the back of her right hand that had started weeping. She turned away from Em but she couldn't hide the graze that showed beneath her left eye. She'd made it worse by scratching because it itched so much. 'I need my job. I can't be a drain on Bob Roberts, you know that! I'm living in his spare room but I'm paying me own way and I don't want to impose on him.'

'I know you want to be independent as long as possible.'

Pixie could see Em didn't like talking to her like this.

'I don't *want* you to go. You're one of my best workers and you know the job inside out. But you're a liability, Pixie. Have you looked in the mirror lately?'

Pixie was flustered. 'My hair's a bit scraggy but . . .'

'Did you know you've got a bald patch at the back?'

Pixie nodded. Of course she knew. Mostly her turban covered it, and she kept that on as long as possible. She was terrified the poison she was inhaling was harming her baby, but she reckoned that as long as she could feel the child moving inside her, everything was all right.

'And how can you walk with your legs and feet like that?' Em pointed at them.

Pixie had begged Bob for a loan of his slippers, which

were what she now wore to work because she couldn't get into any of her own shoes.

'I'm sorry, Pixie, but I'm going to have to ask you to hand in your notice before the management decides to sack you.' Em's eyes were full of tears. 'If anything happens to you the management don't want the responsibility – you get my meaning?'

Pixie did. 'So I've got the sack?'

'No, you've handed in your notice. And by the time I've organized a whip-round for the baby and made sure your wages are up to date, I hope I'll be able to give you a good send-off.' She put her hand on Pixie's shoulder. 'You do understand I'm doing this for you?'

Pixie stifled the tears. 'Oh, yes,' she said bitterly. At the back of her mind, she knew that by giving up the job it would be easier for her to either start again at a later date or find other employment. New employers would think twice about hiring her if she'd been sacked.

As the tears ran down her face, the salt made her skin itch. She watched Em walk away, then turned to Rita. 'I guess that's me told, then.'

'Come on, Pixie, even you can see that you need to give the baby the best possible chance.' Rita mumbled something beneath her breath that Pixie didn't hear. She was glad to hear Rita's voice. It was the most words her friend had spoken to her all morning. She was, if the truth be told, a bit fed up with Rita's moods.

The wireless was playing a medley of dance music now and the girls were humming along as they worked. Pixie saw Rita's hand wobble as she tamped down the powder and more grains spilled onto the table. Rita was about to blow them away when Pixie said, 'Hold on. I'll get Cedric to clear beneath our bench.' He'd taken over Doris's job. 'We can't have that dangerous stuff underfoot.'

'Jesus!' Rita exclaimed. 'Even you won't leave me alone now.'

Pixie decided that, sooner than have an argument with Rita, she'd just go and get Cedric to clear up. They'd be breaking for dinner soon. She got up from the bench and made her way forward. Em was at the end of the hut doing a tour of the machines.

The sudden explosion shattered windows and threw wooden benches across the workshop.

Pixie, dazed, shuffled towards the doorway, grabbing the jamb as support. Everyone knew the drill: they had to remove themselves from the danger as quickly as possible, in case the first explosion set off others.

Daylight streamed in through the roof, which was now simply struts of wood and tin hanging down. Clouds of dust misted the air.

An eerie silence followed the first loud bang.

The second bang came from a machine that no one was operating. All the machinery slowed, then stopped.

Then the noise began, screams, cries and the sound of feet tramping the wooden floors. The smell of cordite, sharp and tangy, filled the air.

'Pixie!'

She heard her name shouted. Then Em, whose face was black and streaked as though water had dripped down it, was trying to propel her out of the doorway that she was still clinging to.

Suddenly, Pixie regained her senses. 'Rita!' she shouted, trying to disentangle herself from Em's strong arms. She twisted her cumbersome body away from Em and ran back to their bench. Rita wasn't there.

'Pixie, come with me,' Em shouted. 'I must count all you girls, check you all for injury.'

'I want Rita!'

'The men are coming for her. You can't do anything.'

Despite all the noise Pixie had heard Em's words clearly. 'Oh, God, is she dead?'

Em dragged Pixie down the steps and practically threw her on to the grass near the train track. 'Worry about yourself, not her! I'm leaving you now. Stay here!'

Pixie saw she wasn't the only woman sitting on the grass. The small gathering was mostly quiet, shocked, she thought. A few were moaning to themselves, vacant-eyed. Some were crying. They huddled closely together for comfort.

Amazingly, a fire engine had already arrived and men were rolling out a long worm of hose.

A pain started in Pixie's groin, an ache, and made its way round to her back. She put her hands beneath the bulk that was her child. Three men leaped from the ambulance that had snaked through the crowd, shouting, 'We're here for Rita Brown. Where is she?' And 'Stand back, everyone.' One man stopped by the destroyed doorway of the hut where the girls had been working. He surveyed the smoking rubble.

Women were still coming out of the broken building, stumbling over shattered wood, rubbing their eyes as they walked into the light of the afternoon.

It smelt like the 5th of November.

Two of the ambulance men had disappeared into the building towing a wheeled stretcher.

Pixie put both hands on the grass and managed to struggle upright just as the stretcher was pushed out of the building. She burst into tears when she saw that the blanket covering Rita was pulled across her face.

Pixie's hand went to her mouth. Was Rita dead? A torn strip of her blue blouse was blood-stained at the wrist where her arm hung down. Rita wasn't moving.

One of the men nodded at his mate and the stretcher started to disappear inside the vehicle.

The ambulance man shouted, 'Where d'you think you're going?' Pixie was hoisting herself up the back steps of the vehicle.

'It's my mate under there. An' I think she might be dead!'

There was sadness in the man's eyes. 'You've got to be a relative,' he said. 'Can't take just anyone.'

'She ain't got no one, so now I'm her sister.' Pixie was pleading with him.

The two men looked at each other, then back at Pixie. 'Looks like we should be taking you in as well, then, in your condition,' the taller one said.

'Okay, but don't touch nothing and keep quiet,' said the other, who was older. Then he turned to the driver. 'There's no one else as badly injured and a second ambulance is on its way so let's get to Casualty.' The older of the two men climbed into the back with Pixie and motioned to a pull-down seat. Pixie sat, glad to be off her feet.

'So she's alive?' The man nodded.

Pixie breathed a sigh of relief. 'Any idea what happened? We've covered her. She's a bit of a mess.'

Pixie could smell disinfectant, mingling with burned flesh. She shook her head. 'One minute everything was all right. Then, boom!'

'Pixie!' The tiny voice came from beneath the covering.

'I'm here, Rita.' Pixie looked at Rita's arm, grazed and grubby, hanging from the blankets. It was so tiny. She held on to Rita's cold fingers, willing some warmth to enter her friend's body.

The ambulance man's voice was severe. 'Talk, but don't tire her.'

Pixie tried to ignore the swaying of the vehicle, which was being driven fast. Rita's face was still covered, but there were no more sounds from her, not even when she was unloaded from the ambulance at the hospital.

There was a long queue of people waiting to be seen, but Rita was pushed through, with the ambulance men shouting, 'Out of the way, please.'

A quick word with the receptionist, and Rita was wheeled through a pair of swing doors. Pixie had to hurry to keep up, her swollen legs and ankles a painful hindrance.

Then Rita and the trolley disappeared from view, and she was barred from the sterile room.

'Sorry. You'll have to wait.' A nurse smiled kindly and

pointed to a room along the corridor. 'Someone will come and see you.'

Pixie sank into a battered chair that had no doubt held many worried people waiting for news of relatives. She could do nothing for her friend but wait.

Twice Pixie fell asleep and was refreshed with a cup of tea brought by a kindly nurse, who had obviously taken pity on her bedraggled appearance. The pain in her lower belly had eased. Anyway, she was more worried about Rita than she was about herself.

Rita's mother arrived in the early hours of the morning when it was still black outside. Hilary Brown was dark-haired, an older, paler version of her daughter. Rather like a floral patchwork quilt that had faded with washing, thought Pixie. Hilary swept Pixie theatrically into her arms. Rita's stepdad looked on, a dour man who didn't want to talk much. He had a swagger about him that Pixie had never liked.

'What happened at the factory?' Hilary released Pixie, who sat down again.

'The doctors won't say anything to me. I'm not next of kin.' Pixie couldn't stop the tears making her voice shake. 'They've been working on her a long time.'

'Not good.' Hilary's eyes were puffy but she didn't look as if she'd been crying.

'Have you seen her?'

'They said they'll let us see her later. She's got damage to her lungs and chest, the rib cage and she's lost the top of the index finger of her right hand. But it's her face, her lovely face . . . They aren't touching that. There's talk of sending her to a special burns hospital. East Grinstead, they said. The Queen Victoria Hospital.'

Pixie stood and opened her arms, and Hilary fell into them again. Malcolm's face was immobile. Pixie could smell the lily-of-the-valley perfume that swamped Hilary. She pushed Hilary away, suddenly aware that she herself must stink of stale sweat, gunpowder residue and burned wood.

'Are you all right?'

Pixie nodded. 'I wasn't near her when the explosion happened. I don't think anyone else was injured. Not badly, at any rate. They had to get everyone out of the workshop in case of further explosions. It was a mess.' Then she was crying, releasing all the tension that had built up inside her.

A nurse, pushing the eternal tea trolley, stopped and offered them some. Malcolm went in search of cigarettes to the nearby pub, although tobacco was in short supply everywhere.

All was silent for a while until a nurse arrived. 'I'll

take you to her,' she said, then added, 'Don't expect too much.'

Pixie and Hilary were shown into a long ward. In the end bed lay Rita. She was quite still. Pixie wanted to walk straight out again.

Rita's eyes were sunken. A pristine white bandage covered part of her head. The burned section of her face melted into her hairline, making it look as though her head had been shaved.

'Oh!' was all Hilary said.

Raw flesh, like minced meat, was what remained of Rita's smooth cheek from forehead to chin. It was like someone had taken a cheese grater to her beautiful face. The skin was tight at the corner of one eye, as if a stitch had saved it from fraying.

Pixie closed her eyes for a moment and took a deep breath. She didn't want to break down in front of Rita.

'It's bad, isn't it?' Hilary said. Her face was crumpling and her eyes brimming with tears.

Rita opened her eyes.

'Hello, you,' said Pixie. She searched for the hand that wasn't bandaged and held on to it. Rita looked at her mother, then looked away. It was obvious she was heavily sedated.

'The police rang to tell us . . . what happened . . .

and we came straight away, love.' Hilary's voice kept catching.

Rita's eyes were swivelling around as though she was looking for something – or someone. She was clearly agitated.

'Pixie's been here all the time. Came with you in the ambulance.' Now Hilary stroked Rita's shoulder and bent to kiss the bandaged side of her head. Tears pooled in Rita's eyes.

A door banged at the end of the ward and Rita's stepdad appeared. He stood at the side of the bed and looked down at her. Pixie caught a whiff of his cigarettes. Disgust registered on his face. The atmosphere around the bed had completely changed.

Rita's fingers tightened on Pixie's hand, her nails digging into the soft flesh. Her eyes flickered wildly. She must have realized Malcolm had arrived.

'I want you to go now,' the nurse said sternly. 'She's distressed and it isn't doing her any good.' In a softer voice, she said to Pixie, 'Come back later. Let her rest for now. She's probably reliving the blast.'

'But she needs *me*. I'm her mother.' Hilary's voice rose almost to a screech.

Rita had closed her eyes but tears escaped from their corners.

'Please go,' said the nurse. 'You too,' she whispered to Pixie, though her tone was much softer.

Hilary walked away quickly, her heels clicking on the floor. Malcolm followed, his steps longer, measured, as though he was glad to go.

'Please come back tomorrow,' the nurse said, putting her hand on Pixie's shoulder.

What on earth was going on between Rita and her mother? Pixie was confused.

Rita was still gripping her hand. When Pixie untangled her fingers, she saw her skin had crescent-shaped cuts where Rita's nails had dug into her flesh.

'I'll come back as soon as I can.' She bent down and whispered, 'You mustn't worry, you're going to be all right.' She smoothed the skin on Rita's good arm. Rita's eyes had closed again.

Walking down the hospital's dimly lit corridors, Pixie thought about Cal. Wherever he was, she hoped he was thinking about her: after all that had happened during the past twenty-four hours, she needed him so much. Something deep inside her told her that the lack of letters wasn't his fault. She'd almost convinced herself that he had been captured, possibly taken prisoner somewhere. She gritted her teeth. Hitler had taken Cal. Hitler had practically destroyed Rita. Had he also taken her own mother? Pixie had never missed Gladys as much as she did at that moment. She laid her hand on the mound that was her child.

'Well,' she said softly, 'old Hitler isn't going to come between you and me, my love.'

As she passed the open door of a ward, a nurse looked up from a desk and smiled at her. Ahead she could see the main entrance.

When Pixie left the hospital the sky was like ink. As she walked carefully down the stone steps, a vehicle's headlights shone dimly in the darkness and its engine purred into life, rolling forward then pulling up beside her.

Bob leaned across and opened the cab door of his van. Pixie was so happy to see him that the tears rose, threatening to spill. 'I thought I'd have to walk home,' she said.

'Get in.' He held out his hand so she could hoist herself up.

'How did you know where I was?' She made herself comfortable on the bench seat. Just when the night was darkest, he'd turned up like a welcoming light. His face was grey with lack of sleep.

'The town's full of talk about the explosion.' He put the van into gear. 'Rita's your mate. Where else would you be but by her side?' He grinned at her. 'Her parents came out earlier, arguing. But her mother said you should be along soon.'

Pixie wondered what the argument was about.

'How is Rita?'

'Not good.' She let out a long sigh. 'Know anything about the Queen Victoria Hospital at East Grinstead?'

'The plastic surgery and burns unit is second to none. Most hospitals can't provide the specialist care that place can. Rita couldn't be sent to a better place, take my word for it.'

'Thanks. I feel better for knowing that,' she said. 'Something's still troubling her, though. I only wish I knew what it was.'

'You should be looking after yourself.'

'Well, whether I want to or not, I can't go to work tomorrow. Until the workshop's up and running again, all the jobs are at a standstill. But . . .' Pixie took a big gulp of air '. . . Em told me I have to give notice. She said I'm a liability.' She put up a hand and scratched the side of her face.

'Thank Christ for that,' Bob said. 'I've been telling you for ages you're in no fit state to work'.

'If I don't work I'll have no money.'

'But I do. The armaments yard won't put anyone's life

at risk until the safety issue's been addressed. I told you, if you really need to work, go back after the baby's born. We'll find a sitter.' He paused. 'I heard there was a second explosion caused by the main one.'

Suddenly she felt absolutely worn out. She yawned then shook her head.

'Everyone was outside,' she said. 'I don't want to be a drain on you.' She saw anger flash across his face.

'I can afford to keep us both,' he said quietly. They were passing bombed-out buildings in Whitworth Road. A bedside cabinet stood shakily on the precipice of half a floor, the other half blown away.

'But I don't want to be a kept woman.'

'Okay, okay. Look after the house, do a bit of book-work for me. You'll have plenty to do when the baby comes.'

'I'm not sleeping with you!'

He grinned at her. 'You seen yourself lately?'

Chapter Twenty-one

Marlene opened the door to a dripping Bob. 'Get in here before you drown,' she said, pulling him inside, then replacing the blackout curtain. She shouted to her mother, 'Put the kettle on! We got a drowned rat here.' She heard the clatter of pots and smiled at him. 'What's brought you out in this storm? You should be in bed asleep.'

In the kitchen she made him sit down in the comfy armchair just vacated by her mother, who had reappeared holding a towel. She passed it to Bob.

'Good towels, those are,' she said. 'My daughter gets 'em off a stall in the market.'

Bob laughed. 'Thought I recognized the make.' He rubbed his hair vigorously. 'I've a favour to ask,' he said, removing his glasses and drying the lenses. 'That auction I was going to tomorrow afternoon.'

'The one at Christchurch, top of Queen's Road?'

Bob nodded as she took the towel from him and hung it to dry over the brass fender in front of the range. 'I'd like it if you'd go instead of me. You've been to enough sales now to know what goes on, what the pitfalls are. Pixie was involved in that bomb blast.'

Marlene opened her mouth to speak, but Bob stopped her. 'She wasn't hurt. But her mate Rita took the brunt of it and is in hospital. Pixie's been given the push from work.' He paused. 'Well, the factory'll be shut for a couple of days anyway while the mess is cleared up, but they won't let her back afterwards.'

'I'm surprised she's still on her feet,' said Marlene. Pixie didn't know how lucky she was to have a man like Bob looking out for her, she thought.

Bob nodded again. 'She's in a pickle, right enough. Worse now that Rita's taken bad. I want to get the last of her stuff into my house so she can hand the landlord back the keys. If I pick you up in the morning, and we set up the stall together, would you mind if I disappeared?'

'Course not. You go off some mornings anyway.'

'I'll be back in time for you to go to the auction and I'll pack away the stall.'

'Fine,' she said. 'So she's finally moving in with you?'

'Yes,' he said.

It wasn't what Marlene wanted to hear. If Pixie was living with Bob, her hope that he might think of her as more than just an employee and friend was dashed. 'How do I get to the auction hall? And if I buy, how do I get the stuff home?'

'Marie from the baby stall is after the nappies and clothing from the fire at Keast's in the high street. Damaged stock. She'll give you a lift and make room in her van for any treasures you buy for me.'

'Tea's up,' said Beth, coming in from the scullery. She put down the wooden tray and poured. The smell of lilac perfume wafted from her. Marlene suspected she'd doused herself in it for Bob's benefit.

'I could murder a cuppa, Beth,' said Bob, making her mother blush.

'Wish I had some nice chocolate biscuits to go with it,' Beth said. She passed a cup to Bob.

'Lovely memories,' said Bob. 'Anyway, where's that little girl of yours? Asleep upstairs?'

Marlene nodded. 'So what have you got your eye on at the saleroom?' Earlier in the day she'd seen him studying the catalogue with Marie.

'The Jolly Sailor on the Hard at Portsmouth took a beating in that dogfight last week. I'd like you to bid on the bedding, sheets, pillowcases, towels and cutlery.' He took out his wallet and began counting notes that he handed to her. 'I don't have to tell you to watch yourself. There'll be a fair few traders there so keep your eye on the profits. No good buying anything we can't make money on.' He finished his tea and set his cup back in the saucer. The wind and rain were clattering against the windowpanes. 'One step outside and I'll be drowned again,' he said, getting up.

Marlene followed him down the passage. It would be so nice, she thought, if she had a decent man like Bob to look after her. Pixie was a lucky woman.

'Sure you don't mind?' he asked, pulling on his overcoat. From its pocket he took a crumpled booklet. 'Here's the catalogue. You'll see the things I've marked.'

Marlene took it from him. 'I'm honoured you trust me with buying for the business,' she said. She held the blackout curtain while he went out into the night.

It wasn't fair, she thought, thinking of Pixie and her love for an American who seemed to have disappeared into thin air. Bob had accepted second best so easily in her affections. Some women had good men and didn't appreciate them at all.

'Bye,' she whispered. Her heart felt like lead.

*

Marie was buying the teas and Marlene had bagged a couple of seats halfway along the hall. Excitement was building now that the auction was about to start.

The number on her paddle was 76 and she put it on the seat beside her. In her pocket was Bob's money and in her purse was all the money she had been able to collect to further her ambition. She had nearly two pounds.

A smell of damp pervaded the hall. Makeshift tables had been placed around three sides of the room to display the items for sale. Marlene was surprised at how many people the organizers seemed to be expecting – the hall was packed with chairs.

'Shift up. Take this mug off me – the handle's hot,' said Marie. Marlene did as she was told, noting that the tea was strong. 'No biccies,' said Marie. 'What I wouldn't give for a half-pound of Nice to dip in me tea.'

'One day,' said Marlene, putting her mug beneath her chair. It was too hot to drink. 'Now you're back, d'you mind if I take another look at the stuff?'

A clatter of rain on the tin roof made Marie shiver. 'Bloody weather. Off you go, then – you ain't got long.'

Boxes of battered kitchen utensils, dog-eared comics and well-used books were each marked with a number. She foraged around and saw with relief that the rolled-up bag of broken jewellery was still in its box of 'odds'.

'You don't want to bother with that rubbish,' came a voice. A smartly dressed man with a moustache and a camel-hair overcoat stood at her side.

'Don't I?'

'Nothing in there to make money on,' he said. A smell of citrus cologne wafted towards her. She looked up into his face. It was a nice face, marred by a scar across his cheek that made him look roguish. He must have just arrived, for there were droplets of rain on his trilby hat.

'You're probably right,' she said, walking along, looking at the display. The man followed. Her eyes fell on a small bundle of bed linen. 'It says here "a quantity of sheets" but there's only a couple . . .'

'The other stuff will be stored elsewhere in this place,' said the man, giving her a white-toothed smile. 'Sometimes the lots are too large to put in the hall. Interested in bedding?'

'You're very nosy,' she said. But she couldn't help herself and smiled back at him. She'd been with Bob at other auctions and he'd told her not to show interest in the lots until it was time to bid.

She fingered a gold bracelet lying in the jewellery cabinet. It was heavy with charms.

'Lovely, that,' the man said. 'My name's Samuel Golden.' He looked at her expectantly as she replaced the bracelet.

'Marlene—' She was interrupted by the ringing tones of a hand-bell.

'Hello,' he whispered. 'Almost time for the show to start. Perhaps we'll meet again?' He treated her to another smile, then walked towards the back of the hall.

A few minutes later Marlene was back in the saleroom. She'd seen all she needed to see in the room next door. She reclaimed her seat next to Marie, and rescued her tea. She smiled to herself and settled down as the auctioneer began talking.

She wondered about the man, Samuel Golden. She thought he was probably in his thirties, smartly dressed, so he had a bit of money. It wasn't easy to keep smart during the war, with coupons needed for everything. She looked around but couldn't see him through the sea of faces staring at the auctioneer, everyone waiting for him to finish speaking about the conduct of the auction.

She nudged Marie's arm. 'All right?' she asked. Marie gave her a grin and showed her a piece of paper with the lots marked that she intended bidding on. The air was full of cigarette smoke and sweat.

The auctioneer began with lot number one, a brass fender that went for seven shillings. Lot number two was a brass carriage clock. For five shillings it went to a woman with frizzy blonde hair. Lot number three, a box of tools, went to a smiley young chap for half a crown.

The sheets and pillowcases were next.

'Some of this Egyptian cotton bedding is marked.' One of the auction helpers picked up a sheet. A large brown scorch mark was visible, making the sheet virtually unusable. But Marlene had thoroughly examined the rest of the bedding lot. 'Who's going to start me off with a fiver?'

There was movement in the hall. The bidding went to six pounds. Marlene sat quite still. The slow bids had gone up in pounds but she hadn't uttered a word. Her heart was beating fast.

'Eight,' said a man in an overcoat.

The auctioneer said, 'Stuff's got to go.' He looked around the room, knowing the lot was too much for an ordinary bidder and traders were thin on the ground. Somehow Marlene knew this was the last room bid.

She raised her paddle.

'Nine.'

Marlene was sweating.

'Nine it is, number 76.'

Marlene let out a huge sigh. 'That's a relief,' she said.

'Good girl,' said Marie, and grinned at her.

They'd make a good profit there, she thought. They

could sell the pillowcases and sheets separately after weeding out any damaged goods. The rough stuff could be sorted for remnants. Bob would be pleased.

She bought cutlery, tin mugs, white enamel with blue stripes around the tops, assorted saucepans and kitchen implements, and four rag rugs that she'd fallen in love with.

The bell went for a half-time break. Marlene counted her money and knew, from the amount she had left, that Bob would be happy with her purchases.

'You going to have enough room in the van for everything?' Marlene eyed two prams, which needed a damn good clean, that Marie had bought. Babies' prams were practically non-existent now and Marie was thrilled to bits.

'I'll make room.' She laughed. 'I was keeping me fingers crossed you wasn't going to bid on them terry squares.'

'Wouldn't do that to you, would I?'

'Some would. Some traders don't care whose toes they tread on as long as they makes a profit.'

'If I had a stall I wouldn't do that.'

'Thought it all out carefully, haven't you, girl?' Marie hitched up her ample bosom. Marlene knew she was well respected on the markets. 'I been working the markets for years. Hard work but honest, the market is, or should be. I got a feeling you wants to sell.'

'Oh, I do. But I want to sell gold. No one else does it at Gosport market, but it's difficult to find the money to buy stock.'

'Well, like the rest of us, you'll have to start small. You want to ask Bob if you can hire a corner of his stall.'

'I'd thought of that. I've seen a couple of pieces here that I'm going to bid for.'

'Good for you, girl. Take a chance. And if you don't sell the stuff you can wear it!'

Marlene felt better about the gamble she planned to make. She told Marie what she wanted and what she intended to do with it. She was banking on the buyers having spent their money.

Marlene excused herself and went to the tea counter. While she waited her turn in the queue, she couldn't help listening to the main topic of the conversation around her.

'Three nights in a row and no bombing. You reckon old Hitler's forgotten about us?'

'Nah,' said the woman serving the tea. 'An Allied midget submarine has torpedoed the battleship *Tirpitz* and put it out of action until it's repaired. Hitler'll be thinking what to bung at us next, you mark my words.'

Marlene had never heard of midget submarines, but

she felt suddenly proud that the Germans weren't having it all their own way in this awful war. She'd ask Bob about them subs. Maybe the shells used on it had been made at Priddy's Hard.

'What yer want, love?' asked the tea woman, interrupting Marlene's thoughts. 'Two teas, please.' The thick brown liquid slopped on the counter top as the woman poured from the huge urn.

When she got back to her seat, the sale started up again. The boxes of odds were being shown. Marlene held her breath. The first one went for two shillings. The second went for a shilling – and it was to her! She'd got the box with some bits of costume jewellery in it. Cleaned up, a couple of the brooches would be worth a bob or two. She was on her way to being a trader!

Then it was the turn of the gold bracelet.

'I'm starting at two pounds.' The auctioneer got his bid and asked for two pounds five shillings. He got it from a woman who was dripping with jewellery and obviously wanted it for herself. Marlene sighed. 'That's me dream shattered,' she said.

'Two pounds ten shillings, anywhere?'

He might as well have asked for a hundred, thought Marlene. In her pocket was Bob's change. But she'd never take from him without asking first.

Marie held up her paddle.

'Right, we've got two pounds ten shillings,' the auctioneer said, 'Thank you, madam.' He looked round the hall. 'Two pounds fifteen?'

Marlene stared at Marie. *She was bidding on the bracelet.*

Marie's eyes narrowed. The flashy woman obviously wanted the bracelet.

'We've got two fifteen. Three anywhere?'

She stared at the overdressed woman, who was looking back at her. The woman shrugged and turned away when Marie raised her paddle.

'It's yours, girl,' Marie whispered. 'A bargain. Gold's a luxury for ordinary people and there ain't no traders here tonight. Pay me back when you make a profit.'

Marlene threw her arms around Marie's neck. 'You did that for me. But why?'

'Cos you remind me of myself when I was starting out. We all need a bit of a hand.'

Chapter Twenty-two

'It won't take long for the copper to heat water for a bath,' Bob said.

Pixie had done nothing but sleep after returning to Bob's house from the hospital and bedding down in the front room. Something fragrant and meaty was wafting from the scullery.

'I didn't know how hungry I was until that gorgeous smell hit me,' she said, rubbing the sleep from her eyes. 'What is it? But you don't want to be bothering about getting a bath for me.' She looked at the clock. 'You'll be getting ready for work soon and I bet you've had no rest during the past twenty-four hours.'

'It's a stew I put together, not a lot of meat, I'm afraid, more gravy cubes. But don't worry about me. I'm not going into work. I'll pick up Marlene and we'll set the stall up – luckily we're at Gosport so I'll be back soon.

You can have a bath, eat and then sleep some more.' He looked sheepish. 'I've taken the liberty of clearing next door completely. I know all the time you hold the key you feel independent, but the landlord won't put up with it much longer. Besides, you need to be with someone now you're getting near your time.' He glanced down at her swollen body. Then he foraged in his pocket and handed her the spare key to his own house. 'All your furniture's in the shed. I've made up the back bedroom for you, and there's a large box upstairs of . . .' he frowned, '. . . personal paraphernalia. I didn't know where you'd like it put.'

In the kitchen the canary jumped from perch to perch, chirruping, and Pixie saw it had clean water and seed. She let her fingers run along the cage.

'Hello, you,' she said. Then, 'And what paraphernalia would that be?' She was teasing him. His face reddened before he went into the scullery, her following closely, as he shook the kettle, lit the gas and put mugs on the small table.

'Make-up, stuff that was in your bedroom on the top of the chest of drawers, notebooks and pencils.' He opened the door to check the stew.

'You didn't look at it?'

He put down the tea towel he was holding and closed

the oven door. 'I opened one book, saw it was full of your writing – well, I presumed it was yours. I then had the feeling that it was all very private and I swear I never read so much as a word.'

She breathed a sigh of relief. 'Thank you.' She believed him.

'Are you going to tell me about it?'

Pixie shook her head. She looked up into his eyes then smiled. 'Maybe one day,' she said.

The kettle was steaming and Bob poured the water into the teapot.

'If you want to go up and see your room, everything's ready for you.' He shrugged himself out of his jacket. Pixie wandered back into the kitchen. She knew it was useless asking if he wanted help. He had everything under control and she'd be as much use as a chocolate teapot.

Wearily she climbed the stairs and went into what was to be her room. Her own patchwork quilt covered the comfy-looking double bed next to which was a dressing-table with a frill around its base and three mirrors on top. Everything in the room was fresh, clean and pretty. In the corner there was a cot, painted white with a bunny sketched on the headboard. A pile of small blankets and a tiny patchwork quilt lay in readiness for her baby. On the floor was a bright new clippy rug. She was overwhelmed by his kindness.

Pixie sniffed away the tears that threatened to fall and went downstairs, taking with her a nightdress, slippers and an old dressing-gown that had once belonged to her mother.

Bob had brought in the tin bath, which sat in front of the range. Places were set at the table for them to eat.

'Thank you,' she said. 'You don't know what this means to me.'

'The cot's not new – it came from Marie's stall – but I've painted it.'

'Did you draw the bunny?'

He nodded, and blushed.

Suddenly Pixie felt a great wave of tiredness over-whelm her. She turned to him and held onto his shoulder for support.

'Not surprised you're worn out. You've been through a bomb blast and seen your best friend shattered. Drink some tea and I'll put the water in the tin bath, then you can do what you want. Help yourself to food.'

Bob went back into the scullery and Pixie remembered she needed her toothbrush and toiletries. Back upstairs she took a closer look at the rag rug. It was all brightness, in contrast to the war's dull colours. Just looking at it made her feel happy. She lifted a corner to see how it had been made. The material was pulled through a canvas backing with some kind of hook. It looked quite simple. Perhaps she could make one.

Her clothes were in an open suitcase on the floor. On top of the pile were a couple of framed photos that had hung on her bedroom wall next door. One was of a little girl with a bow in her hair and a crooked fringe. The other was of her mother. She was arm in arm with her friend and they were enjoying a day out in Southsea, on the pier.

'Oh, Mum,' she said. 'I'm so sorry I couldn't pay up *all* the debts. Now it's my fault we've lost our home.' Pixie wiped the back of her hand across her face. 'I've done the best I can,' she said. 'But being here, I'll be able to wait for when you come home again.' She clutched the small frame to her chest. 'Please come back soon.'

She set that photograph by the side of her bed. She was about to leave the room when Bob called, 'I should only be about an hour. Leave the water in the bath and I'll empty it. Don't you dare try to do it yourself. Don't forget: eat, then sleep.'

Before she had time to answer, he was gone, the front door banging behind him. She heard the van start up as she entered the kitchen to see the tin bath steaming, a clean towel hanging over the back of a chair, a jar of mauve bath salts and an unused bar of soap in a saucer on the rug. She draped her nightdress over the arm of a chair near the range where it would warm. As she set the mug down she saw Bob had mixed up the powdered shampoo with water and left it in a cup next to an empty jug for rinsing her hair.

The fire in the range was burning brightly and Pixie grasped the end of the bath to pull it nearer the heat.

'Ouch!' It was too heavy. Well, now she *would* have to do as she was told and leave Bob to clear up after her. A sharp pain dug into her back, but she wasn't going to spoil this lovely bath worrying about that. She eased her cumbersome body into the tub.

She forced herself not to think of Cal.

She picked up the soap and smelt it. 'Mmm, lilac.' Soap was in such short supply. Lots of people saved slivers to make usable bars.

Pixie sat relaxing in the water. Bob had put the wireless on and popular music issued forth, 'Brazil', 'You'll Never Know', 'My Heart And I', as she soaped her body.

The siren wailed its long monotonous song.

Oh, no!

As quickly as she could, Pixie finished washing.

'Oh!' She felt as though she was urinating in the water and was unable to stop herself. She thought back to Doris and the way her waters had broken, signalling the start of her labour. Was it happening to her now, during a blasted air raid, and while she was alone? Surely it was too early for the baby to be born.

She knew she mustn't panic.

Bob had said he'd be about an hour. A first baby's birthing took a long time, didn't it?

Holding tightly to the sides of the bath she pushed herself upright. A sudden sharp pain had her bent double, like a hairpin. When it had gone, she got out of the water and towelled herself. Another pain hit her before she managed to tug on her nightdress.

'Damn!'

The house shook, following a terrific bang that reverberated around the kitchen, sending cups sliding across the table, pictures falling from the walls and a loud crack as a windowpane broke.

Something was wrong with her head. She couldn't think straight, but she knew she had to act on all the safety issues in case the house took a direct hit. She hoped the fuse box, water and gas meter were in similar places to next door. With one hand cradling her stomach, which seemed to be as solid as iron, she turned off the electricity at the box near the front door. Then, using the torch she found there, she managed in the half-light to turn off the water beneath the sink and the gas below the copper. That was the hardest and she had to lie on the floor to do it. After rolling up painfully, she grabbed the canary's cage and stuck it in the corner of the Morrison shelter.

She found a change of sheets in the scullery that she also pushed inside the shelter. If she was going to give birth, she didn't want to ruin Bob's blankets.

Pixie thought about Blake's Maternity Home at Elson. Back in the summer she had signed papers to use it for the birth of her baby.

Another window broke, upstairs this time. Now she could hear planes droning overhead. Searchlights flickered, glowing through the curtains. She suddenly felt sick and very afraid.

She would never get to Blake's. How could she, with no transport and no one to help her? A sharp pain seared her from back to front. She cried out and doubled over, but even if she managed to make her way to the front door there would be no one around. Already her neighbours had clattered past on their way to the nearest public air-raid shelter.

Better to stay here. Yes, that's what she must do. Make

the Morrison shelter more comfortable. What would she need? She couldn't make a flask of tea because the gas was turned off, but she could fill the jug with the water left in the pipes.

She thought of the stew in the cooling oven. Another pain shook her. Hungry as she'd felt before, she was in too much pain to eat.

Another crash, and dust fluttered around the kitchen. The cream and green food cabinet slid forward and fell against the table, exposing a large cobweb. She screamed and realized it was time to scramble into the shelter.

She lay, sweating and moaning, awaiting the pains that came quickly now. Floating in and out of consciousness, she tried to remember if she'd done everything she could to keep the home safe.

She didn't think Bob would come back soon. Once the air-raid siren had warned of imminent danger, he'd have had to sort out the stall, then get himself and Marlene to safety.

She sipped some water and, using a corner of the sheet, sponged her forehead and neck. The pain was like nothing she'd experienced before and all she could think of was that the child should be all right because she wanted it so much. Again she slipped into unconsciousness.

*

'Get the quilt off my bed!'

Hands were pulling her from the shelter and she was being wrapped up and carried.

Another voice, Marlene's, yelled, 'I've got her dressing-gown and coat. We can get her other stuff later.'

Pixie opened her eyes to find Bob was carrying her, 'Sit with her,' he said to Marlene, who was now beside her. Was she in a vehicle?

'Pant,' Marlene said firmly. 'Don't push.'

Pixie obeyed. She heard the engine fire up and felt the vehicle moving just as another spasm tightened and gripped her. She wanted to vomit. 'I'm going to be sick.' She got no further before she was heaving into the foot-well. The smell rose and she gagged again. A hand was caressing the side of her head, pulling her hair away from her face. Everything swam out of vision again.

A male voice shouted, 'I can take it from here. She'll be fine.'

The vehicle was now stationary.

She was rolled on to a hard surface and another pain tried to saw her body in half. Pixie opened her eyes and looked down at herself. She was covered with blood.

She screamed.

Through her own noise she heard a woman's voice, 'You the father?'

'Yes.' That was Bob's voice. She should right this wrong – but the sickness had come back and a container was placed near her.

'The baby,' Pixie yelled, in a rare moment of clarity. 'Is it all right?'

'We'll soon find out,' came the woman's voice, calm and quiet.

A mask that smelt of rubber was placed over her mouth and nose and the woman said, 'Stop pushing, dear. Wait until I tell you.'

She could smell disinfectant. She was being probed and the soft voice spoke again. 'Good girl, push.'

Pixie was floating as she heard the voice say, 'You have a beautiful little girl.' She tried to smile but instead her eyelids closed.

Chapter Twenty-three

'You going anywhere for Christmas, Gladys?' asked Cora, a busty blonde twenty years her junior.

'I don't know yet. You?'

Cora tipped the filled measure into the glass. 'Den's asked me round to his house but I'm not sure I want to cook for the old bugger.'

'Don't mind taking his money, though, eh?'

Cora winked at her. 'He gets plenty in return.' She set the glass of whisky on the bar and put the water jug beside it so her customer could have his drink the way he preferred it. She took the man's coins and counted them, 'Just right, Percy,' she said. Then she opened the drawer of the till and put in the money.

Gladys patted her permed hair. 'I've already asked to be put on the rota for extra work. I could do with the money.'

'Must be horrible not having a man at your age,' Cora said.

'Oh, I don't know,' she replied. 'There are compensations, like having the bed to yourself and not having to wash out skid-marked underwear!'

Cora started laughing, a big belly laugh from a big girl. 'You are a one,' she said. She opened a packet of Smith's crisps, sprinkled the blue bag of salt, then started eating after shoving the bag at Gladys, who declined. Cora offered a crisp to the orange cat asleep on the counter. It opened one eye, also declined, but licked her hand.

'You and that bloody cat,' Gladys said. The last time there was an air-raid Cora had risked her life searching for Mogs in the back yard while the planes screamed overhead.

There weren't many people in the bar and it looked like being a quiet night as there was no mild ale. Neither the brewers nor the black market could provide it. Gladys looked around the White Swan, known locally as the Dirty Duck. It was a dive of a place. She mopped the floor at nights with bleach but still the tiles looked filthy. The air was thick with cigarette smoke and the smell of stale beer, even though there were barely twenty people standing around drinking.

The door opened and in came a well-built man. For

a second, Gladys's heart stopped. But it wasn't Del. She began breathing again.

Cora asked, 'How come you ended up working here?'

'Told you. I got bombed out and saw the notice in the pub window offering a room.' Cora nodded and went on talking to Percy, who was never seen without his flat cap.

'I'm going outside for a break,' Gladys said. She knew Cora wouldn't mind. It would give the girl a chance to fish out a couple of bottle tops from the rubbish and sit them next to her legitimate bottle-top pile representing the drinks the customers had bought her. At the end of the evening she could either redeem them for money or have the drinks. Cora liked money.

In the lavatory's mirror Gladys studied her face. She looked old, she thought. She pulled away her collar. The marks where Del had tried to strangle her had almost faded now. She didn't like wearing high-necked blouses and jumpers, but she didn't want anyone knowing about her past and feeling sorry for her.

It was cold in the back yard. A fine drizzle was falling but it made the air feel clean. A sharp thud startled her, then the rattle of the dustbin lid. But it was only Mogs – he'd come out of the bar for a bit of affection. She bent and stroked his soft fur, making silly noises at him while he twisted around her legs. She picked him up and he began purring.

Two months had passed since she'd run away from Del.

She remembered it as though it was yesterday. She shuddered.

They'd been in a Brighton pub. From the windows there was a fine view of the sea and pier. Well, there was when the blackout curtains weren't shutting it out.

'Stay here while I talk to Henry,' Del had said. 'I got myself in deep with another bookie.' Full of drink, he had walked unsteadily over to the three men standing outside the Gents. Gladys had sipped her gin.

They were like an unhappily married couple now. All the fizz had gone out of their relationship. If she'd had any proper money of her own she'd have got a bus out of town ages ago. But she was stuck in a loveless union where she paid with her flesh for every single thing she was given. She had the bruises to show for it.

There was a lot of shouting going on. One of the men pushed Del in the chest and he stumbled. When he staggered back to her table his face was like thunder.

'Let's get out of here,' he said. His sausage-like fingers dug into her arm. 'I owe that bastard three hundred pounds. I can't afford to pay, but if I don't cough up I'll get stuck with a knife.'

'What are you going to do?'

'What are you going to do?' he mimicked.

The usual row ensued in the street outside. The roads were slippery with frost. He kept shrugging her off as she tried to hold on to his arm to stop herself slipping in her high heels. Gladys was scared of going home to the poky house in the cobbled street. When Del's temper escalated, it was almost worse than a raid.

They'd hardly got indoors when he sat down and put his hands over his face, saying in a very small voice, 'I can save my skin if you'll help me.'

Gladys, near the fireplace, asked fearfully, 'What d'you mean?'

'Mick said he and a few mates would like to party with you. He's got some big-shot coming down from Birmingham he needs to get on the right side of. For that he'd forget about the money.'

She knew what he meant all right. She'd be taken to a house somewhere and the men would be like beasts with her. One after the other – if she was lucky. Any kind feelings she had left for Del disappeared. 'I'm not prostituting myself for you,' she said.

That had been when he had leaped out at her, thrown

her against the wall and begun squeezing her throat. When she was losing consciousness she managed to croak out, 'All right.'

'Good girl,' he'd said, sighing with relief.

Then he was solicitous. He pressed her to his body, muttering how sorry he was for hurting her and that he'd never, ever hurt her again. She played along, too scared to do otherwise, closing her mind when he lifted her skirt and forced himself into her.

Afterwards, locking the front door, he left her while he went back to the pub to tell the bookie the deal was on.

All she could think of was that he might bring the men back immediately.

Gladys, more dead than alive, managed to summon the strength to heave a chair through the window. She climbed out, was over the front wall and off like a scalded cat.

Terrified she might bump into Del round every corner, she ran, her heels crippling her, towards the edge of town. The frost crunched beneath her shoes as she moved through the undergrowth in the allotments.

The sheds looked safe, like small houses.

The one she'd spent the night in had a paraffin stove and everything a gardener might need for a restful afternoon away from his missus. The next morning she was well set up with a cup of tea and a biscuit before she walked painfully to the main road and hitched a ride into Portsmouth.

She walked along the sea front, looking at the barbed wire strung across the beach to deter German raiders, and turned into Old Portsmouth. She could see Gosport across the harbour. Her heart constricted with pain: she would have loved to go home but couldn't face Pixie and the mess she'd left her in.

But if she had money, she thought, she could return. Alas, the little she had in her purse might buy her a bed for the night or food, not both. She *wouldn't* go home empty-handed.

She knew she'd been a rotten mother, flitting in and out of her daughter's life since Pixie had been old enough to get her own breakfast. Leaving the girl to clear up after her, while she followed men who would treat her like a queen for a while then cast her aside. Ever since Pixie's dad had gone, Gladys had needed to know she was attractive and desirable.

Tears had filled her eyes. She had brushed them away, staring at the choppy water of the harbour and the Channel, where boats and ships of all kinds were moored. In the distance she could see the *Victory*, Nelson's flagship. She could even just make out the armaments yards, beyond Camper & Nicholsons' shipyard. The keen wind blew her hair across her face and she tucked it behind her ear.

The incident with the tango dancer had shown her how she'd fooled herself. She'd thought she was still a young woman. He'd thought she was an old tart.

Last night when Del had made his suggestion it had underlined the fact that men thought she was nothing but a whore to be passed around, as you'd share a packet of fags. All the time she'd been looking for love, Del had been using her.

At home she had a beautiful daughter, who loved her despite her neglect. Maybe Pixie would allow her to make up for all the lost years when she had pushed her aside.

If she got a job she could save some money, take it to Pixie and beg her forgiveness.

A couple of young girls walked by, leaving the smell of perfume and youth in their wake. Gladys watched them. One glanced back and giggled. They probably thought she was on the game. This area of Portsmouth was well known as a pick-up point.

There was a pub on the corner near the entrance to the harbour. She looked down at herself. Was she presentable enough to go inside and ask if they had any bar work or cleaning jobs?

Without another thought she went in.

She froze beneath the eagle stare and puffed-up hair of the woman behind the bar. 'We don't need any more staff,' she said curtly

Within ten minutes she was standing in the public bar of another pub, the White Swan.

An hour later she was bathed, had eaten a curled-up fish paste sandwich and been taken on by a man called Jeremy, who looked as though a puff of wind would blow him over. He had taken pity on her and given her a job. 'If you mess me about, dear,' he'd said, 'you're out on your arse in the morning.' He'd shown her around, introduced her to his friend Stephen and given her the sandwich with a cup of tea. While she was eating he handed her a couple of pretty jumpers, a black skirt and a large man's shirt. 'These have been left behind. Maybe you can make use of them.' Then he pushed a tube of Pan Stik into her hands. 'Hide the bruises, dear. Heaven forbid anyone thinks I've done it.'

That was how it had happened.

She had a room with a single bed, scruffy but clean, and a lovely view of Portsmouth and the harbour.

Now Gladys put Mogs down and watched the cat slink away. Stephen doted on it.

She looked up at the sky. There were no stars and she

wondered if it might snow. The back door opened with a creak and Cora poked her head out. 'Come and give us a hand, Gladys. The bar's full of Canadians.'

Bob couldn't remember when he'd ever been so happy.

It was three in the morning and he'd lit the fire in the kitchen range. It warmed the house. Coal was hard to come by but he'd managed to get a couple of bags off Alfie, who lived near the coal yard, in return for lending him his van at the weekend. 'Supply and demand,' he muttered, and nearly spat out the nappy pin gripped between his teeth. On the table there was a bag with a couple of sandwiches in it and he'd made tea in the blue flask ready for work at Fareham market.

Across his lap was a little girl in a tie-around vest, who was kicking her legs and making a fighting motion with her tiny fists. She was gurgling to herself while he wrestled with a terry-towelling nappy and what seemed to him the ridiculously small curved pin. Talcum powder covered the two-week-old child, the chair, the floor and Bob.

'There,' he said. 'That's you fresh and sweet. Now we need a clean nightie so you can go back upstairs with your mum.'

He'd been woken earlier by Sadie's soft whingeing.

He'd padded into Pixie's room and picked her up, hoping she hadn't woken her mother. He reckoned the more Pixie rested, the quicker her TNT-poisoned body would heal.

He pulled the warm white flannelette nightie off the wire fireguard and dressed the small wriggling figure. Then he picked up the bottle of milk he'd already warmed, settled back with the baby in his arms and tipped the bottle at exactly the right angle. For a baby who had arrived unexpectedly early, Sadie had soon made up her birth weight.

Bob was captivated by her – she had stolen his heart.

Once upon a time he had hated coming home to an empty house. Now there wasn't room to swing a cat in the two-up and two-down. The child had completely taken over his house and his life.

He removed the bottle to give Sadie a breather. He listened carefully. There was no sound from upstairs. Pixie cleaned and cooked, as if she was his wife. Well, without the bedroom benefits. But he wasn't one to press her. The baby's birth had drained her. And she still mourned Cal, even though she knew he wasn't likely to return.

Bob wanted Pixie to think of him as more than a

friend. As yet that wasn't happening. He decided for his own sake he would distance himself from her.

Yes, he would bide his time.

Sometimes, though, she spoke about the American as though he was still alive. Bob wasn't going to be the one to tell her that a man who never contacted the woman he professed to love obviously didn't love her very much.

He suspected Cal was dead, though. Or possibly taken prisoner. He didn't bring the man's name into a conversation unless Pixie did. He preferred her to think about the people surrounding her now, the child, her friend Rita and, more hopefully, himself.

He'd offered to take her to Chichester to find Cal's sister. Ruth surely would know what had happened to her brother. Pixie agreed, but Bob knew she was putting off the day because she didn't want to find out the truth about the man she loved. Either he had perished in the war or he had found someone else. A bitter pill for anyone to swallow, let alone a woman recovering from childbirth and the complications caused by working with cordite. But every day she was stronger, and looking more like her old self.

Okay, so she wasn't as pretty as some of the girls he'd bedded. But Pixie was the woman he wanted to build a home with. And if he had to wait, he would wait for however long it took. But Pixie had to want him for himself. He wasn't going to be runner-up to any Yank. Jesus, he thought, those Americans had a lot to answer for – they were even changing the English language. How many times in a day did he now say 'okay'?

When Sadie had taken her fill of the bottle, Bob rubbed her back. Then he carried her upstairs, treading quietly so as not to disturb Pixie. But she was awake.

'Hello, you.' She smiled and held out her arms for the baby. Bob sat on the edge of the bed. The room smelt of clean baby and talcum powder. 'This is a nice surprise,' Pixie said.

'Better than the surprise I had after I got back from an auction yesterday,' he said. It still amazed him that Marlene had the cheek to do it.

'What was that?'

'My *assistant* had put a flat, glass-lidded box at the front of the stall and was selling gold charms and antique brooches. She'd already got rid of three, so she told me.' He saw Pixie sit up with interest. 'Those three charms had paid for the amount the rest had cost so the remainder was profit. Though she did admit she owed Marie some money.'

He knew Marlene could do no wrong in Pixie's eyes

ever since Sadie's birth. That night Marlene had insisted Bob go straight back to his house to check on Pixie with the bombing. Had he taken her home first, God knew what would have happened.

'What did you do?'

'Do? I told her she should have asked me first.'

'And what would you have said?'

'That it was okay for her to do that.'

Pixie laughed. 'What are you moaning about, then?'

He shook his head. 'I've always known she wanted to start up on her own.'

'Then help her,' Pixie said. 'No one else will. It's hard enough people looking down on her for being an unmarried mum . . .'

'Don't I know it? *I* get sick of the pointing fingers she has to put up with. I lose money because she works for me. But she's a good worker, better than some blokes I've had in the past.' He was telling the truth. Marlene was a damned good worker and he didn't want to lose her. He smiled at Pixie and her sleeping child. 'There's tea in the pot. I'll bring you up a cup. Then you should sleep while she allows you to.' He got up. 'We ought to start thinking about Christmas,' he went on. 'There's no hope of a turkey, though. According to the wireless only one home in ten will have one this year.'

Chapter Twenty-four

After the explosion, Rita had been moved to the Queen Victoria Hospital in East Grinstead, which specialized in dental and jaw injuries. She was in Ward One.

'The lower half of your face is coming along nicely,' Sir Paul Elkins told her. He was Australian by birth and smartly dressed in a grey suit. Gently he re-laid the cotton and gauze dressing, containing *tulle gras*, a Vaseline-like substance, over the side of her face and treated her to a smile. He picked up the clipboard from the end of the bed and studied it. His dark moustache was extremely glossy. 'The teeth have been screwed into place. Two top and three bottom. When they've settled I can guarantee no one will realize they don't belong to you.' He put his fingers to her chin and pain shot through her head. 'That shows your jaw is healing nicely.' Obviously he had noted her discomfort. He stared into her eyes. She blinked.

The haze that blighted her sight was lessening with each day. 'You're lucky you weren't blinded. Probable full sight recovery.' He didn't wait for her to speak. It was difficult for her to move any of her facial muscles. She was sure he knew this, and was thankful she didn't need to make an effort.

'I've taken skin from your abdomen and replaced the area that was lost from below your hairline to your cheek. I don't want you looking at yourself in a mirror yet because there may be more work to do.' He patted her hand, the one that wasn't bandaged. 'Your hair will grow again where it's been shaved due to the operation, but you may have to arrange it in a different style to cover the scarring.' He looked down at her. 'Don't worry about that. We have a beautician who will show you a few tricks.' He smiled and studied his clipboard. 'Enough information for now, I think. Do you want to ask me any questions?'

She shook her head by moving it slightly. Not when it hurts so much to talk, she thought.

His eyes held hers. 'You girls know the sacrifice you're making working with chemicals like these. Sadly, I lost a woman who protested until the end that she was happy to die for such a worthy cause. You aren't going to die.' He seemed to relax. Then he said, 'Couldn't save your finger, I'm afraid.' Her hand was swathed like a huge white lollipop. 'The rest of the hand is fine, no tendon damage. Broken ribs will mend. I'm having you moved into Ward Two where the women are.'

And then he was gone, his entourage following.

Sir Paul Elkins, her surgeon, had made the facts quite clear. She thought of the other girls at Priddy's Hard risking their lives to win this war. She thought of Pixie and her baby, the damage the poisons in the factory could do. Pixie's skin and hair were discoloured, and she was tired all the time: another symptom of the poisoning.

The little nurse with the short dark hair, who seemed able to communicate with Rita despite Rita's silence, tucked back the whiter than white sheets. It was almost visiting time, though visitors seemed to turn up when-ever they liked. The nurse, asked, 'Anyone coming in?'

Rita formed her lips into a 'No.'

'Never mind. You'll have to put up with me fussing about, then. My name's Joannie. You'll need to be got ready for your move once the visitors have gone. Open your mouth. Something to ease the pain.' Joannie popped in a couple of tablets and gave her a small cup of water. Rita dutifully swallowed. 'But you never know, your mother might come,' she added.

Rita could have told her she didn't want her mother

anywhere near her, and that her best friend was about to have a baby. She might even have had the baby by now, for all Rita knew, so she wouldn't be able to travel all the way to East Grinstead in Sussex. She prayed she'd hear soon, but it would be difficult for Pixie to contact her while so much was happening to them both. And during the past months Rita had been so miserable and bad-tempered that any friendships she'd cultivated at Priddy's Hard had withered away.

Rita had no idea how long she'd been there. She slept a lot. She swallowed all the pills she was given. She was in the Plastic Surgery Burns Unit, the best place in the country to be after her accident, so she'd been told.

But *had* it been an accident? Or had she really thought so little about herself that she hadn't bothered to be careful when filling the shells?

She turned over and slept.

'This is your first Christmas, my darling.' Pixie gazed down at the sleeping child, whose arms were stretched above her head, the cot's covers kicked aside. Their bedroom was above the kitchen and the heat from the range warmed the small space. Pixie's heart swelled with pride and love as she gazed at the marvel that was her daughter.

Finally, she tore herself away from her child and bent down to pull the long package from beneath her bed.

Would Bob like it? Or would he think it a silly present for a man? But how could she buy him a gift when she had no money of her own and was reliant on him for everything? She lifted the package onto her bed and opened it. The bright colours cheered her at once, and that was what she wanted it to do for Bob, make him feel happy when he got out of bed in the mornings and put his toes into the softness of the rag rug.

Surprisingly, it hadn't taken her long to make. The rug hook had seemed to fly in her hands, and while Sadie slept during the day when Bob was at work, the rug had taken shape. The pieces of material had come from old clothes, some hers, some Bob's. And a trip to a local jumble sale had provided colourful cottons for just a few pennies. The backing was an old potato sack, washed and hemmed. Pixie stood admiring the rug, a smile on her face. Then she rolled it up again, tied it with a piece of red cotton, making a bow, and carried it into the front bedroom, laying it carefully on the end of Bob's bed along with the simple card she had made and signed from her and Sadie.

He was deep beneath the bedclothes, the downy quilt keeping him snug. She bent down, kissed his forehead, inhaling the male sleepy musk of him, then turned to leave the room. As she got to the door his voice called softly, 'Gotcha!'

Pixie stopped. 'I tried so hard . . .'

'I'm a light sleeper. Anyway, where's your red coat?'

She was confused.

'Father Christmas outfit?' He was sitting up in bed, his eyes on the package.

'Silly,' she said. 'Do you want to open it now?' She hoped not. She was embarrassed.

'I think not. We'll open our presents together later in the morning, shall we?'

'Like a real family.' The words were out of her mouth before she'd had time to think.

'Yes,' he said, so softly she almost didn't hear him. Then he said brightly, 'Now I'm awake I think I'll make some tea.' He got out of bed and pulled his dressing-gown over his pyjamas. When he reached the doorway he kissed her lightly on the forehead and said, 'Merry Christmas.'

He was off down the stairs and she followed. It smelt Christmassy in the kitchen. Last night, they'd prepared the dinner for today. There was no turkey, but Bob had managed to get hold of a small chicken. He'd proudly presented her with the bird, which she'd had to pluck and gut. They were both excited about cooking and eating a lovely Christmas this was going to be, she thought. In the afternoon, Marlene, her mum and the little one were coming over for tea. Pixie had already planned on saving as much white meat as she could from the bird to make chicken sandwiches. It was to be a lovely treat, along with the cake that she'd made. Not exactly a Christmas cake, because she couldn't get half the necessary ingredients, but she'd substituted carrots for some of the fruit, extra dried egg powder and some cocoa to darken it. And there was real sherry in it, quite a lot. It smelt delicious.

Pixie had made a rag cushion cover for Beth, and hoped she'd like it. She'd had a go at making a cloth rabbit for Marlene's little girl, Jeannie, stuffing it with all the scraps of cotton she'd accumulated. She'd spent ages trying to get the ears right. Its eyes were two buttons from one of Bob's old shirts and its tail was a pom-pom fashioned from the white wool of one of Sadie's first matinée jackets, which she'd grown out of now. For Rita, Pixie had wrapped up a necklace of her own that Rita had always loved. Green glass beads that would glint against Rita's skin, bringing out the dark colours of her eyes and hair. Rita wouldn't need to borrow it from her any more. Pixie would give it to her when she was able to visit her. Marlene's had been the hardest gift to find. She had no money, even supposing there was much in the shops to buy. She finally decided to give her a silver brooch in the shape of a half-moon. Pixie's mother had given it to her – an unwanted gift from one of her admirers. Pixie felt it was too pretty to wear every day, and if Marlene didn't like it, she could sell it on her jewellery venture.

For Sadie, Pixie had sewn a whole menagerie of animals.

She looked around the kitchen. Holly was pushed behind pictures and a piece of mistletoe hung in the doorway. They'd have some fun with that when Marlene and her family arrived, she thought.

'Pixie!' called Bob from outside. 'Come and help.'

She ran to the front door to find he had the back of the truck open.

'Go on, bring it out.' Pixie's eyes grew accustomed to the darkness as she looked inside the van, which held Bob's stock that wasn't piled in the front room of his small house. Bob had his hands on the handle of a large object. She couldn't believe her eyes. It was a pram!

'Oh!' she said. It wasn't just any old pram, but a high one. She pulled it out into the half-light of the morning. 'Oh, it's beautiful.'

There weren't any prams to be had in the shops. Children's stuff was in short supply – the war again.

'It's not new,' Bob said, 'but I've cleaned it up and there's not a mark on it.'

'Oh, Bob, it's wonderful,' she said.

'I'm glad you like it,' he said. 'C'mon, let's get it inside before any nosy parkers see us in our nightwear and think bad thoughts.' He pulled the pram backwards until it stood on the pavement and she was able to push it up and over the front doorstep. Meanwhile he hauled out the coal and closed the doors.

She was still admiring the navy blue and white pram, imagining herself pushing Sadie along the road, head held high, when Bob returned.

'Thank you,' she said. 'It's such a lovely Christmas. If only I could find out how Rita . . .'

'I'll take you to see her,' he said. 'I know how much you've been worrying about her. But you've got to remember she'll be a different Rita from the one you knew.'

'What d'you mean?'

'It's not just the scarring. I've had mates come back from the war with their personalities changed . . .'

'Em's husband changed and not just because he lost the use of his legs.'

'You know exactly what I mean, then.'

'It wasn't her writing on the letter,' she said.

'I expect she got a nurse to write it for her. But the main thing is, the letter was for you and she's still your best friend.'

Pixie thought for a while. Then she smiled. 'And I feel strong enough now to see Cal's sister. Can we go to Chichester together?'

He stood facing her, then put one hand on her shoulder. 'I'll take you. But I think it's better if you see her on your own. I don't want her to believe you've jumped into bed with—'

'But I'm not sleeping with you!'

'Other people don't know that. I've already had a few sly digs from some of the women customers. The last person you need to think you're not a good woman is your child's father's sister, right?'

Pixie nodded. 'I see what you mean,' she said.

'Tell his sister whatever you want but let it come from you. Maybe he's in a prisoner-of-war camp somewhere. Maybe he's dead. But I'm sure she'll be pleased about the baby and I'm glad you feel able to cope with seeing her.'

'But what will you do while I'm with her?'

'Don't worry about me – there may even be an auction—'

He didn't even get to the end of the sentence before Sadie's lusty cry interrupted them. 'I'll go and get her, you pour out the tea. It'll be well and truly mashed by now,' he said.

Chapter Twenty-five

'Joannie, can I have something to ease the pain? My head's throbbing.'

'You've got a hangover – put up with it!'

Rita looked away from Joannie's laughing face. The ward was decorated with paper chains, bells and balls the residents had made. In the corner a tree was covered with tinsel. An angel topped it, her wings made of silver paper. The air smelt of excitement instead of disinfectant and she thought she could smell dinner cooking somewhere.

Christmas at home with her mum and *him* had been something to be got over as quickly as possible. Usually she went dancing on Christmas Eve with the girls, got up as late as she dared, then went for a walk. If there was a Christmas dinner, she ate it, washing up afterwards. She'd spend the evening with Pixie and her mum, if Gladys happened to be there. She always felt her own mother was glad to see the back of her.

'You are the meanest nurse ever,' she said to Joannie, who was stripping the bed next to hers. They both knew she was joking. Christmas Day or not, the work in the wards went on as usual.

She thought back to last night, Christmas Eve. Seven o'clock and she was reading a book by Richard Llewellyn, sitting in the day room.

'Coming down the Speckled Hen?' Arthur was an airman who had lost a leg, the sight in one eye, and had facial scarring. People were sad for him. Except Arthur was anything but sad. He made you laugh with the things he got up to, and the specialists laughed along with everyone else. Sir Paul Elkins had said, 'These men and women have been through hell and out the other side. If the staff can't take a few high jinks, they should change their jobs.'

Arthur insisted on paying for Rita's drinks. An allowance from his father who rarely visited him should be disposed of as soon as possible, he said.

Whitey Summers, Den Allan and Pru Lavant were her new friends. Pru had a two-year-old daughter. She was hoping to see her at Christmas, but the little girl couldn't take to her mother's burned face, and cried when she saw her. A gas cylinder had blown up during an air raid and Pru had taken the brunt of it, throwing herself across her child so that the little one was unmarked.

Inside the pub a huge log fire blazed, but sadly there was no mild and no brandy, only cider. Some locals were playing dominoes, shove halfpenny and darts. Carol singers were chanting old favourites so the little gang of patients could join in lustily.

By the time they left after the lock-in, they were full of the Christmas spirit and it was four in the morning.

At the hospital door they were greeted by the starchy matron, who said, 'Merry Christmas. Going out? Or coming in?'

Rita couldn't remember the last time she had laughed so much. The best thing was that she was surviving the horror of what had happened to her. And she wasn't alone. Others had suffered like her and were surviving too.

Rita grabbed hold of Joannie. 'I vaguely remember we came back with lanterns from the roadworks where that bomb left a crater . . .'

'Don't worry,' Joannie said. 'I arranged for Eddie to take them back so they wouldn't be missed.'

Eddie was an ambulance driver.

'He never took them in an ambulance?'

'With its lights flashing in the daylight,' she said. 'And the answer's still no. Nothing for your hangover!'

Rita stuck out her tongue at the nurse.

'I can see you're feeling better,' Joannie said, as she plumped up the pillows and moved away.

And Rita was. She hadn't had a reply to her letter to Pixie. She so badly wanted to know her friend was all right. Joannie had written what Rita had dictated. Her own hand wasn't stable enough to keep the paper still but she knew that soon she would master the constant shaking. Pixie would come and see her when she could. She was sure of that.

She would never forget that Pixie, after the blast at the factory and despite being poorly herself, hadn't left her until the very end. She had even lied, telling them she was her sister to enable her to stay close.

Would Pixie bring her baby? Rita thought the child must have been born by now.

Rita also hoped Pixie had managed to go to her mother's house to collect some of her clothing. She'd arrived at East Grinstead in old things that the War Memorial Hospital had provided. The trouble was, her memory was hazy and she wasn't sure she'd even asked Pixie about her clothes. This hospital was wonderful but it couldn't work miracles where clothes were concerned. Even the WVS had its limits.

Joannie was back again as a buzzer sounded. 'All those who can walk, come along to the canteen.' She wore a Father Christmas hat with a pom-pom on the end. 'There's home-made crackers,' Joannie said, tucking her arm through Rita's.

Eight roast potatoes, a few sprouts and other vegetables from old Mac's allotment, two nice chops, and apple pie to follow with more apples than pie, but that was how Jack liked it. No cream or custard, but the top of the milk would do nicely. It didn't seem much of a proper Christmas dinner but it was what Em's husband fancied and she hoped to God he'd eat it. The chops had been hard to come by. There were many families eating less than that today. Em closed the oven door, trapping in the heavenly smell.

Em sighed. She was worn out. She looked down at the new slippers her lovely elder daughter, Lizzie, had bought her for Christmas and smiled to herself. Her girl was happy living away from home and that made Em happy, too.

'Where did you say they was taking Doris and the little 'un?' If Jack called to her one more time she'd kill him.

'The New Forest, a picnic,' she shouted back.

'A picnic this time of the year?' His voice was full of sarcasm. 'What about their dinner?'

'Tonight they'll be eating at Eliza's.'

Em put a hand to her head. The two aspirins she'd taken didn't seem to be working. She went to the knife drawer and took out cutlery for the two of them, setting the kitchen table.

A loud crash sent her scurrying into the front room. 'Oh, my God!' Her husband was sprawled on the floor, staring at her accusingly. One of the wheelchair's wheels was spinning.

'Don't make a fuss. I was trying to reach my pipe. Why do you always put it where I can't get it?' There it was again, the accusation that she was to blame for his fall.

Em tugged the wheelchair upright, then grabbed him beneath the arms and managed to haul his bulk across the seat of the chair, where he was able to wriggle back into a sitting position. She could see he wasn't hurt. She didn't have the energy for the argument that would start if she said, 'You left the pipe there yourself, Jack.'

She moved and winced. She must have pinched a nerve.

'Where's Doris?'

She repeated resignedly to him, 'The New Forest. They've gone to the New Forest.'

It was an act, his forgetfulness. He was trying to catch her out in a lie. As if he even *cared* where Doris and James were.

'For the day,' Em said, making sure the chair's brake was on. 'The baby won't know much about it but Doris will be thrilled to bits to see the ponies.' She handed him the pipe, his tobacco pouch and a box of matches. Then she went back to the kitchen, took the lid off the boiling sprouts and hummed along to carols from the wireless. They settled her nerves.

Eliza Slaughter adored Doris and the baby. Em had no worries about them being with Harry and his son Cedric: Eliza would kill the pair if either laid a finger on them.

'Em, did you take the matches?'

As she put the saucepan lid back on the sprouts, her knuckles were white with anger. She counted to ten in her mind and went back to pick up the matches for him. They had either fallen or been thrown on the floor. As she handed them over he grabbed her wrist.

The sudden sharp pain of his fingers nipping her flesh made her gasp.

'I think you like me confined to this house, dependent on you, so you can go off to work and mess about with the blokes there.'

She pulled free. 'Don't, Jack. It's Christmas Day.' She

sighed. Then she rubbed her skin. Her wrist was already darkened with fading bruises.

'I know you're getting it somewhere.'

'Jack, stop it. I'm going back into the kitchen to dish up the dinner and you and I are going to sit and eat it together. After I've washed up, we'll listen to some carols from Winchester Cathedral on the wireless. Maybe have a sherry or two.'

Em thought of the next two days, glad that Doris would be back home with her tomorrow. And her grandson, that wonderful little boy: he was her last thought at night and her first in the morning.

Jack was staring at her.

'There's never been anyone but you, Jack. And never will be.' She hated herself for the lie, but remembering Sam's long-ago gentleness gave her the courage to carry on.

His hands dropped back into his lap. 'I'm sorry, Em.'

He wasn't sorry. They both knew that.

'Come out in a few minutes,' she said calmly. 'It'll be on the table.'

Back in the kitchen, draining the vegetables, Em thought back to the year before Jack's accident when he was virile, good-looking and had sent her cards from every foreign country he had been sent to. Jack had fought for his country and for her. She'd repaid him in the worst way possible and now she was paying for it. And deserved to go on paying.

She thought of Sam down the Fox. It was over now, all over. Gone but not forgotten, never forgotten. The afternoons when she hadn't been working she had spent in Sam's bed, safe and warm and cuddled in his strong arms, while outside the rain lashed against the windows. She had been happy then.

'I never thought the place would look like this.'

Bob was peering at the rose bushes pruned to within an inch of their lives and the neat rectangular gardens with just a sprinkling of frost. The ground and grass were crunchy beneath their feet. Bob looked up at the two women watching him.

Rita laughed and touched the bandage covering part of her shaved head. Her face was red and scabbed. 'I suppose you thought I'd be in a dark and dismal ward, all bandaged and miserable.'

Pixie took a deep breath of air that was crisp and clean. She shifted Sadie from one arm to the other. 'I don't have to ask if you're happy here.' Rita had put on weight and there was a certain calm about her. It had shown in the way she'd held Sadie, cooed at her and been loath to hand her back.

'As happy as one can be after having their face mashed.'

'Oh, Rita, I didn't mean . . .'

'I'm being honest with you, Pixie. For the first time in a long while I'm happy.'

'But no mirrors,' said Bob.

Pixie glared at him. If looks could kill he'd have shrivelled away for his thoughtless words.

'I don't need a mirror to know a friend likes me for who I am, not what I look like.'

Pixie smiled at Rita with admiration. 'Even I expected Queen Victoria Hospital to be full of miserable patients.'

'I hadn't been here twenty-four hours when I was told, "It's your face that's taken a beating, not your feet. Get out of bed and do something." I've had a couple of ops, but some people here have had up to thirty. I'm one of the lucky ones.'

Pixie felt very humbled by the new Rita.

Bob put out his arms to take the child and Pixie passed Sadie to him. She was gaining weight every day and had dimples in her cheeks.

'I'll take a walk and leave you two to your women's talk,' he said.

'See those double doors?' Bob looked towards the main building. Rita carried on: 'Just inside there's a tea place for visitors. There's homemade cakes baked earlier today. And the bread pudding – I don't know how they do it but it's lovely and moist. We'll meet you there in about half an hour. Don't want that gorgeous baby to get cold.' Rita tapped the side of her head. 'I forgot, a friend of mine, an airman, said he'd love to meet you. You won't miss him. He's dishing out the teas.'

Pixie watched Bob walk across the grass, leaving footprints in the frost.

'You do look well, you know,' she said. Rita tucked her arm through Pixie's and they continued walking.

'So do you. Your legs and ankles are the normal size again and your skin looks like you've been on holiday in the fresh air. But was it very bad, the birth?' Rita asked.

'I'm not here to talk about something that's over and done with. Anyway, it's surprising how quickly you forget the pain. Every woman must feel the same else the whole human race would have died out years ago. How's your mum? She been up to see you?'

Rita shook her head. 'I told her to keep away from me.'

For a moment there was silence. Then Pixie drew Rita towards an oak tree that had a circular metal seat at its base. She used her handkerchief to wipe it free of frost and pushed Rita down. 'She's your mother. What's going on?' Pixie remembered the strangeness between Rita and Hilary at the War Memorial Hospital back in Gosport.

Rita's eyes swam with tears. 'I'm safe here,' she whispered.

'Safe from what?'

'Safe from him.' Rita was twisting her skirt, bunching it, setting it free, then starting the procedure all over again.

Pixie remembered how the nurse had picked up on Malcolm's peculiar behaviour and practically ordered Rita's parents away from the hospital.

Across the grass a small pond was surrounded by winter-dead brown rushes. Pixie stared unseeingly at it. There was something different about Rita here, like she wasn't scared any more. And she certainly didn't smell of booze. She looked up into her friend's eyes and felt for her hand, the one that wasn't bandaged.

'It was him. Malcolm. You were scared of him, weren't you?'

A tear dropped from the edge of Rita's eyelid and travelled down her scarred cheek. 'He used to come into my room.'

'What d'you mean, come into your room?'

'Do I have to spell it out?' Rita seemed angry that Pixie didn't understand. 'He'd stand over the bed, looking down at me.'

'But you're not a child. Why didn't you tell him to

bugger off?' Immediately the words were out, Pixie saw Rita clam up. 'Oh, my love, I'm sorry.' She'd suddenly grasped with clarity what Rita was trying to tell her.

'You think I didn't?'

'No, of course I don't think—'

'He was everywhere. Opening the kitchen door when he knew I was having a strip wash. But I started putting a chair beneath the handle. That fooled him.' Rita was getting even angrier. 'He started coming down to the outside lavatory when I was in there. One day I caught him touching my underclothes in my bedroom drawer. I felt sick. I tried not to be alone in the house with him. When I wasn't out with you or down the Fox I used to buy drink, usually a small bottle of whatever I could get to dull the pain, and sit in the park until I had enough courage to go home and face him.'

Rita laid her head on Pixie's shoulder. 'I've missed you,' she said, and sniffed.

After a short silence, Pixie asked, 'Why didn't you tell your mum?'

Rita sighed. 'I finally plucked up the courage to do just that. She said I was making it up because I fancied him. You know what hurt the most, Pixie?'

Pixie shook her head.

'That she believed I'd fancy *him*. That *I* would do such

a thing to hurt my own mother. I don't want to see either of them again, ever.'

'Why didn't you talk to me?'

Rita pushed back her hair. 'I wanted to, but you hadn't heard from Cal and you were pregnant. I thought you had enough on your plate without me adding more worries. And I honestly believed that my mother knew what was going on but closed her eyes to it.'

Pixie smoothed Rita's dark hair. It hurt that she hadn't known she was in such pain. She was supposed to be her best friend, wasn't she? Yet Rita had had to carry this awful burden by herself. 'So what happens now?'

'Eventually I'll be able to leave here. I'll have to get a job. It's been a while since I had any money in my pocket, though if I do a bit of shopping in the village for the patients who can't get about, they often slip me a few bob. I haven't been able to buy you a Christmas present in return for those lovely beads.' Rita sniffed again. 'People have said I should get compensation from Priddy's Hard for what happened. But I've made a few enquiries and apparently not. I'd already had warnings about my clumsy behaviour and the smell of drink on me, so it's my own fault. Pixie, I'm just so pleased I didn't seriously harm anyone else.' She looked at Pixie with her huge dark eyes and said, 'Except you. I'm convinced

Sadie came early and you had such an awful time because you were running around after me.' She tightened her grip on Pixie's hand. 'I'm not going back to my mother's house.'

Pixie said, 'You don't need to worry about me or Sadie. We're both fine and that's all that matters. But where will you live?' She frowned. Then her eyes lit up. 'Maybe you could live with us.'

'One day at a time, Pixie. This place is one of a kind. I'm happy and safe here, but when I get out, it'll be different. I'll feel different. The wonderful doctors here have even thought of that. There are special sessions designed to help people like me get their confidence back. I'll need to come to terms with myself and the way people react to me. Who knows what the future holds?'

Pixie squeezed Rita's good arm. 'How did you get to be so clever?'

'Enough about me, except I need you to get some of my clothes for me. Could you do that? Could you also try to put Mum off coming to see me? Deep down she knows the truth, but she'll fight to the end to protect Malcolm.'

'I'll send Bob round to your mum's,' Pixie said. 'He's good with people. Comes of working on the markets, I expect.'

Rita laughed. 'Promise me you'll come again, and not just to bring me clothes.'

'You try and keep me away,' said Pixie. Then, looking towards the main buildings, she said, 'C'mon, let's go and get a cuppa. I can tell you all the gossip on the way. About Marlene, Bob's assistant, she's got a little kiddie. And Em and little James – he's the light of her life. Babies certainly bring their love with them, Rita. And I ain't seen hide nor hair of me mum.' She sighed. 'I don't half miss her.' Then she brightened. 'I'm going to see Cal's sister tomorrow.' With her arm still tucked into her friend's, Pixie walked towards where Bob and her daughter were waiting.

Chapter Twenty-six

Bob helped Pixie climb into the front seat of the van.

'I'm so excited about this,' she said, as he passed her the sleeping child, wrapped up against the cold. 'Do you think Cal's sister will like me?'

'Of course she will.' He got in beside her and started up the engine. 'Are you sure you're not too tired after the visit to Rita?'

He was fond of Rita, had enjoyed her company and was relieved she and Pixie had at last seen each other after the factory blast, but he was not looking forward to this visit to Ruth.

'I'm more worried about you taking time off from the market.' Pixie was looking at him.

He brushed his fingers through his wayward hair. It was a sunny day, cold, but the sun more than made up for all the frost they'd had lately. 'Marlene can handle the stall. She only needs a bit of help with setting it up and I've done that. If she was three or four inches taller she'd do the lot herself. I must teach that girl to drive,' he said. Marlene was a woman in a million, he thought.

'You think a lot of her, don't you?'

He glanced at her with a smile. 'Yes, but I . . .' He stopped. There was a sudden silence between them. Damn! He'd nearly told her he loved her. This wasn't the right time to be declaring his feelings. He was second best to a man he believed to be dead. Why couldn't he accept that?

'Bob, I don't take your help for granted,' she said. 'One day I'll pay you back for everything you've done for me.'

The problem was she still loved Cal and she was finding it difficult to get over him. He was silent as he drove out onto the main road. In bringing Pixie to meet Cal's sister he hoped the American woman would be able to clear up the mystery of Cal's disappearance. Pixie would then be able to move on. Life was for the living. Bob sighed. The dead mustn't be allowed to take first place in his and Pixie's relationship.

Bob watched the traffic passing and saw the devastation the bombs had wreaked. Lines of houses, then a gap like a pulled tooth. Streets piled high with rubble, impassable.

There'd still been parties to celebrate the New Year, though. Spirit of England, Bob thought. Always hope for the future. But what about his future, with Pixie and Sadie?

Lying in bed on New Year's Eve he'd heard the fog-horns blowing from the tugs, ships and boats in the harbour, heralding 1944. From the street had come singing: 'Roll Out The Barrel', 'Auld Lang Syne'. There'd been laughter and children shrieking joyously.

In the morning Pixie and he had wished each other a happy New Year. He'd handed her a small package and waited excitedly while she opened it. It was a silver necklace. A heart-shaped locket on a chain.

'You can put a photo of Sadie in it and keep her close to your heart,' he'd told her. 'I didn't buy you a Christmas present – you can't call a pram a proper present – so I hope this makes up for it.' He'd looked at her expectantly. 'You see, I never expected that lovely rug you made for me.'

Now she was fingering the necklace. It looked lovely around her slim, pale neck.

It seemed that in next to no time they were on the outskirts of Chichester and he could see the spire of the cathedral.

'Do you know where to go?' Pixie asked.

'More or less. At least, I know where Oak Road is. Old Oaks Guesthouse can't be far along that road. When we get there I'll wait until the door opens, then leave. I'm sure you'll both have a great deal to talk about so I'll pick you up from the end of the road at four.'

She nodded. He could see her nerves were taking over now.

The house was large, terraced, with huge front windows and a gravelled front garden. A sort of shooting-break with wood around the windows and back door was parked on the gravel. A sign swung from the centre of the porch. The house looked clean and inviting. The whole road seemed to take in lodgers, for Bob had noticed more than a few guesthouses, their signs swinging in the light wind.

'It'll be all right,' Bob said, holding the still sleeping child while she alighted onto the pavement.

'I wish you were coming in with me,' Pixie said, taking Sadie from him. Then she waited while he passed her the bag containing the baby things that had to travel everywhere with her.

'That wouldn't be right,' he said. 'I'd be an outsider and a distraction.' He pushed his glasses up on his nose and turned away.

*

As Pixie faced the front door she saw the curtain at the side window drop back into place. At least someone was in. The door opened. She heard the van glide away and she was left facing a woman with a tired face but a welcoming smile.

'Come in. I'm Ruth and I want you to know you're very welcome, Pixie. I was so glad to hear from you, as Cal had told me all about you. He didn't give me your address, though, so I had no way of contacting you.'

All the while she was talking, in her soft American accent, she was pushing Pixie through a warm, carpeted hall towards a large kitchen at the back of the house. Pixie sat on a chair with what looked like a home-made cushion on it.

Ruth lit the gas beneath the kettle and took down bone china cups. Sadie began a thin wail.

'Oh, let me take her.' Ruth's face lit up as she looked at the baby.

Pixie handed over her child. 'Sadie's getting to be quite a little lump.'

Ruth didn't answer. Pixie could see she was captivated by the child, touching her fingers and talking to her in hushed tones. The baby stared up at her and stopped snuffling.

'She's so like Cal,' Ruth murmured.

Pixie looked about her. Everything shone. You could see your face in the polished table. The carpet beneath the dining area ran to about a foot from the edge of the gleaming wood floor. Pixie could smell lavender polish. A Welsh dresser overflowed with blue and white crockery and fine bone china. It was a kitchen out of a dream, Pixie thought. The woman had put her heart into her home.

When Ruth looked up, Pixie saw that her eyes were moist. 'My husband's in the air force, an Englishman. England's my home now. We've been trying for ages to have a child. That's why I run the guesthouse. Takes my mind off things.' She suddenly looked guilty. 'Oh, I'm sorry. You don't want to know about me. You came because of Cal.'

She gave Sadie to her mother, then left the kitchen to return moments later with a letter. She handed it to Pixie, after taking back the child so Pixie could read it properly.

It was from the United States Navy. Cal's ship had been torpedoed by a U-boat. The destroyer had broken in two. There were survivors. Cal was not among them. He'd been awarded a Purple Heart.

Pixie sat with the letter in her hand for a long time. At first the words swam around in her brain, like tadpoles in a pond. When the tadpoles eventually settled into words, she knew this piece of paper signalled the end of everything she'd hoped for.

'Would you like to drink this?'

Ruth, the baby on her hip, had made tea and was holding out the cup to Pixie, as though she was a child.

'At least I know now,' Pixie said. Her head and heart felt as though they were being crushed in a vice.

'I wish I could have saved you some pain.'

'Every day I waited for letters,' Pixie said. 'I didn't approach you before because I kept hoping . . .' And then it was as though she had come out of a dream. She looked at Ruth, took the cup and drank slowly.

'I know,' said Ruth.

'I worked at Priddy's armaments factory. Towards the end, near her birth, I was in no fit state . . .'

'I didn't find out until recently,' Ruth said. Then, 'Look, this has been a terrible shock. Why don't you go upstairs and lie down? I can look after Madam. When I first had the news I wanted to be by myself. We were very close, you know, my brother and I. When I knew he was going to spend time in England – did you know he planned on coming back after the war?'

Pixie shook her head.

'I came over here to be with him. I met Roy, my

husband, never dreaming this place would end up being my home.'

Pixie allowed herself to be led upstairs to a room at the back of the house, all blue chintz.

'I'll give you an hour or so, then we'll have something to eat and we'll talk.'

Pixie nodded. How very like Cal his sister was, kind, sensitive. The door closed and she took off her shoes, then lay on a quilt that also smelt of lavender.

She slept.

Later, when they were sitting together in the front of the van, Bob saw that Pixie had dark circles around her eyes. 'Are you more settled now you know what happened?'

'I am. She's a nice lady, Bob, but I wish I could have met her in better circumstances. She told me to visit whenever I want. She loves Sadie – they haven't been lucky enough to have children.'

'What about the parents?'

'Ruth's going to write and tell them she's met me.'

'Will Ruth visit you?'

'Probably not. She's busy all the year round – the guesthouse can't be left. Even now, in January, she has only one empty room. Her husband's in the RAF in Yorkshire. She works hard. She used to have a woman come in to help, but war work pays better wages than cleaning so now she does everything herself.'

All this was small-talk, thought Bob. He wanted to know if Pixie was ready to move forward with her life. Sadie needed two parents, ready to grab the future with both hands.

He turned to her. Her face was white, the tears silently running down her cheeks. Bob knew he should try to comfort her, but his eyes went towards the road ahead.

Pixie stared out of the window. She could just make out the chalk hill at Portsdown. She knew Bob didn't dare drive fast – it was dark and all vehicle lights were dimmed due to the blackout – even though he had to get up early for the market at Gosport tomorrow. He'd already told her he couldn't afford not to go but it was doubtful he'd get much custom. The couple of months after Christmas were always slow. People didn't have the money after spending what little they had on the festivities.

She wiped the back of her hand across her eyes and looked down at her sleeping child. Ruth would have made a lovely mum. The silence in the vehicle was heavy with unspoken thoughts.

'I thought I heard someone next door in my old house,' she said suddenly.

'That would be the owner,' Bob said. 'Your former landlord. He's had some bomb damage in that posh house he lives in so while it's being fixed he's decided to stay there.'

Pixie said, 'How on earth do you find out these things?'

'By keeping my ears and eyes open.'

Pixie smiled. 'In that case, I don't suppose you know where my mum is?'

'I noticed there was no Christmas card from her . . .'

'I couldn't send her one either because I didn't know where to send it.'

'I've no idea where she is. She'll have a surprise seeing Sadie, though.'

They were passing the bottom of Ann's Hill now and soon would be home.

She'd cried a lot in that comfy bed in Chichester. Then she'd slept until Ruth had brought her a cup of tea. At the bottom of her heart she'd known she'd never see Cal again.

She stared at Bob's profile. He seemed withdrawn. He needed support now that the lean buying time had arrived. Her going around with a miserable face would help neither of them. She'd make him a sandwich and some cocoa before he went to bed as a thank-you for taking her to see Ruth and Rita. In the morning she might even bake him a Victoria sponge, his favourite, if she could find the ingredients.

Tomorrow she decided to surprise him by walking to the market to visit him, pushing Sadie in her new pram.

Chapter Twenty-seven

The wolf-whistle from the lad on the building site at the top of Parham Road added to Pixie's joy at being out on such a lovely morning. She wore her black tailored coat, which fitted her again now that her bump had gone, and her favourite black high heels, thankful that her swollen feet and ankles had magically disappeared after Sadie's arrival. Her broken skin had healed weeks ago and she'd rinsed her hair with a chamomile shampoo to help mellow the harsh poisoned yellow and restore her own blonde tones.

She took pride in the beautiful pram and her lovely baby asleep inside.

When she reached the market running through the high street it wasn't as busy as usual. Some of the regular stallholders had disappeared. The space near the bombed town hall, where the fishmonger usually plied his trade, was empty. And the man and his wife who sold bedding near the Gas Board weren't there.

There was a crowd of people waiting for a lorry to turn in the middle of the road and Pixie had to wait. Two large elderly women weren't helping matters, blocking the pavement as they gossiped. The women's voices were strident.

'It's called the Jungvolk, and it's ten-year-olds being brainwashed for the Hitler Youth. I tell you that man is evil.'

'Course he is – else we wouldn't be at war with him, Marge.'

'But there's men round here being un-god-like just the same, Ada.'

'Whatever do you mean?'

'Him as got that Marlene girl working for him, the one no better than she should be,' said the taller of the two.

'Her with the kiddie?'

'Unmarried.' The woman sniffed. 'Shouldn't wonder if she ain't his fancy piece. And now he's got another young bit into trouble. Living with him.'

Pixie felt her cheeks burning. It was Bob they were discussing, and herself. She tried to see what the women looked like.

The woman wearing the scabby fox fur was all ears and asked, 'And they ain't married?'

'Why pay for the goods when you've already sampled them, Marge?'

'No!'

'She had her baby just before Christmas.'

Pixie was feeling sick. She couldn't move. And the lorry was now backing onto the pavement.

'I know all this for gospel because my Petey lives at the end of their road. Christmas Day they was all together, laughing and joking. Well, I'll tell you this for nothing. I wouldn't buy another thing off the dirty bugger, not even if it was the bargain of the season. And I shall tell everyone about him lowering the tone of this market.'

'Get out of the way!' A man's voice cut through, immediately silencing the crowd. Pixie felt the pram handle wrenched from her hands and pulled back, nearly knocking down the canvas side-wall of the wool man's stall. Skeins of wool fell to the ground and Pixie stumbled on her heels, holding on to an upright pole to steady herself.

'You all right, love?' The lorry driver was peering out of his wound-down side window, his face ashen.

'Yes,' said Pixie. A young woman holding on to a small child's reins was grabbing at the pram. 'Thank you,' said Pixie. 'I don't know what would have happened if you hadn't taken control.'

'He shouldn't have come down so far into the town when the market's here,' came the woman's reply. 'No room to turn, them lorries. You sure you're all right?'

Pixie smiled at her gratefully and composed herself.

'Could have knocked your pram over,' said the young woman, as the little boy managed to twist the reins tightly around himself. She bent to unravel him.

Pixie looked for the two women who had been talking about the Hitler Youth but they had disappeared. 'Thank you,' she said again to the woman.

Sadie had slept peacefully through the drama, and as Pixie looked down at her, her heart swelled with love for her daughter.

She stood for a moment amid the noise and bustle. Then, instead of making her way down to Bemisters Lane where Bob had his regular pitch, she walked, this time more slowly and thoughtfully, back past the rubble that had once been Gosport's town hall, turned into Spring Garden Lane, then Forton Road and went home.

The wireless was playing 'Don't Get Around Much Anymore' by the Ink Spots and Gladys was humming along. She'd finished mopping the floor, had dusted the shelves at the back of the bar and checked the evening's float money. She looked at the wall clock: she had forty minutes to get changed before opening time. A nice cup of tea first, though, she thought, and maybe take the weight off her feet for a while.

There was a bang from upstairs and glass shattered. Voices were raised in anger – Stephen and Jeremy at it again, like cat and dog. Gladys laughed to herself as she climbed the stairs. She was used to the petty arguments between her employers, but working together in the bar, they were polite and considerate towards each other. By the time Cora arrived for her evening shift they'd be like a couple of lovebirds again. Gladys was very fond of both of them.

Sometimes, late at night from the window of her room, she stood watching the dark waves and the outlines of the ships moored in the Dockyard. The car ferry, the shipyard and her daughter, whom she longed to be with more than anything else in the world, were across the water. But she was scared of rejection. Just once too often she'd left her daughter to clear up her debts. Suppose Pixie didn't want to see her? She was a ferry boat ride away – so near yet so far.

There was a monster of a stove in her room and a huge stone sink, almost big enough to bathe in. She filled the kettle and put it on to boil, hearing the pop, hiss and splutter of the blue and yellow flames as the gas ignited.

She'd already done the morning shift and, if the truth be told, wanted to curl up on the bed and sleep like a hedgehog, hibernating, for the rest of the winter.

She opened the wardrobe door and took out a battered shoebox. Her ration book and birth certificate were on top but beneath them was her post office savings book.

That, she hoped, was her way back to Pixie. She'd need to work hard to deserve her daughter's love and forgiveness.

The sums paid in were growing nicely. She was working this evening because Colin, the night barman, wasn't in, and she would have more money to save. The drinks she had been bought this morning she had taken in money instead. A few months back she would have swallowed anything offered her.

The kettle was boiling and she made a pot of tea. Another crash rent the air. A squeal, then silence. Gladys loved her employers. They'd given her a chance when she was down and out. She opened her door, walked quietly along to the end room and listened. Both men were talking softly now. She gave a small sigh of relief and went back to her own room. She scooped up her personal items and put them back into the shoebox. A photograph caught her eye.

A little girl in a blue dress, her hair cut with a crooked fringe, sitting on a bench. Her daughter, Pixie.

What a rotten mother she had been, she thought once more. All her daughter had ever wanted was to be loved and she had pushed her aside for a string of no-hopers, men who didn't care about her but had exploited her. She hadn't been there for Pixie, as any decent mother should.

Well, this time it would be different. Much as she wanted to, Gladys wasn't going within a mile of her daughter until she could show her she'd changed. And the first thing she had to do was pay Pixie back for all the debts she'd have settled since Gladys had left. She didn't mind how hard she had to work, but she would do it. She kissed the photograph. 'I'll make it up to you, my love, if you'll let me,' she whispered. She put the photo safely inside the savings book and closed the wardrobe door on the shoebox.

She was hanging a blue dress for that evening over the back of a chair when a knock on the door startled her. She opened it to find Jeremy with a puffy, tear-stained face.

'Have you got a cup of tea for a wounded warrior?' He was gazing longingly at the teapot and the steam curling from the spout.

'Come on in,' she said. 'I'm about to soak my feet so

you'll have to pour it yourself.' She collected the enamel bowl from beneath the sink and the packet of salt from the cupboard. Using the rest of the kettle's water with a dash of cold from the tap, she placed the bowl on the floor.

Gladys sat on the upright chair and put both feet into the bowl of salted hot water. 'This'll set me up for the evening shift,' she said.

Jeremy ran his long fingers through his red hair and then began pouring the tea. He smelt of woodland scent. He pulled his silk dressing-gown around him, tying it tightly around his slim waist.

'Well, did you come for a cuppa or to moan about Stephen, who's too good for you?'

'Gladys, you have no idea how that man aggravates me.'

'I've seen you flirt with that young sailor. Then you get the hump when the one man who cares about you gets cross.' She took a sip of her tea and murmured, 'Aaah.'

'Other men don't matter. It's Stephen I love and deep down he knows that.' He shifted from one foot to the other. 'I've . . . well, we have a favour to ask. Stephen has suggested a weekend in the country. It would give us a chance to iron out a few of our difficulties.'

He paused. Gladys grinned at him. She knew, in her,

both men sensed a friend who didn't judge them the way the law did. A homosexual relationship was illegal. But this was Portsmouth and men working together for long periods often formed attachments that were frowned upon. Gladys and her 'live and let live' attitude made her a trustworthy ally.

'Yes,' she said.

'Yes it would do us good, or yes you'll look after this place? It would mean extra money for you.'

Gladys knew then that the Fates were on her side and willing to help her reunite with her daughter. 'You'd better tell Cora – she's been here longer than me and I don't want any arguments.'

'Believe me, Cora won't want the extra work.' He stirred his tea and put the spoon on the saucer. Gladys breathed a sigh of relief.

Later, Gladys asked Cora if Stephen had been down to talk to her about the proposed weekend.

'We'll be all right, you and me,' Cora said. Strands of platinum hair were falling from her Victory Roll. 'Oh, look.'

A man was striding towards the bar, looking at Gladys. He ordered a pint and she served him. He took his drink and sat in the alcove. Every so often Gladys could feel his eyes on her.

'He fancies you,' Cora whispered.

Gladys felt the old stirrings. He was possibly a bit younger than her, and good-looking. Most men were in the forces and what was left were old men or young boys. Gladys thought of the current song, 'They're Either Too Young Or Too Old' and smiled to herself. She wondered how this one had escaped.

'You could have him,' Cora whispered, after he'd been to the bar and bought Gladys a drink as well as ordering another half for himself.

All the chat-up lines had come out, including 'When do you finish?' She'd had to lean across the bar to hear him above the noise made by a crowd of sailors, laughing and joking.

It had been so long since she'd been with a man. Surely a bit of a kiss and a cuddle after work wouldn't harm anyone. Barmaid's perks, that was.

She was weighing up the pros and cons when Cora said, 'You working here or are you just gonna stand in the way?'

The evening went quickly. Stephen and Jeremy didn't come down, and when the man came to the bar to buy her another drink and have a chat, he said, 'I'll wait on the corner.'

Gladys looked at his sensual lips and strong hands,

imagining them roaming over her body, then surprised herself: 'Don't bother. I expect you've got a missus at home. I'd get back to her if I was you.'

She walked quickly away, closely followed by Cora, who said, 'I can't believe you just did that.'

Her aim in life now was to get back to Pixie, not go out with any man who chatted her up.

Cora was looking at her as though she was mad. She pushed against the bar's stable door and flounced out into the room, where she picked up Mogs, who was asleep on a chair.

'While you're out there messing around with that cat, you could empty the ashtrays,' Gladys said. Sometimes Cora drove her mad playing with Mogs when she should have been working. She looked along the bar to where the bloke who had tried it on with her was still staring at her. He was certainly a good-looking man, but that stuff was behind her now. She wanted to get back to Pixie. Gladys knew that her refusal had brought her one step closer to a reunion.

Chapter Twenty-eight

The front door flew back so hard that it smacked against the wall. Pixie hauled the pram over the doorstep and pushed it into the front room. Sadie was still asleep.

'Just you stay like that while I get some things together,' she whispered, wiping her own tear-stained face.

In the red phone box at the top of Spring Garden Lane she had made a telephone call to Ruth, begging her to come to Gosport and collect her. She'd been cool and calm, and had only broken down once she had walked away.

Ruth would collect her from outside the Criterion picture house within two hours.

'I can work for you,' Pixie had said, 'if in return Sadie and I can stay in your spare room.'

Ruth had had to phone her back, for Pixie had no money, only a few pennies. It had surprised her that Ruth had agreed so quickly. After all, they didn't know each other that well.

As Pixie walked around the house that had been her home she felt very tearful. But the sooner she'd packed up what she needed for herself and her child, the sooner she could leave. The last thing she wanted was to meet Bob, face to face, as she was fleeing from his home. There was no time to sit down and write him a letter – she would do that later.

With Sadie's things packed into a large holdall, a change of clothes for herself in a carrier bag and the baby in her arms, Pixie walked down the street and out of Bob's life.

Near the Criterion there was a café. Pixie ordered a cup of tea from the harassed waitress and waited, keeping an eye on the front of the picture house.

When Ruth drove up she asked no questions, simply stowed the bags in the boot of the car and ushered Pixie in with the baby on her lap.

Pixie managed to hold back her tears until they got to Fareham. Then she knew she had to be honest with Ruth. 'Bob's losing money because he's taking care of me. It just isn't fair. He can cope with the nasty insinuations people make about Marlene – she's an unmarried mother, too, and works for him – because they don't live together. But now people are saying my child belongs to him and we're living in sin. His customers are leaving him. I have to go. I'll ruin him otherwise.'

Ruth didn't speak for a long time. Then she said quietly, 'It sounds to me as though you're more than just a little fond of Bob.'

'No!' Pixie said quickly. But memories returned of him standing by her bed with a cup of tea in his hand, of him being there when her precious baby was born and always making sure she had something to eat. And she realized she did care for him. Not in the giddy way she'd loved Cal, but in a safe, settled way. Did she really want to leave him? No, she didn't. Did she want to ruin him by living in his house? No, of course not. She had to leave, had to stand on her own two feet.

'Cal wouldn't want you and his baby to be alone for ever, you know,' Ruth said.

How understanding she was, Pixie thought. Ruth ran her fingers through her hair, reminding her that Cal used to do it in exactly the same way. 'I have to do what I feel is right and proper,' she said. 'I can't bring my daughter up at the expense of other people's welfare.'

'Well, if you really want to work for me, it won't be easy. But I'd be glad to have you.'

Pixie looked down at her sleeping child. It was going to be a hard road ahead.

But she was a woman, not a little girl. She pushed back the tears. She was a mother to this lovely child. So why, oh, why did she so want to feel her own mother's arms about her?

'You can hear the band from here,' Rita said. 'If enemy planes come over I hope the Jerries don't hear the music in the village hall. We'll all be goners if they do.'

'Wait up,' said Harry. 'I've just trod in a bleeding cow pat.'

'Is it your real foot or the false one?' asked Joannie.

'It don't matter, does it? Still smells the same!' Harry was bending down trying to wipe off the mess with a handful of grass.

'Whose idea was it to come over the fields instead of walking along the lanes?' Joannie wondered.

'Whose do you think?' They looked at Rita, who couldn't stop laughing.

'Oh, stop moaning and let's get to the village. I never realized how dark it gets out in the country.' She strode off. 'Last one pays for the lemonades.'

Eventually, arm in arm, the three discovered the five-bar gate that led to the church hall where the weekly dance was in progress. RAF Copington was hosting and the American airmen had provided refreshments.

'First, the lavatory – I need to tidy up – then a drink and a dance, in that order,' said Rita. As they piled inside she could smell perfume and body odour amid the excitement.

Joannie pulled her along, shouting to Harry, 'You fill the plates with some of that gorgeous food.'

Rita looked at the two trestle tables laden with bread, jacket potatoes wrapped in clean tea towels, plates of sliced tinned ham and dishes of tinned fruit. There was also bread pudding and apple pie. Rita licked her lips. She was being fed very well at the hospital and knew that the effects of the TNT she'd been handling at Priddy's Hard had now practically disappeared. But rationing had taken its toll and she was always hungry. The Americans brought in tinned foods that were no longer in the shops and Rita had spied a dish of pineapple.

The large hall was crowded with servicemen and girls, the ceiling and walls covered with bunting. Rita liked the look and sound of the band, a group of middle-aged men and a stunning young singer in a red dress. They were giving their rendition of 'That Old Black Magic'.

In the lavatory Rita peered at her face in the fly-specked mirror. She remembered the first time she'd been allowed to look at herself after the accident. She hadn't recognized herself. For weeks afterwards she'd despaired and was given medication to sleep and help her through the day. Gradually, with the aid of Pixie and her friends at the hospital, she'd come to like the person in the mirror, the new Rita, older, wiser and glad to be alive.

Soon she would be able to leave the hospital permanently. She was scared, but every outing gave her more confidence.

Joannie said, 'You really do have the prettiest hair, you know.'

Rita had allowed it to grow and wore it hanging down one side of her face, like Veronica Lake. After the blast it had grown back soft and wavy, and wearing it like that disguised the scarring that remained.

Pan Stik blended with her skin tone, and she'd got quite professional at drawing her high arched eyebrows. Her natural eyebrows had been burned off and now refused to grow back.

Her hand, minus an index fingertip, caused her no problems at all, for she'd learned to use her third finger as her main digit. As now, when she smoothed a little blue eye shadow on her lid. Rita glanced at Joannie brushing her hair free of tangles. They had become close friends and Joannie was teaching her to laugh at herself, as Harry did about his lost limb.

'Your hair's nice, too,' Rita said. Long and dark, it

complemented the strawberry wool dress her friend wore. Rita, in pale blue, with shoulder pads and box pleats, stood sideways to look at the line of her body.

'Well, now we've finished admiring each other,' Joannie said, 'let's go and get an American to dance with – after we've eaten, of course.'

Harry was standing at the end of the table with three plates, one already filled, and was munching a sandwich. He pointed to a table and two empty chairs. 'Got us seats,' he said. 'Look after my food.' He went in search of another chair. Near the plates were three glasses of what looked like fruit punch.

Three young American soldiers were joking and larking about. Joannie stood behind them, waiting her turn to add food to her plate.

'Come to the front, darlin'.' The red-haired one had a cheeky face. Another didn't look old enough to be in the services, with his beautiful blue eyes and blond buzz-cut hair. He saw Rita behind Joannie and stepped aside to make space for her, so she, too, could choose her food.

'Thank you,' said Joannie and Rita, simultaneously.

A tall, dark-haired man picked up a plate of biscuits. 'We call these cookies. You call them biscuits.'

'I suppose so,' said Joannie. He was looking at her as though he could eat her.

'Would you like to dance?'

'Why, yes.'

Rita watched her friend put down her plate and sail off onto the dance floor in the American's arms. The red-haired man sidled up to Rita and asked her to dance.

'I'd love to,' she said, putting her plate on a chair. He took her arm and when they were on the floor he stared hard at her face beneath the fall of her dark hair. His face burned suddenly red. They were dancing to a slow song. Rita wanted to talk to him but didn't know how to, for it was obvious the scar had upset him. She wasn't sure if he was repelled by it, so she tried to keep as far away as possible while going through the dance steps mechanically. She felt a wave of relief wash over her when the music stopped and he returned her to her friends.

Immediately he let go of her she pushed through the straggling dancers on the floor and made for the lavatory.

In the cubicle she cried, her forehead pressed against the cold white tiles. The hospital had done everything it could for her and soon she was to leave. She'd thought she would be immune to how others reacted to her, but the young American had shown her this wasn't so. She was far from immune.

Through her tears she heard Joannie's voice, 'Where are you? Don't make me kick open every cubicle door to find you. Joe's just told me about the dance. He didn't know what to say to you. It's the first time he's ever seen scarring on a woman and he's eighteen years old – a child, Rita. He's as upset as hell!'

Rita wrenched open the door. 'So I'm to be the strong one and make small-talk about my ugliness?'

'Don't be daft,' said Joannie. 'Of course you have to be the strong one! If you just go on telling yourself that you're ugly, you'll get nowhere at all.'

'I want to go home.' Deep down she knew she was being childish.

'No. We'll all go home, back to the hospital together.' Joannie put her arms around Rita. 'Have you thought that that lad may go to the war and die? You have your whole life ahead of you. And despite the scarring,' she turned Rita around to face the mirror, 'you're a very attractive woman. If you can't see that you must be blind.'

Rita saw her glistening hair, her good features and trim figure.

Joannie was right. Even with the scar she was good-looking. 'I should have said something to him,' she said. 'Made it easy for him. I . . . I just lost my confidence.'

'You'll need confidence to go back to Priddy's Hard.'

Rita wiped fresh tears from her eyes. 'I'm not going back to work there. I can't. I don't want the girls' pity.'

Rosie Archer

'You won't be pitied. It'll be the bravest thing you'll ever do. Besides, Priddy's Hard is the main supplier of ammunition, shells and mines, along with Bedenham and Frater.'

'I know that,' said Rita, wondering why on earth her friend was yakking on about the work she'd been doing when the accident occurred.

Joannie pushed open the cubicle doors, making sure they were alone in the lavatory. She came back to stand in front of Rita and put her finger to her lips, signalling silence. 'Because of where I work and what I do, I've been privileged to hear information that's about to change the course of this war. You mustn't breathe a word about this and I'm only telling you in the strictest confidence.'

Rita waited.

'Gosport is about to play a leading role in what's to be called D-Day.'

'D-Day?'

'Ssh,' said Joannie. 'Walls have ears. Whisper!' She leaned in closer and spoke quietly. 'I can't go into the details but men and supplies are leaving the south coast to cross the Channel as an invasion fleet.' She paused. 'So men and women who did good jobs at Priddy's are needed for more twelve-hour shifts. The factory is pulling out all the stops. We're going to get that bloody Hitler!'

Rita stared at her. Was this privileged information really true? But Joannie wouldn't lie to her. 'How d'you know?'

Joannie leaned in closer. 'Our hospital will be needed for those who come back from this operation in a damaged state. We're trying to get current patients home as soon as possible.'

Rita felt as though her safety net had broken. 'Do you know how terrible it will be for me to go back to the place where this happened?' She pointed to her face.

'Yes, but your carelessness caused that. Your confidence is going to make you stronger.'

Rita digested her words. 'Are you sure?'

Joannie nodded. 'We've done all we can for you, Rita. It's your turn now. Get back in the world and enjoy your life.'

Rita put her arm through Joannie's and took a deep breath. Together they opened the door and went back into the dance hall.

Joannie deliberately steered her towards the end table. Rita gulped. The Americans were drinking punch and chatting amiably to Harry. Which meant, of course, that Rita had to face the red-haired young man once more.

'Confidence,' whispered Joannie.

'Ah, here they come.' Harry eyed Rita, who smiled at him to let him know she was all right. The dark-haired American immediately claimed Joannie to dance again.

Rita sipped her drink, which was mostly orange juice. The red-haired man, Joe, stood beside her.

'Look, I'm sorry about the silent treatment. I'd really like to start again. Will you dance with me?' He took away her drink and put it on the table. She looked at Harry for reassurance and he winked. 'My name is Joe, and I don't want any cracks about GI Joe,' he said.

He put out his arms and Rita slid into them.

'There, am I forgiven?'

He had a fresh cologne smell mixed with the earthy scent of his uniform. Rita began to relax. 'I'm Rita . . . The misunderstanding wasn't all your fault,' she said.

She looked around the crowded noisy room but it was like they were cocooned in each other's company and other people hardly existed.

The band was playing another slow tune. Rita had thought her days of being held in a man's arms were over, yet here she was, dancing close to someone who wasn't really much younger than her and she was enjoying it immensely.

A sudden memory came to her of her stepfather,

breathing heavily outside her bedroom door, wanting to enter, yet guessing she'd probably wedged a chair behind the handle – pushing it open would wake his wife. Rita shivered. She'd almost let her fear of him destroy her.

Perhaps it would be nice, after all, to go back to the armaments depot. It would be good to think she could help with the exhausting and dangerous work at Priddy's Hard and be among her friends again.

When the music finished and Joe took her back to her friends, they were ready to leave.

'Why don't I take you home to the hospital? We've got a jeep that'll drop you off.'

'Fine,' said Harry. Rita was quite content to do what the others wanted as long as she didn't have to step around any more cowpats. She looked up and caught Joe staring at her. She felt herself blush.

'In that case we can have another drink and another dance,' said Joannie, and was immediately whisked away. Harry looked rather pleased, as he was talking earnestly to a local girl with long dark hair.

'What are we waiting for?' Joe had handed Rita a drink that looked like lemonade but tasted of water. She put it down, and he whirled her around to a fast Glenn Miller number.

Rita thought the minutes passed too quickly. Soon she

was arm in arm with Joannie, and Harry was walking along, trying not to limp, with the village girl, Bess.

The jeep was outside. Laughing, they all crowded into it. Rita was glad of the jeep's cover as the winter wind had sharpened and a few flakes of snow were floating around. She shivered and Joe put his arm around her.

They dropped off Bess first. She waved, then ran up the path to a small cottage. Harry tucked a piece of paper that had her address on it inside his wallet.

Rita hadn't seen the American who was driving the jeep but he had a pretty girl sitting at his side. The girl was quiet and didn't contribute to the chat and laughter.

When they drove through the hospital gates, Joannie showed her pass so the vehicle could ferry her and the dark American to the nurses' quarters.

'You want dropping off somewhere quiet, I can pick you up in half an hour,' the driver suggested.

'I'll make you coffee in the ward's sitting room, Joe,' Rita said. 'We won't be discovered if we keep our voices down.'

'I never heard that.' Joannie laughed. Rita knew the sitting room was out of bounds after dark. Two minutes later Joannie and her partner were dropped off. At the next building, Rita and Joe got out.

Rita was trying hard not to giggle as she walked up the

steps, her arm through Joe's. Once inside, she threw her coat onto an armchair and lit a small oil lamp after making sure all the blackout curtains were drawn. She was about to go through to the kitchen area when Joe grabbed her and said, 'I don't want coffee. I'd rather have you.' His hat lay on the table. He pulled her towards him and together they fell onto the sofa where he began kissing her. Gently he placed his fingertips on her breast. She could feel the heat of his hand on her body, through the material.

'If you want me to stop, you only have to say,' he began, but Rita silenced him with another kiss. It had been so long since a man had desired her. He held her tighter, stretching his arms and legs around her body, enfolding her. His tongue met hers and her fingers explored the unexpected silkiness of his hair, the width of his shoulders. Then he was kissing her eyes, the tip of her nose, his tongue exploring her mouth. A warm sensation shot up from deep inside her as she realized just how much she wanted him.

Their mouths met again, this time with no reluctance, as he pulled her dress over her head. His kisses were as familiar to her as if she had been kissing him for years.

Rita wanted him inside her. She opened her eyes and saw him above her, his face smiling, his eyes tender. He came into her gradually, carefully, his body poised, his face buried in her hair, and they lay together, still, for a moment, until his movements began.

The pleasure rose furiously inside her. She felt completely at his mercy until the swift spasm of his passion ended. She heard him whimper and call her name and then he wetly kissed her eyes, her mouth, and flopped beside her, exhausted.

Rita wanted to thank him. He had made her whole again.

She lay with him, hating that at any moment he would have to get up and go.

'We're leaving tomorrow afternoon,' he said. 'I don't know where. All I do know is it's down south to make the beaches secure. Can I write to you?'

'I'd like that,' Rita said. He looked at his watch. The moment she had been dreading had arrived. Without him saying another word she got off the sofa and dressed herself. He leaned back and watched her and she felt his eyes devouring her. Then he tidied himself.

'You will write, won't you?'

Those were his last words before Rita heard the return of the jeep. She walked hand in hand with him to the door and watched him climb into the back of the vehicle.

She was still watching long after it had left, her smile reaching deep into her heart.

Chapter Twenty-nine

'Hello, I'm home.' Bob put down the bunch of blooms. There was a sprig of Michaelmas daisies, some sprays of red berries, a few late bronze chrysanthemums and, mixed in with the greenery, some early daffodil buds. He thought Pixie would like the gift. He took off his coat and hung it on the hook behind the front door.

It was cold in the kitchen. Pixie had let the range go out. He left the flowers on the table and looked around. The house felt different. 'Pixie?'

There was no answer. Bob went into the scullery, opened the back door and called again. The thin layer of snow outside was unmarked. Something felt wrong.

She hadn't told him she was going to be out, although, of course, she didn't have to tell him of her movements, did she?

He lit the gas beneath the kettle and switched on the

wireless. 'The White Cliffs Of Dover' was being sung by that other girl singer, not Vera Lynn. He liked Vera Lynn best.

Bob ran some water and began a cold strip wash. Wearing so many clothes to stave off the chill down the market had made him sweat. One of his first chores was to clean himself up. He began singing along to the music and only stopped to clean his teeth.

Then he made some tea and tackled the range. A few firelighters made of paper and some kindling soon brought it back to life. He wondered how long Pixie had been gone. It wasn't like her to let the fire die down.

He wondered whether to put the flowers in a vase or leave them in a bunch. Best to leave them: Pixie would like to arrange them her way.

Bob went back into the scullery to peel some potatoes. There were sausages under the meat safe in the cupboard. Sausage and mash, gravy and peas. Pixie liked mash the way he did it with a bit of marge, milk and a shake of pepper. She'd need something inside to warm her up when she got in. He hummed along to the wireless.

His eyes fell on the Victoria sponge she'd baked for him. He didn't dare eat any for fear of spoiling his main meal.

He thought about his day at the market and while the potatoes went on to boil he emptied his money-belt. The notes and coins spread across the table and he began to count them.

It wasn't long before he'd put back the float for tomorrow and set his profits aside in a tin. He needed more stock.

He thought about Marlene selling six blankets to one buyer. She was a treasure, pretty, too, with her auburn hair trailing down her back, like some fairy-tale princess. If he hadn't had his eye on Pixie for so long he'd have made a play for her long ago. He knew she liked him. Perhaps not in that way now, but at one time it might have worked. All she ever did lately was natter on about that Samuel Golden she'd met at an auction.

Bob swallowed the dregs of his tea and got up to pour more before the pot went cold. 'You can shut up, mate,' he said to the canary. It was busy jumping from one perch to the other, then pecking at its bell.

In the scullery he turned the gas right down beneath the potatoes. He looked at the clock. Ten past seven. Pixie was very late. She didn't like being out in the dark with Sadie. Not even with the pram protecting the little one. The thought of Sadie warmed his heart.

Something worried him.

The pram was in the front room. Surely he'd noticed it when he'd come in.

He went along the passage and pushed the door wider. The pram held only the mattress and pillow. He frowned.

His throat was dry as he took the stairs two at a time and tumbled into Pixie's room. The pile of clean nappies wasn't there. Opening the drawer, he saw it was empty of the usual baby clothes.

His heart thumping wildly, he wrenched open the wardrobe door and saw empty hangers. Pixie had little finery, but her best clothes and decent shoes were no longer in their usual places. Then he pulled open the dressing-table drawer and saw her notebooks were missing. She'd never go anywhere without *them*.

He sat down on her bed and put his head in his hands. She had left him.

But why?

Bob stifled the tears that threatened and tried to recall if he'd done anything to cause her to run away. He shook his head. On the contrary, Pixie had shown her caring side by baking him a sponge cake as a thank-you for taking her to see Rita and Ruth.

So, why had she left?

To the best of his knowledge she had very little money, despite his attempts to give it to her. So who, possibly, had taken her in?

Without the pram, she would need a lift for herself, Sadie and their clothing.

Rita, her best friend, would be unable to put her up at the hospital.

Would someone at Priddy's Hard have offered her a room?

But why hadn't she said something to him? Why hurt him like this?

He'd hoped that after Cal's sister, Ruth, had shown Pixie the letter as proof that he was dead she'd understand the time for mourning was over, and she'd do better to look to the future.

Sudden anger flowed through him.

What more did she expect him to do for her?

He'd done his best to show her he loved her. A deep sigh wrenched at his heart. He'd given her time to get over the death of her lover and she'd played him for a fool.

There wasn't even a note explaining her actions and whereabouts.

Damn the woman! He got up, slammed the door to her room and stormed down the stairs. In the scullery he turned off the gas beneath the potatoes, gathered up the flowers and dumped them in the dustbin in the yard.

In the mirror above the range he looked at himself.

There were dark circles beneath his eyes. He said, to his grim reflection, 'What a bloody idiot you are!', and then, 'You let her get under your skin and then she discards you like a bit of rubbish!'

His mouth tasted dry and sour. He went to the sideboard. Using the opener, he took the top off a bottle of Newcastle brown ale and put it to his lips.

'There you are, love.' Bob folded the blanket, wrapped it in newspaper and passed it across the stall to the elderly woman, at the same time as taking her money. 'Better to keep you warm in bed than a strapping six-footer.' The white-haired woman in her seventies giggled like a girl as she thanked him and walked away.

He picked up his mug of tea and slurped the last of it. God, the weather was bitter today. This morning, setting up the stall, his breath had frozen on his scarf. He looked at Marlene, who was wrapping a gold bangle in a small piece of parachute silk. Paper supplies were still bad and every shop asked the customer if they needed their goods wrapping. Marlene had come by a few yards of silk and hit on the idea of making her gifts look pretty. They were selling well. But she wouldn't take a chance and spend more money than she could afford.

She must have felt Bob looking at her because after

she'd given the man his change she smiled at him and came down to chat.

'Won't be sorry to finish today,' she said. 'Heard from Pixie?'

He sighed. It had been weeks since she'd left him worrying and wondering what he'd done to make her leave. 'Had a letter yesterday,' he said. He served a man with a paperback book, putting the coins in his money-belt.

'She explain why she upped and left?' Marlene stared at him.

He thought for a moment. He wasn't one to bare all to everyone where feelings were concerned, but Marlene was the nearest to a mate he had because he spent all his time working with her. And he needed to unburden himself. He was fed up with being unable to sleep night after night for thinking about Pixie and the little one.

'Said she'd overheard some women saying they were boycotting my stall because of the way I allowed her and the baby,' he coughed, 'and you, to live with and work for me when it ain't right and proper. Apparently this woman was going to tell everyone I was a menace to society.'

Marlene took the money for a set of three place settings. 'Going well, that cutlery,' she said, slipping the cash into her money-belt, then blowing on her fingers. 'I bet the woman was that Marge Sidebotham. You remember

I had a word with her for running off with a paperback under her coat and not paying for it? I caught her up by Walpole Park. There was a big crowd around us and she was shouting about me not being married, though what that had to do with her stealing I don't know. Since then she's been a pain in the arse running me down left, right and centre.'

Marlene bent to a cardboard box beneath the stall, took out the flask and refilled two mugs with tea. 'Should warm us up,' she said. 'But Pixie don't know about some of these customers what make life difficult. I'm used to it but she took it all to heart.'

Bob sold two blankets. His fingers were freezing. After he'd put the money away he cupped his hands around the hot mug for warmth. 'She should have spoken to me before she went. I remember telling her we weren't doing well. I suppose she remembered that, too, blamed herself.'

'Every business suffers after Christmas. It's the way of it,' said Marlene. 'Oh, I wish I'd known what she was up to – I'd have told her the truth.' Bob saw she had her eye on a woman who was looking at the gold trinkets and trying to lift the lid. Marlene put down her mug and went down to see to her. Bob sold a paraffin stove.

Pixie had hurt him. He had thought he was getting

through to her, easing her sadness about losing Cal. When she'd learned that Cal would never come back, he'd begun to feel truly hopeful. He'd tried in a million ways to show her he loved her, and she'd repaid him by running off. He could see she'd meant it for the best, because she didn't want him to lose customers and money – but bugger the customers and money! He wanted her!

Oh, she was safe enough where she was. He didn't need to worry about that. Her and little Sadie would be well looked after. From what he'd seen and heard of Cal's sister, she was a good woman. But he wanted to go to Chichester and bring Pixie back. He wouldn't, though. This time his pride wouldn't let him. He wasn't a puppet on a string. On the other hand, if she came home of her own accord, because she'd decided she loved him, he'd be over the moon. In the meantime, of course, he'd make it his business to keep an eye on Pixie from afar, and if anything went wrong, he'd be there like a shot. The silly woman had even said she'd pay him back everything she owed him! He didn't want Pixie's money, just her. He drank his tea and stamped his feet to keep warm.

Bob watched the passers-by. They were all muffled up against the cold, breath steaming as they stood and chatted. He waved to Len on the next stall, selling umbrellas and handbags.

Marlene came and stood next to Bob.

'You're doing well, aren't you?' He said to her.

She smoothed her golden hair back beneath her bobble hat. 'Well enough that I've paid Marie what I owed her,' she said. 'And I got some money put by for more stock. I was going to ask if I can come along with you when you go to another auction.'

He nodded. 'Good idea.' He stared into her eyes. 'What d'you say to me teaching you to drive?' He saw the excitement on her face.

He laughed. 'If you can drive I'll get another stall, one you can manage on your own. You can spread out a bit with your pretties and gold, and sell for me as well. What d'you reckon?'

'I'd throw my arms round your neck and kiss you, but old Marge Sidebotham might be looking,' she said.

'Don't do that, for God's sake. I've been thinking about expanding for a while. Thought I'd get a lad around Easter, free myself up for travelling and buying. I'd thought if I got more help, I'd have more time to spend with Pixie and Sadie but . . .'

'Go up to Chichester and talk to her.'

'No! She's got to come back because she wants *me*.'

He felt himself blush – he'd been talking quite loudly. There was a lump in his throat as he noticed a man peering at the paraffin heaters. 'Don't just stand there drinking tea, Marlene,' he said gruffly. 'That bloke wants serving.'

Pixie threw the blue counterpane over the immaculately made bed and smoothed it flat. She looked around the Blue Room, as Ruth called it, noting that there wasn't a trace of the couple who had stayed two nights. The few coins that were the cleaner's tip lay in her apron pocket. Ruth had told her cash and gifts from clients were her own business. Pixie was surprised by some of the items she'd been given. It was the clothes she liked best, though. Visitors bought new holiday clothes and discarded old ones. The other day a rather large lady had asked her to 'get rid of' a two-piece suit. Pixie had altered the brown wool jacket and skirt to fit her and now they hung in her wardrobe. Of course, sometimes visitors left behind articles they hadn't meant to leave. Watches, rings, bracelets, cigarette cases. These she put securely in the safe behind the desk.

'I keep stuff like this for a year. If I have the home address I can send it on,' said Ruth. Pixie realized why the Old Oaks Guesthouse was so popular.

The weeks had passed quickly for Pixie. She enjoyed the work, which wasn't as hard as filling shell cases at Priddy's Hard. But she missed the chatter of the girls.

Ruth was the kindest person to work for. Every day she took Sadie out in a pushchair she'd bought from a second-hand shop in town. 'It gives you a chance to get on without the little one under your feet,' she'd say to Pixie. And Pixie would watch her cooing over the child or dressing her in the new clothes she'd managed to buy for her. Sometimes Pixie hated herself for feeling jealous that she wasn't able to do the same for her daughter.

Roy, Ruth's husband, came home as often as he could. Pixie was surprised to find he was younger than Ruth. With his blond moustache and broad shoulders he seemed barely old enough to fly a Spitfire. One evening when, for once, they were without guests and the three sat around the table, he told Pixie how he had met Ruth.

'She was sitting in the Chichester Arms, waiting for Cal, who was on leave, He was among the first of the GI's to arrive in England. I arrived with some friends. I took one look at her and knew she was the girl for me. But Spitfire pilots have an unhappy knack of getting themselves killed so I didn't do anything more than buy her a drink, surprised to find she wasn't English. She'd come over here to be near her brother. When Cal arrived with his mates, some of the locals decided to spice the evening up with a fight, starting with the usual jibe the English lads make to the Americans – "Overpaid, over-sexed and over here."' He reached for Ruth's hand. 'I got pulled into it but fought against the locals. We scarpered before the police came and the three of us, Cal, Ruth and I, ended up in another pub. We became friends and later I persuaded her to marry me. The icing on the cake would be for us to have a child of our own. Two years and no luck.'

Pixie saw him look at Ruth with such tenderness. And Pixie knew then that Sadie could quite easily become the child that Ruth had never had.

But Sadie was lucky to have an auntie who loved her so much, wasn't she?

'Are you happy here?' Roy had asked. The smell of Woolton Pie lingered in the air.

'Yes,' answered Pixie, truthfully. She didn't say the guesthouse would never feel like home, though. She didn't say she missed Bob either. There were times when she wished she hadn't been so hasty in running away.

'Rita, my friend, tells me Gosport's to play a part in the D-Day landings.'

Pixie was horrified: she'd done the unforgivable. She'd passed on information that she should have kept to her-self. She knew she was blushing furiously.

'Ssh. Walls have ears!' Roy put a finger to his lips. Then he smiled. 'But you only have to visit the town to feel the excitement in the air, and if you can get past the guards you'll discover the special slipways being built and beaches being hardened to accommodate the heavy traffic.'

Pixie nodded. 'Haslar Hospital at Clayhall is one of the hospitals selected to take the casualties. Rita told me training's going on at HMS *Daedalus*, and Priddy's Hard is working like the clappers, producing rockets, mines and such. What will the airmen be doing?'

She knew she shouldn't be talking about things like this or asking questions, but they were on the same side, weren't they?

'I'm guessing I might be flying sorties over the coast of Normandy. We'll be providing protective air cover for the ground troops making their way inland. Though, of course, we mere airmen aren't told what will happen until the last moment. Most of the information we get is pure speculation. Spies can lurk anywhere, Pixie.'

Ruth frowned. Pixie knew she was terrified for the safety of the man she loved so much. After all, she'd already lost her brother, hadn't she?

After Roy had gone to the pub to meet a couple of his pals, and Ruth and Pixie had cleared away the remains of the meal, Ruth went upstairs to check on Sadie. When she returned, Pixie had already got out her material, scissors and clean sacking and was sitting by the fire hooking strips of fabric to finish her latest rug. She looked at Ruth, noting how much more relaxed she was since she and Sadie had come to live at the guesthouse.

Roy had also managed several home visits, so Pixie thought this was another reason for her chirpiness.

'I miss Cal so much,' said Ruth. 'We were so close as kids and as grown-ups.'

'What was it like growing up on a farm in America?'

'Happy.' Ruth's face took on a faraway look. 'Though we lived miles away from anywhere, our friends would cycle over and we'd spend hours playing hide and seek in the old sheds and empty silos. I think that's why Cal wanted to join the Navy. We were so far from the sea he talked about it endlessly. Sadie is so like him – she reminds me of him so much.' Ruth picked up a log and stacked it on the fire. 'Our winters were colder than they are in England, but I feel it more here because everything is so damp.' She used the tongs to pick up a piece of burning wood that had fallen on to the hearth. 'I had a letter from my parents this morning. They want to come and see us, you and Sadie, too, but not until after the war,' she said.

Pixie decided that Ruth was quite a lonely person and that the guesthouse helped to alleviate the pain of being on her own when Roy was away.

'Still, I'm not alone in missing my brother, am I?'

'Hardly,' said Pixie. 'It wouldn't be so bad if there was a grave. I could at least go and talk to him.'

'I think, Pixie, that wherever he is, he knows about his beautiful daughter, and as he loved you so much, he wouldn't want you to be unhappy. You're too young to stay single, and although you never speak about him, I'm sure Bob owns a chunk of your heart. I also believe you didn't realize this until he was no longer in your life.'

Pixie put down the hook she was using to thread a piece of material through the sacking. 'The thing is, Ruth, there's too much water under the bridge now. I've not treated Bob well. He's been so generous to me, but when the going got tough, I ran off without giving him the benefit of the doubt that he could sort out his business. I know I've been a fool. But the good that's come out of this is meeting you, and Roy, of course.'

'I think you've also forgotten that you're making quite a little business for yourself, selling those gorgeous rugs to that little shop opposite the market entrance.'

'That's all down to you.'

Pixie thought back to when shopkeeper Emily Wright had stayed a couple of nights at the guesthouse when a stray incendiary bomb had landed in the passage at her home. Her husband had wasted no time in putting on a new door and making good the damage, but as Emily ran the shop, it was easier for her to stay out of his way and let him get on with the repairs. 'No, Emily saw the rugs and fell in love with them. It had nothing to do with me, Pixie. I'm just happy that you can put money by, doing something you like. I guess you're determined to pay Bob back. Am I right?'

Pixie nodded. She didn't add that on the days when the weather was sunny she often remembered her and Rita sitting on the wall during tea break at Priddy's Hard, the chats they'd had and the laughter she'd shared with her best friend. Sometimes she sat in bed while Sadie slept and wrote down all of her thoughts in one of her exercise books. The pile of filled ones had grown considerably now.

Soon the snowdrops would be out and spring would arrive, but everything had changed. Letters between her and Rita were full of chatty stuff but it wasn't the same as sitting on that tumbledown wall at Priddy's and laughing because they had Spam sandwiches for lunch yet again.

*

'Busy night tonight, Gladys.' Jeremy smiled at her. 'Will you be able to manage if I go and lie down? I've one of my "heads".'

Gladys knew her boss had been quite poorly lately and, as Cora was in, she'd cope.

'Would you like me to make you a cuppa or something?' His face was white, and she knew Stephen was worried about him – he seemed to have lost all his enthusiasm lately. Gladys glanced at Stephen, who was eyeing them. He slid off the bar stool and came over.

'Go and have a lie-down, dear,' he told Jeremy. 'We'll manage.'

Gladys left them to it to serve a sailor in his blue bell-bottoms and tight top. When she'd finished, Stephen and Jeremy had disappeared. Lately there had been a bit more in her wage packet for all the extra work she did.

She was about to serve another customer when the siren went. 'Bugger it!' She had a choice: run for the air-raid shelter and leave the pub in the hands of the customers, who would think that Christmas had come and help themselves to drinks, or stay and look after everything. By now Stephen would have Jeremy tucked up in the Morrison shelter.

Gladys looked around. Already most of the customers had run for the air-raid shelter near the docks. Half-empty glasses stood on the bar and the tables. Gladys rang the bell and made the announcement that the pub would close, but remaining customers were welcome to stay.

'Cora! Sort out the utilities, love,' she shouted, then went round to check the blackout curtains and make sure the doors were locked. She emptied the till, intending to put the takings away safely. Any drinks would be on the house until the bombing stopped.

The slow buzz of the planes could be heard now. Accompanied by explosions. The Germans would be trying to destroy the Dockyard.

A small voice asked, 'Gladys?'

Gladys, on her way out the back with the takings, paused. She recognised the voice and saw a dark-haired young woman reaching out to catch her arm. Surely she wasn't about to steal the bag of money. Then Gladys recognized Rita. When the girl turned her face to the candlelight, Gladys saw, hidden beneath her mane of beautiful hair, the scars.

A big bang, close enough to make everything in the pub rattle, threw the two women into each other's arms.

'Get in here,' shouted Gladys, pulling Rita behind the counter and beneath the heavy wooden flap that had to be lifted each time someone left the bar.

Dust was falling. Flakes of dirty brown ceiling

distemper covered Rita's hair. She grinned at Gladys. 'I just washed it!'

Gladys laughed. 'You ain't lost your sense of humour, then?'

'Not much point, eh?'

'How did it happen?'

Rita told her about the accident and that she had been negligent.

'So you're not due a pay-out?'

Rita shook her head. The drone of the planes discharging loads had filled the air with the stink of burning. 'I can't get free of the smell,' she said, gripping Gladys's hand. 'How long is this war going to last?' Rita wiped the beads of sweat from her forehead. She was shivering.

'This time next year it could be all over,' Gladys said. 'Don't be scared, love, hold on to me.' She put her arms around Rita – the explosions outside must be making her relive the one that had destroyed her face. 'Stay there.' She got up and went to the back of the bar. Another bang, and just as she was pouring a measure of whisky into a glass, the wall seemed to move sideways, giving more than a good measure of spirit. Gladys took a deep breath, reached for another glass and put gin in that, followed by a slosh of orange.

Scrambling back to Rita she said, 'Down this in one.' She gave her the gin, and drank the whisky.

'You remembered my tipple,' said Rita. Gladys could see she was calmer now, despite the falling debris.

'You're my girl's best friend,' she said. 'Of course I'd remember.'

'Never thought I'd meet you tonight when me and Harry decided to drive down south from East Grinstead,' said Rita. She peeped through the hatchway and waved to Harry, who waved back.

'Looks a nice bloke. Is he . . .'

'No, he's a friend. Like me, he's recovering.'

Gladys nodded to show she understood the situation. 'Long way to come for a drink?'

'Harry wanted to see his sister. She got bombed out last week and is in a hostel. She'd have been with us tonight but she's got little kids and told us to get out from under her feet. She's at Eastney. Harry got her a flat so we're going to help her move in. Then we'll go back to the hospital.'

'Not going over to Gosport to see Pixie, then? Ain't fallen out, have you?'

Another crash, and Rita threw her arms around Gladys. When the noise had settled she said, 'She's not in Gosport no more.'

Gladys's heart started to thump. Surely something bad hadn't happened to her girl. 'What d'you mean?'

'She's living in Chichester with Cal's sister and young Sadie.'

Gladys had never heard of these people. Who were they? She must have looked very confused, for Rita said, 'Get another couple of drinks. We're both going to need them.' She started to open the clasp of her handbag.

Gladys stilled her hand. 'I don't want your money,' she said. Getting up from her crouching position, she refilled the glasses with spirits. She looked around the bar: the other half-dozen or so people there were looking at her expectantly. Gladys filled some glasses with good measures, then said, 'I ain't bloody waiting on you lot. Whisky's on the bar, folks!' She scrambled back to Rita. 'I think you'd better fill me in on what's been going on since I been gone.'

Half an hour later Gladys had heard all about her daughter and the granddaughter she'd known nothing about. Happiness bubbled inside her when she thought about Sadie. Rita told her she reckoned Pixie was a bloody fool for leaving Bob.

'He's a good man. And I got to see her,' Gladys said. 'Will you give me her address?'

Rita frowned. 'At first I wasn't going to because you broke that girl's heart, and if it wasn't for you spending money you never had, she wouldn't be in the dire straits she's been in.'

Gladys looked the girl straight in the eye. 'I know, love. But I've been sorry for it all ever since. I was a selfish cow. But the reason I'm working here instead of living off some bloke is to save money so I can settle debts. Hopefully, if Pixie will let me, I can start anew and be a proper mum and grandmother,' she said quietly.

'I believe you,' said Rita. She fumbled in her bag, then scribbled on a piece of paper.

Gladys took it and put it safely into her pocket. 'You don't know what this means to me,' she said.

The noise of planes and the thwump, thwump of falling bombs had stopped. It had been replaced by the sound of voices and running feet outside on the cobbles. She heard a policeman's whistle, and inside the pub, the few customers were moving about. The smell of dust was in the air and she realized it would take her and Cora ages to clean up. Cora. Where was she?

Had the girl gone down to the air-raid shelter without telling her?

Rita was making her way over to her friend. When they got to the door, she turned and waved.

Gladys moved from the bar to the hall and came face to face with her two employers . . .

'Have you seen Cora?'

They shook their heads. 'No, and we've already looked in the rooms to see what damage . . .'

Without listening to Stephen she ran down the steps into the cellar, calling Cora's name. Cora wasn't in the pub. Just then the all-clear sounded. Gladys hauled open the heavy rear door, surprised to find it unlocked.

The stink of bomb smoke hung heavy in the air. Fires were burning in the distance sending an orange glow into the sky, almost like an early sunrise. Gladys saw a crater and masonry rubble.

Cora was lying on the cobbles, her lower half free of the bricks that covered the rest of her body. Gladys felt her heart constrict.

'Is it her?' Stephen's voice was quiet. Gladys hadn't heard him following her outside.

'Yes.' Gladys knelt down and began lifting some of the lighter stones from Cora's body. Blood covered them. She couldn't shift the one that had killed the girl.

'Best leave her for the experts.' Stephen had bent down and was feeling for Cora's pulse. He looked at Gladys and shook his head.

Oh, Cora my love, thought Gladys, a lovely girl like

you and this is how you end up, dead in a stinking alleyway.

'I didn't know she'd gone out,' Stephen said.

'I bet she went to call the cat,' Gladys said. She could feel the tears running down her face. She put her hand on the young woman's cold arm. 'Oh, love,' she wept.

Chapter Thirty

It helped to keep busy. Gladys dusted the dressing-table in her bedroom, then sorted through the drawers, throwing out clothes she knew she'd never wear again. It was a miserly pile: she'd bought very little since she had dedicated herself to saving her wages. Clothing restrictions had been lifted and she was fed up with recycling garments that had become so worn the material was almost see-through.

Cora's funeral had been a low-key affair, paid for by Jeremy. Stephen had closed the pub for the day. Their grief was genuine, as was that of the rest of the staff. Cora had been well liked by all at the White Swan.

Jeremy was ill again, thin and bad-tempered. He clung to Stephen, spending a lot of time in their room listening to music.

Gladys had not expected the death of Cora to affect

her so deeply. She had become almost hardened to friends arriving in the bar and telling her of people she'd known who had lost their lives. Portsmouth was a moving population due to the forces and war was cruel. The cat had disappeared.

She knew now she had to find Pixie as soon as possible. She or Pixie could die tomorrow and all the money she had saved for reparation would be useless if her daughter was gone.

In the evening, Stephen opened up. The first half-hour or so was always quiet and Gladys had intended to speak to him, but he had something on his mind when he poured her a whisky and asked her to sit down at one of the small tables.

'I'll come straight to the point,' he said. 'You're so different from the scruffy woman we took in and we both think the world of you, but Jeremy's ill and wants to move to the country. Would you be prepared to run this place?'

She looked into his green eyes. He wouldn't have asked her if he didn't think she could do it.

At first her heart soared. There were so many changes she'd make if she was in charge. Then excitement took over: she knew she could double the profit in next to no time. But it would mean being here twenty-four hours a day. And putting away all thoughts of looking for Pixie and her grandchild. Of course, she had no guarantee that Pixie would want anything to do with her, after all this time. Especially as she'd left Pixie with debts that had nothing to do with her.

Now Stephen was giving her a chance to do something with her life. He was willing to take a chance on her work and her honesty.

'I expect you wondered why I didn't advertise for more staff after we lost Cora, but I wanted to make the right decision.'

Gladys drank her whisky in one go. She put the glass on the table. 'No,' she said, with a deep sigh. And for the next ten minutes she told him that finding Pixie meant everything to her.

His hand enveloped hers. Her eyes met his. 'We'll keep in touch,' he said. 'Wherever I am there'll be a job for you, should you need it.'

The seagulls whirled around the ferry boat, their squawking loud enough to waken the dead. Gladys stood near the funnel where it was warmer and watched the fine flakes of snow fall and immediately melt on the hot surface. Across the water was the wooden jetty of the

Gosport pontoon. Around her, in the choppy sea, were ships, yachts, sailing craft and the motor torpedo boats built by Camper & Nicholsons. The boatyard had been heavily bombed in 1941 but had set up other premises in North Street.

When she had disembarked she carried her small case through the Ferry Gardens towards the bus station, looking at the front of the buses to see their destinations.

Inside the Provincial bus she sat next to the door.

There had been little point in staying any longer at the pub. She'd made up her mind to leave, so it had made sense to go as soon as possible. Gladys couldn't get out of her mind the sight of Cora lying dead. One moment she'd been laughing, the next the life had been taken out of her. Gladys couldn't risk this happening to her or her daughter.

'Single to the Criterion, please,' she said. The conductress gave her a smile. Before the war men had taken the fares and driven the buses. Now women worked at men's jobs while the men fought.

It had been a while since she'd been in Gosport and the fresh bomb sites saddened her. She got off at the picture house and walked along the road, then into the street where she'd lived for many years. She was aware that Pixie wasn't there any more, but she needed a base where she could stay for a while until she had the courage to go to Chichester, the place she believed Pixie to be.

Since she'd met Rita in the White Swan she had written to her and Rita had written back. Gladys was aware that Rita would soon have to leave the Queen Victoria Hospital at East Grinstead. Rita had explained that the surgeons had done all they could and now the rest was up to her. Every day new patients were being admitted with war wounds and burns, and beds were at a premium.

Somewhere at the back of her mind Gladys wanted to carry on the hospital's job of looking after Rita, rebuilding her confidence and giving her a home. Which was all very well, but she needed a home for herself first.

Living next door to Bob had given her an insight into the hours he kept at the markets and when he'd be at home.

She took a deep breath and knocked on his door. When it opened she could hear the Ink Spots coming from the wireless.

'Well, this is a turn-up for the books,' said Bob. He was obviously in the middle of shaving, for he had puffs of soap on his chin. He opened the door wider so she could enter.

'Don't worry, I know Pixie's not here,' Gladys said. She

felt quite peculiar going into his kitchen. Memories of her own house, next door, came flooding in.

'I'll put the kettle on,' he said. 'Won't be a moment. I'll just finish shaving. Make yourself comfortable.'

She watched him go into the scullery. His shoulders were broad and his back strong beneath his white vest. Not only was he a good man but he was quite an eyeful, she thought. The canary was singing and Gladys crossed the floor to the cage. 'Don't tell me this is the bird I left Pixie?'

'It is,' he shouted. 'We decided the poor thing had had enough travelling so it's with me now. So, Gladys, what's this all about? What do you want?'

The kettle must have already been on the boil for when he came into the kitchen the teapot was on the tray with steam curling from its spout, a couple of mugs and milk. 'No sugar, I'm afraid,' Bob said.

He had stuck a small piece of paper on a nick in his chin and had put on a blue shirt. Gladys thought he was probably as nervous as she was. He began to pour the tea. She opened her handbag, took out an envelope and put it on the table.

'What I want is my daughter back. I know where she is. I think you do too.' She paused. 'Do you mind if I take my coat off? It's trying to snow out there and I don't want to feel cold when I leave.'

'Sorry, Gladys, I was a bit taken aback to see you. Forgive my manners.'

He took her coat and went to hang it in the hall. She sat down in the chair by the range. As he stepped back into the kitchen, she said, 'I've behaved more like a trollop than a mother for far too long, but I've come to my senses.' She nodded towards the envelope. 'In there is enough money to cover whatever Pixie owes you.' He began to speak but she waved his words away. 'The debts were mine. She got herself into all kinds of trouble trying to sort out my bills. Rita's filled me in on a lot of things. I know you lent Pixie money. Now we're square.' She picked up her tea and began to drink it.

He didn't speak, simply sat and stared at her.

Gladys put down her mug. 'I'd like to ask a big favour of you.'

'I knew there'd be a sting in the tail.' He refilled her mug from the teapot. 'What is it?'

'Would you let me stay here a couple of days? I'll go to Chichester to talk to Pixie and then I'll be gone.' There was amused astonishment on his face. She knew she was taking a chance asking him but she dearly wanted to talk to him about Pixie and Sadie, and the possible outcome of her proposed visit.

He took a deep breath. 'I worry about her all the time

but I had to give her time to decide what she wanted. Not being able to see her is killing me.'

She could smell the freshness of his shaving soap and cologne. Gladys got up and went over to him. 'I know you care about her. Which is why, if I stayed just for a couple of days, I could let you know first-hand what she wants. Besides, Bob, I've never set eyes on that baby. Yes, I know it's my own fault but this past year has taught me a lot.'

He ran his fingers through his hair, the ends of it still wet from his wash at the sink. 'Okay, a couple of days. You can stay in her room. It's just as it was when she left. I haven't had the heart to clear it out, not with some of the baby's stuff still there.' He looked at the envelope on the table. 'I don't take back gifts from people I care about. I told Pixie that but she's as determined as you seem to be to pay me back.'

'It's a good feeling, Bob.'

He went to the scullery. 'You hungry?'

Gladys hadn't until that moment realized how hungry she was. 'I am,' she replied. She heard a noise, something heavy bouncing down the stairs of her old home. 'New neighbours?'

'Not really,' he called. 'It's your landlord. He's been staying while his own house is repaired after a bomb blast. He told me he'd be off soon. It'll not take him long to find someone to move in with all the homeless in Gosport.'

At his words a smile lit her face. Gladys let a thought run around her brain. 'Rita said you've got our furniture in your shed. Is my old landlord on his own in there?' she asked, waving towards next door as Bob came in with two plates of stew and dumplings.

'That's right,' he said, to both questions. Then, glancing at the table, 'Haven't you got the spoons out of the sideboard yet?' He put the food down. 'Supposing Pixie's had enough of living with you and doesn't want to come back to Gosport? I know what you're thinking, Gladys. What if the landlord doesn't want you back?'

Gladys laughed. 'What are you – a mind-reader? Those are chances I have to take. If she won't come back for me, she might come back for you.'

'I'm not begging her.'

'If she loves you, you won't have to.' Gladys went over to the oak sideboard, opened the drawer and took out some cutlery. 'That stew looks delicious,' she said. She gave him a spoon and a fork.

She finished before him and told him she'd be back in five minutes. Then she picked up her purse and, after outlining her lips with a bright red lipstick and fluffing up her hair in the mirror over the range, she opened the front door.

It seemed funny knocking on the door of what used to be her own house. Gladys ran her hands down her shapely body. Being on her feet all the time in the pub had kept her slim and supple.

She didn't have to wait long before a grey-haired man in a navy-blue cardigan opened the door. At first he looked perplexed, then recognized her. 'Well, I'm blowed, Gladys!'

'You going to invite me in or do I freeze on the doorstep?'

He stepped aside and she swept past him, noting the new paint in the hallway. 'I heard your house took a bomb.'

'Yes, but the builder's put it back together again and I'm leaving soon,' he said. 'You look well, Gladys. Life treating you good?'

She turned her back on him, bent forward and ran a hand over her seamed stockings, a gift from one of the Americans who frequented the bar. 'Damned things are always going crooked on me. They look all right to you?' Gladys was very proud of her shapely legs and neat ankles. She let him study them for a moment, then turned back to face him. 'Life would be treating me better if I had a place so I could have my girl living with me.'

'Ah, yes. Lovely pins, Gladys. I mean, yes, your stockings are straight.' He coloured. 'But you left and she caused me a problem with the rent.'

'That was my fault, not hers. Look I won't beat about the bush, I need a place to live.'

'And you want me to be daft enough to let you live here again?' He looked bewildered.

She glanced around the kitchen. 'You've made a lovely job of painting the walls in here.' She went up to him and stroked back a strand of his hair. 'You wasn't always so nasty to me, Gerald.'

He coughed, and she saw beads of sweat on his forehead. 'Cor, that were a few years back, Gladys.'

'You're as young as you feel, Gerald. You're still a fine-looking bloke, you know.'

No way was this man going to lay a finger on her, Gladys thought, but his ego wouldn't let him believe that. She knew the little fling they'd had years back had meant more to him than it ever had to her. She opened her bag and took out a large brown envelope. She counted two pound notes and put them on the old table he'd been using for painting materials and for eating off. The rent before had been twelve shillings a week.

'Let's be business-like. It's best if I pay a deposit, Gerald. I know you'll treat me nice. And I'll do the same for you. A deposit means you got money up front if anything happens, which it won't, this time,' she assured him, with a dazzling smile. She went on putting down another pound note. She wasn't stupid, she knew the value of money. 'Pick it up, Gerald. You don't even have to advertise for a new tenant because I'm here.'

When he had the money in his hand, over a month's rent, she knew the notes would do the trick. Cash in the hand can't be beat, she thought.

She put her bag on the table, her arms around his neck, and gave him a whopping kiss on the cheek. She knew he was breathing her in and was glad she was wearing her favourite perfume, Evening in Paris. He'd smell it on the air and remember her when she'd gone.

She broke away and picked up from the table two keys on a piece of string that she decided were the spare set. 'I'll be needing these,' she said. 'Shall I move in this weekend? Don't want no tramps in here spoiling all your lovely work, do we?

'You still got your little car, Gerald?' He nodded. She could see he was trying to keep up with her questions. 'Might be nice for you to take me out in it, one of these days.'

She saw the gleam in his eyes. Dream on, Gerald, she was thinking. All you'll ever get from me is the rent, regular as clockwork. But now I've got a home for Pixie to come back to. It crossed her mind as she walked down the passageway and out of the front door, her front door, that Pixie might not want to come back to Gosport. She pushed that thought away.

As she opened Bob's front door, which she'd left on the latch, and walked up the passage, smelling the homely scents of cooking and polish, she felt very pleased with herself. A year ago she'd never have taken charge of her life in the way she'd just done. She'd had no confidence then and had hidden behind her latest man, trusting that he would look after her. Wasn't it good to be able to decide things for herself? She hadn't been fair to Gerald, though, she'd led him on to get what she wanted. It wasn't honest. She decided she *would* allow him to take her out for a drive to a pub somewhere. *But only as a friend.*

Bob was in the scullery washing up the dinner things. He had the kettle on for tea. She went up to him. 'Meet your new neighbour.'

Bob's face broke into a big grin. 'How the hell did you do that?'

She touched her nose. 'Me and Gerald go back a long way. Now I need a job.'

'That won't be difficult. Priddy's Hard are crying out for labour.'

Everything was falling into place, Gladys thought, but was it happening too quickly? She was banking on Pixie bringing her baby home. What if she didn't want to come back? Well, if that happened, she still needed a home and a job, and she'd be able to fulfil her promise to Rita that when she left the hospital there'd be a home waiting. 'Of course. It's all hands to the pump for more ammunition, mines and rockets, isn't it?'

He nodded. 'I suppose you'll be wanting me to help you back with the furniture?'

'If you would? I'd like the canary and all,' she said, 'if you don't mind.'

He laughed at her. 'Of course, and Pixie'll need the rest of her stuff from this house. If you can persuade her to come back. I can't bear to go past the room with all the kiddie's stuff in, it cuts me in two.'

Gladys opened the front-room door and gasped at the pram. 'That's a smasher,' she said. He stood facing her. One look at his stricken face and she closed the door again. 'You want her back, don't you?'

'More than anything.'

Chapter Thirty-one

'Didn't you offer to take her to Chichester? The forecast reckons the snow will fall deeply later today.'

'Course I did, Marlene. Gladys wanted to go by herself on the train. And I'm not sorry. If I saw Pixie, actually saw her, and she didn't want to come home it would just about finish me.'

He walked the length of the market pitch noting how her jewellery was set out to catch the eye on a large piece of black velvet. The gold she kept in the glass-topped box. 'You'll have the whole stall decked out with your stuff soon, won't you?'

He was teasing her. She'd learned how to drive in no time at all and now he had an eight-hundredweight Bedford van. It was nearly ten years old but his mate Ron hadn't been able to use it during the war, due to the petrol rationing, and had kept it in good condition, garaging it in the enormous lock-up where he kept his stock.

Marlene was a different person now, he thought. Along with the van, he'd bought a ten-foot stall off a bloke who'd found the going too tough, and over a weekend he had painstakingly sawn a couple of inches off the main supports so Marlene could throw the canvas sheets over it with ease. She made money for him and money for herself. He thought about the bloke at the auctions who had taken her out once or twice.

Bob asked, 'How's young Mike coming along?'

Michael was sixteen and learning the trade, helping Marlene.

'I like him, and he's got the patter off to a T with the old ladies. But he's got some mates that sometimes hang around and I wouldn't trust them as far as I could throw 'em,' she replied, tossing her bright hair away from her face.

He was a nice enough lad, thought Bob, and you have to give the young ones a chance. Another couple of years and he'd get his call-up papers. He'd left Mike on his own a few afternoons and there hadn't been any breakages or bother.

'He's got a good head on him for adding up. Right quick he is,' Bob said.

'You work too hard,' Marlene said. She was drinking a cup of tea, and handed one to him.

Every so often a few flakes would fall from the leaden skies. It wanted to snow – Bob could feel it in the air. 'Yes.' He took a mouthful of thick black tea.

'What are you going to do if you don't get back together?' Marlene was muffled up against the cold, wearing layer upon layer of clothes and a bright red scarf tied round her neck.

'You mean with Pixie?'

She nodded.

'I'll work even harder, Marlene,' he said. 'To be honest, I don't know what I'll do.'

'You should have gone to Chichester with her mother.'

'If I had, I would have picked her up, stuffed her in the van and kidnapped her. No, the answer is, if Pixie's missed me half as much as I've missed her, she'll come back without my interference.'

Pixie dried the plates. There had been six guests for breakfast that morning. Four people had left and the last couple were packing. She wiped her hands and gave Sadie a piece of dry toast, which she happily banged on the tray of the high chair. Pixie dropped a kiss on her daughter's fluffy bird's nest bed-hair.

The large kitchen was warm and smelt of frying. From the wireless came the seductive sounds of Glenn Miller's music. As Pixie looked through the window she saw snow settling on the grass at the back of the guesthouse. She hummed along with the tune.

Ruth was in the lavatory outside the back door, heaving her heart up, and no one was happier about it than Ruth.

Pixie wiped down the gas stove. Two days ago she had accompanied Ruth to the doctor's surgery and sat in the waiting room. For several days Ruth had been tired and sickly. Then she had fainted in the greengrocer's and Pixie had been sure. When the manager had found a chair for Ruth to sit on, she'd said, 'You're pregnant.'

Ruth had looked at her as though she was daft.

Pixie was busy counting up the weeks since Roy had had leave. 'It's early days but I reckon I'm right. Make a doctor's appointment and I'll come with you.'

Ruth had been let down so many times during their marriage that she'd given up all hope of conceiving.

Ruth and Pixie left the surgery with leaflets to read and practically danced down the street. When they got home Ruth wrote to Roy straight away.

'Don't go overdoing things,' said Pixie. She knew Roy would be thrilled – he'd want to wine and dine his wife and shower her with gifts on his next leave. She'd keep herself out of the way when he came home – she wouldn't want to be a gooseberry while they celebrated.

'I was told by my doctor to carry on as usual. Hard work, healthy food and exercise are good for me.'

'Can't argue with him,' said Pixie. But she'd make sure that Sadie didn't wear Ruth out.

Now she glanced out of the window at the snow and hummed along to 'String Of Pearls'.

'No one told me being pregnant was like this.' Coming back into the kitchen with more colour in her face than she'd rushed out with, Ruth grimaced. 'Not that I'm complaining,' she said. 'Let me finish the wiping up.'

Pixie heard a knock on the front door and went to answer it, wondering if one of the visitors had forgotten something.

'Ooh!' Pixie held on to the door frame for support. The cold air coming in from outside made her cheeks tingle while at the same time her heart began to pound.

Her mother was wrapped in a brown coat with a fox-fur collar, and her snug bootees were exactly the same colour. Pixie was speechless. Somehow Gladys looked younger – she was wearing less make-up. That was it. Her cheeks were pink with the cold and Pixie smelt Evening in Paris wafting towards her. Memories flooded back.

'Well, do I stand here all day and you let the cold inside the place, or do I come in?'

'Oh, Mum!' Pixie was stunned.

'Let's get inside, love.'

With tears in her eyes, Pixie melted into her mother's embrace. Together they walked through to the kitchen where Ruth was busy with Sadie, exchanging another dry crust of toast for the soggy remnants of the previous one.

Gladys went over to the child and looked down at her granddaughter. 'Sadie?'

Ruth nodded, clearly bewildered.

'Can I pick her up? I don't want to disturb your routine.' Gladys looked at Ruth for affirmation and touched Sadie's silky hair.

'Of course. She's sticky and messy,' Pixie said. Sadie's dribble confirmed it.

'I don't care about that.' Gladys scooped the child from the high chair and held her close. That was something Pixie had never dreamed she'd see. Gladys closed her eyes, evidently overcome with emotion at holding her granddaughter in her arms.

'Who's a heavy girl, then?' she cooed at the baby. For

a moment there was silence in the kitchen broken only by Sadie's noisy gurgle as the now wet toast caught in Gladys's hair. Gladys was laughing. 'She's beautiful. Oh, Pixie, I should have been here for you.'

Ruth was staring at Pixie, who lowered her eyes, 'Meet my mum,' she said. 'Mum this is Ruth, Cal's sister. Cal was Sadie's dad.'

Everything was all right. Pixie had often wondered how she would feel seeing her mother again. Yet it seemed quite natural for her mother to be holding Sadie as though nothing unusual had happened. There was something different about her . . . a kind of calm she hadn't possessed before.

'I'll make some tea,' said Ruth, suddenly springing to life. 'You two must have lots to talk about. One of them being your return to Gosport, I would imagine. Why don't I take Sadie shopping with me?' She glanced out of the window. 'There's snowflakes falling. She'll love that.' Ruth shook the kettle to make sure there was enough water and lit the gas.

'Thanks,' said Pixie. She caught hold of Ruth's arm. 'You don't have to go out because of us . . .'

'No, I don't, but there are things I need to do and you'll be able to relax.'

'If you're sure?'

Reluctantly Gladys passed the child to Ruth, then began disentangling bits of toast from her hair and the fox-fur collar.

'Take your coat off, Mum.'

Ruth went out of the room, taking Sadie with her, as Gladys put her coat over the back of a chair. Pixie finished making the tea while listening to the sound of Ruth dressing the child in her thick outdoor clothing and putting on Sadie's bootees with the usual accompanying struggle.

It was funny, she thought, how many times she had so wanted her mother with her, but now she was unable to think of a single thing to say to her.

The front door closed. With the tea on the kitchen table, the women sitting facing each other, a wave of deep silence engulfed the room, until Gladys said, in a small voice, 'I'm so sorry.'

It was as if a floodgate had opened.

'I'm not angry, Mum. I got over that ages ago. But I needed you when the baby was born. Bob was there for me but I cried for you.'

'And it's my loss I wasn't there.' Gladys put her hand to her eyes, as though she was pushing away a headache. 'It took me a while to grasp that you're worth more than that constant stream of no-hoper blokes I put my trust in. I want you to come home.'

Pixie looked at her mother as if she'd grown three heads. 'Come home? Where? Our home was repossessed. And I can't leave Ruth – she's pregnant.'

Gladys seemed to curl in on herself. 'And what about you? Don't you have a life? What about Bob? And I have a home.'

'You mean you had a home! Even I couldn't hold on to that house. And I did Bob more harm than good! I couldn't bear his customers thinking he wasn't a good man because he'd taken me in out of the goodness of his heart, and not buying from him.'

'You're wrong, Pixie. You should have spoken to him. Every trader goes through bad patches, especially after Christmas.'

'So he's well?' More than anything Pixie wanted to talk about Bob. Did he hate her for what she'd done to him?

'Of course he's well. But he deserves more from you. Come home with me.'

'Where will we live?'

Pixie listened in amazement as her mother told her how she'd saved enough money to pay off her debts and to put a rental deposit on their old home.

'It'll be so different from before,' Gladys said. 'And I

have something else to tell you. Rita's coming to stay at the house.'

Pixie looked confused.

'She came to the pub where I was working, Pixie,' she explained. 'She needs a home. She's going back to Priddy's Hard. They're crying out for workers. I've got a job there, too, now – I went round to see Harry Slaughter about the night shift.'

'That took guts,' Pixie said. Her mother really was full of surprises. She shook her head. It was courageous of Rita to apply for a job at the armaments yard as well, she thought.

'We all need guts to carry on. We need to help each other as well as this country of ours.' Pixie saw the tears glisten as her mother said, 'I wish I'd been here for you when Cal . . .'

Pixie took the tea cosy off the flowered teapot and refilled Gladys's cup. She told her mother of the anguish of not knowing what had happened to Cal until she'd found Ruth.

Gladys was listening intently. 'Ruth will manage without you. You do know that, don't you?'

'She's been good to me. I don't want to leave her in the lurch.'

'Does that mean you'll come home?'

'I'd like to.'

Gladys rose from the chair and put her arms around Pixie. 'You won't regret it, I promise you.'

Pixie began clearing away the tea things. 'I'll have to talk to Ruth,' she said.

Her mother was smiling at her. 'And I'll make it up to you.'

Pixie believed her. She knew that for her mother to work and put by money to settle her debts, then come back to Gosport, showed she had indeed changed.

'I never expected you to agree, you know,' Gladys said.

'Well, if it doesn't work out I'll still have some money behind me. Oh, Mum, it always seems to boil down to money or the lack of it, doesn't it?' Pixie's eyes lit up. 'But I've an income of my own now, as well.'

'Is it the rugs you've been making?'

Pixie laughed. 'That Rita can't keep her mouth shut, can she? She never could! Come and look.'

She put the tray of dirty crockery on the draining-board and took Gladys into the front room. She opened a large cupboard and pulled out two of the smaller rugs. One had a tiny square left for her to finish. The colours seemed to fill the room with light.

'Did you really make these?'

Pixie could see Gladys was impressed. 'When Sadie's

in bed it's lovely to be quiet and work on different patterns. It not only relaxes me but I was surprised how much people are prepared to pay for them. I work here, helping out in the guesthouse, but that's for bed and board. I wanted to pay Bob back, you see.'

Gladys fingered the rugs. 'They're lovely. But you've no need to worry. As I've said, I've settled up with Bob. But if I know him the money is still in the envelope on his mantelpiece. We're out of debt and out of danger.' She laughed. Then, more seriously, 'You could sell these anywhere.'

Pixie heard the telephone and went into the hall to answer it.

When she came back she said, 'That was a couple wanting to be booked in for two nights next weekend. I've entered it in the ledger. Look, Mum, I will come home but only once I've made sure Ruth can cope.'

She'd hardly finished the sentence when the key in the front door and a sudden gust of cold air announced the return of Ruth and Sadie.

'Oh, let me get in,' said Ruth, bumping the pushchair over the step. 'The snow's settling and it's freezing.'

Pixie unstrapped her baby and began taking off her coat and leggings. She snuggled her face into Sadie's warm neck. The little one giggled. Pixie passed her to

Gladys. 'Make yourself useful,' she said, going out into the kitchen. She was back in moments with a terry-towelling napkin and talcum powder. 'Time to change your granddaughter,' she said.

Ruth had already taken off her coat and boots. 'Guess what I've done,' she said. There was a glint in her eye. 'I've been putting cards in the newsagent's window and as many other notice-boards as I can.'

'What for?'

'I think it's time you went home, Pixie, so I've advertised for someone to help out here, in the guesthouse.'

Chapter Thirty-two

'It's amazing how we can make so much out of so little,' said Pixie, looking at the homemade banner, which said 'Happy Birthday Jeannie', strung across the mirror. The table was set with a pile of plates and cutlery at the ready, and an assortment of cups, saucers and enamelled mugs were stacked ready for use. 'Pity we can't all sit around the table,' she said, 'but there's not enough room.'

She smiled at the jellies wobbling, and the fairy cakes, made with marge and the meanest quantity of sugar, which looked delightful and tasted delicious. The tinned fruit in her best glass dishes had come from an American friend of Rita's and the centrepiece of a large chocolate cake, made by Em, relying heavily on cocoa, looked scrumptious. The ham, also from the American forces stores, was sliced thinly beneath greaseproof paper and sitting on another of Pixie's best dishes. Milk and orange juice courtesy of welfare foods were on the sideboard for the children to drink. Salad stuff was hard to come by in April because the lettuces were only just peeping from the earth, but a large tin of beetroot had been sliced to go with the ham, and Gladys had boiled some potatoes.

'Kids don't want to sit around.' Bob was staring at little Tommy Winters from over the road who had already sampled the jelly with his fingers. 'It might be a birthday party for Jeannie and us grown-ups,' he added, glaring at Tommy who had now smeared chocolate all over his face. The glare turned to a smile as Tommy gave him a cheeky grin. Bob liked the little blighter. Pixie had insisted he should come, even though he was a handful. 'But five minutes after they've finished eating,' Bob said, 'they'll be off playing and we can have their chairs.' He slipped his arm around Pixie's waist. 'It'll be like eating in shifts,' he said. 'And where's Em?'

Pixie smiled up at him. 'She'll be along later. Her Lizzie's come home and she's bringing her. Do you think it's too warm in here? I don't want Ruth to feel too hot.'

The range was giving out a satisfying heat. She turned the wireless down so that Harry James and His Orchestra were in the background.

'Stop worrying.' He kissed the back of her neck and, as

always when he did that, a tingle ran through her, making her feel warm, loved and ready to fall into his arms. How she had ever run away from this man she never would understand – she'd fight tooth and nail to keep him now.

'Do I look all right?' She had on a grey woollen dress with shoulder pads and a peplum that flared over her hips, accentuating her small waist.

'All right? You look good enough to eat.' He grinned at her, then ran his fingers through the lock of hair that fell across his forehead. 'You'll have a great deal to write in your notebooks for today, won't you?'

Pixie blushed. That she'd kept a written record of the war years was no secret. But what she hoped to do with those notebooks when the war was finally over was a secret that she was unwilling to divulge to anyone. Not yet, anyway. Bob gave her neck a tiny nip and she giggled, but before he could kiss her there was a sharp knock on the front door.

Pixie gave a final look around the room as Marlene walked in, dragging a disgruntled little girl. 'Honestly, you wouldn't think it's her birthday – she's got a right fit of the miseries today.'

"Ommy!' cried Jeannie. She adored Tommy. Marlene took off her child's coat and untied her hat strings. Pixie waited until Marlene had taken off her own coat, then carried the outdoor clothes to Rita's room, which had once been the front room. She knocked on the door.

'Come on, you,' she said to Rita, who was patting Pan Stik over her scars, standing on tiptoe in front of the mirror over the fireplace. A glorious smell of violets filled the room, perfume, also a present from an American friend.

'Do I look all right?'

'That's the self-same question I've just asked Bob. What d'you think I'm going to say to you? That you look like the rear end of a pantomime horse?'

She peered at Rita. 'Actually it's not until you sweep back your hair that anyone notices the scars. But we love you for you. We don't care about them. Get a move on!' Rita made a face at Pixie's reflection in the mirror and Pixie left her to it, after telling her the grey slacks and grey knitted jumper fitted her curvy body perfectly. Rita had finished knitting the jumper the evening before and Pixie had sewn the pieces together because she was better at sewing than Rita.

Rita was fine in her own surroundings and at work on the line at Priddy's Hard, but her confidence went haywire whenever she ventured to new places or met new people. Pixie noticed the letter from Joe on the end of Rita's bed. 'What's he got to say for himself, then?'

'He's got leave coming up and wants to see me.' Rita blushed.

Pixie knew the young American had been regularly writing to her. She put her arms around Rita. 'That's good,' she said. Rita was never short of admirers, but Joe was special.

Marlene, following Pixie, asked, 'Where's your mum?' Pixie waved towards the back garden. 'Lovely spread,' gushed Marlene. 'Looks a treat. Gosh, that colour suits you, Rita.' She was looking at the grey sweater and Rita's curves. 'If your hair was a different colour you'd look just like the "Sweater Girl", Lana Turner!'

'Mum's bringing in the washing,' Pixie said, after Rita had finished posing and the three of them had stopped giggling.

They trooped into the kitchen. 'The weather forecast said it was going to rain,' said Beth, Marlene's mum, as Gladys came in from the back garden with a basket of clothes from the line.

Jeannie was happier now and sat on Beth's lap cuddling her teddy bear. Tommy was sitting next to them.

'Want Sadie,' Jeannie demanded, shoving her teddy at Tommy.

'She asleep?' Beth asked.

'Yes. I'll wake her in a moment, else she won't sleep well tonight,' said Pixie.

'Is Ruth's husband coming today?' Beth asked, smoothing a lock of sweaty hair off Jeannie's forehead, then removing Tommy's fingers from the potatoes.

Tommy's mother had died in an air raid and his dad had taken it badly. The little boy spent a great deal of time with Pixie and Gladys.

'Yes, he's home on leave,' said Pixie, as she tweaked straight the sheet that she'd used as a tablecloth. She then began folding the dry washing, her mother helping with the larger items. Jeannie climbed down from Beth's lap to retrieve her teddy from the floor.

There was another knock on the front door. Rita called out, 'I'm getting it. It's Ruth and Roy.'

Pixie heard footsteps in the hall, then Ruth came in, closely followed by her husband in civvies.

'You look *so* well, Ruth. Oh, my, you got a little bump!'

'Being pregnant certainly agrees with you,' said Bob, coming down to greet them. 'Hello, mate,' he said to Roy, shaking his hand. 'Thank goodness you're going to save me from this gaggle of women and kids! Get your coats off.'

He went to the sideboard and took out a bottle of Brickwoods Light Ale and found the opener.

'That looks good,' said Roy. 'Nice to see you again, Bob.'

'How's tricks?' Bob returned.

Pixie saw Roy gesture towards Ruth. 'What can I say, Bob? In a few months I'll be a daddy and I couldn't be happier.'

Bob had poured out the beer into two tumblers and passed one to Roy.

'What d'you reckon to what's happening in Gosport nowadays?' Roy asked.

'It's like a forces building site, with all the preparations for the invasion. Still I don't have to tell you that, do I?' Bob said.

'No,' said Roy, 'and it's still very hush-hush. But we're going to get Hitler this time, you mark my words.'

The women were talking quietly among themselves until a cry from upstairs cut the air.

'I'll get her,' said Gladys. 'I want to put some of this dry washing away.' She left the kitchen with an armful of folded clothing.

'She's lost ten years since you and Sadie have been living with her,' said Ruth.

'She's a wonder, my mum.' Pixie grinned. 'Can't believe she's turned out to be the mum she has. And at work she's been made up to line manager. Never thought she'd stick to working in the armaments factory. But she gets on a treat with the girls there. Best mates with Em, of course.'

'You should see them in the mornings going in for the day shift,' said Bob. 'Arm in arm, the three of them, Rita, Pixie and Gladys, striding down the road to Priddy's Hard – talk about that Gracie Fields song, "Sing As We Go".'

'Yes,' said Beth. 'Bob brings Sadie round to me. I love having her and she's company for Jeannie.'

'You seen that bloke you met at the auctions, Marlene?'

Marlene blushed almost as brightly as her red hair at Roy's question. 'Once or twice,' she mumbled.

Bob winked at Roy. 'He hangs about like a lovesick puppy,' he said.

Gladys came in with a bleary-eyed little girl in her arms and put her in her high chair. 'Come on, love,' she said, turning to Jeannie. 'Hop up on this chair. It's your birthday do.'

Marlene helped her daughter onto a chair with a cushion to make it higher so the little girl could reach the table more easily. Then she settled Tommy next to Jeannie.

'I'll go and stick the kettle on,' said Pixie.

'I'll do that,' said Rita, grabbing Pixie's arm so that she

wouldn't disappear into the scullery. She looked at Bob. 'You ready for your speech, then?'

Pixie asked, 'Speech? What speech?' She heard the hiss and pop of the gas being lit.

Bob's face was bright red.

'You didn't think this was just a birthday party, did you?' said Gladys. 'Though Jeannie is important enough for us to give her a party and presents on her birthday.'

Rita returned from the scullery with two brown carrier bags full of wrapped parcels. 'These are for you, little girl.' She bent and kissed Jeannie's cheek. 'And so this little girl and boy won't feel left out, we've got presents for them as well.' She bent towards Sadie and put a parcel that looked suspiciously like a hand-made rag dolly into her hands. Sadie immediately opened her mouth and clutched at the toy. Tommy had a smile a mile wide at his five-piece cowboy set and promptly jammed the hat on his head.

Bob took hold of Pixie's arm. 'You'll have a lot more to write about in your notebooks tonight, won't you?'

She smiled at him. One day when the war was over, perhaps she'd share them with him.

'This woman has driven me mad,' Bob said, with a broad grin.' She's been through a lot this year, as have all of us,' Again he brushed his hair off his forehead. He was still blushing and gave a small nervous cough. 'But you've been invited today, being some of our very best friends, because a couple of weeks ago I asked Pixie to marry me.' He coughed nervously again. 'She said yes.'

The clapping started, but he waved a hand to quieten everyone, then delved into his trouser pocket and took out a small box.

Pixie was staring at him. This was something she knew absolutely nothing about.

The kitchen and its occupants were hushed. Bob snapped open the box.

Inside, glittering like a star fallen from the velvet heavens, was a ring. Diamonds glittered against the gold background.

'We're going to do it all properly now, Pixie my love,' Bob said. 'I thank you for agreeing to be my wife. You have only to set the date. It's up to you.'

He took her small hand in his. Pixie felt suddenly very safe, very cared for and very happy. He slipped the engagement ring on her finger. Pixie thought that until that moment she had never known what true love was. She looked up into his eyes, full of promise, full of love.

'Oh, I do love you,' she whispered. He kissed her and everyone started clapping again.

And the canary, on the sideboard, sang its heart out.

Acknowledgments

Thank you Juliet Burton, my long-suffering agent, and thank you Jane Wood, my editor, for believing in me. Also Katie Gordon and Joel Richardson. There are many people who have helped me at Quercus and I can't do without any of you. Thank you.